Hiss H
for
Homicide

A Nick and Nora Mystery

T. C. LoTempio

BEYOND THE PAGE
PUBLISHING

Hiss H for Homicide
T. C. LoTempio
Copyright © 2021 by T. C. LoTempio
Cover design and illustration by Dar Albert, Wicked Smart Designs

Beyond the Page Books
are published by
Beyond the Page Publishing
www.beyondthepagepub.com

ISBN: 978-1-950461-94-3

To Mary Krol Foster and her children,
Nicole "Niki" Staples and Douglas Martel.
Miss you guys too!

Acknowledgments

As always, thanks go to my incredible agent, Josh Getzler, and his assistant, Jonathan Cobb, without whom the Nick and Nora series would not be continuing! Thanks also to beta readers Emily Hall, Laura Roth, Shelley Guisti, Barb Weismann and Denise Waechter! Your input helped make NN4 so much better! And kudos to the entire Beyond the Page editorial team, and especially to Bill Harris. Your eyes caught what mine did not!

A big thank-you to all my friends who support me in this venture, you know who you are! To all the amazing authors who have appeared on Rocco's blog and who I am proud to call my friends, especially the amazing Carole Nelson Douglas, without whose encouragement there might never have been a Nick and Nora. And, of course, Rocco, the real-life Nick! Any mistakes in this book are totally my own! Read and enjoy.

Prologue

"After Tuesday there will be a lot of unhappy people around. I'm sure they never expected me to actually go through with it. Maybe I should invest in a bulletproof vest, ha ha."

Marlene McCambridge leaned back in the overstuffed leather chair and propped one elegantly clad foot against the polished wood desk. One perfectly manicured hand reached up to brush a lacquered, expertly dyed blonde curl off her high forehead, while the other gripped a half-empty glass of Scotch. Raising the glass to her lips, she took another sip, swallowed deeply.

Her soon-to-be ex-partner wasn't a happy camper, no, not at all. Desiree had never been able to harm anything, not even a spider. Although in this case, she might make an exception.

Marlene downed the rest of her drink in one long gulp. She'd miss Desiree, in a way. After all, they'd had a good long run, but like all good things, it was time for it to end. She couldn't speak for Desiree, of course, but if she had to write another line like "my clasped hands made my cleavage seem almost buoyant, straining against the thin fabric of my dress," or "his chocolate hair and eyes reminded me of hot fudge, and I leaned against his hairy chest, feeling his muscles ripple beneath me," then holy moly, she'd have to slit both her wrists. After all, how many different ways could one describe a hairy chest? Desiree would probably disagree, but she was positive they'd exhausted them all, and then some.

Well, at two p.m. Tuesday, the world would know two things: the writing team of McCambridge and Sanders was no more, and Marlene McCambridge was no person to screw around with. Or tell your innermost secrets to.

Everyone loved a good scandal, right? And she was going to pull the plug on some real juicy ones. Sometimes it paid to be the person people confided in. In her case it paid very well indeed: two million big ones, to be exact. And that was only the beginning . . .

She pushed herself up and out of the chair and lurched toward the well-stocked bar at the other end of the den. The person she'd rented the house from had encouraged her to not be shy about drinking the large quantities of liquor on hand and she had every intention of depleting his supply before her ninety-day lease was up. Cruz was a quiet little town, the perfect place for her to hide out from the media storm that was sure to follow her announcement, to put the finishing touches on the project that would assure her financial independence.

It wouldn't be long now. Once everything was set, she'd take off, maybe head to Rio, or maybe somewhere else in South America. She'd always had a weakness for men with Spanish accents. Too bad they always ended up ripping her off and vanishing.

She splashed more Johnnie Walker Black into the glass, added ice and a splash of tonic water, and had barely taken a sip when every nerve in her body began to tingle.

The unmistakable creak of a floorboard reached her ears. Now, how could that be? She was alone here, or at least she was supposed to be.

Shake it off. This is an old house. Old houses always have noises. It's nothing.

The floorboard creaked again.

"Hey," she called out. "Anybody there?"

Silence.

Marlene flung open the den door and moved cautiously into the narrow hallway. She inched her way forward, peering this way and that, until she finally approached the large sitting room. Her sharp eyes took in the area, narrowing as they settled on the bay window over to the far left. One window was cracked open. Her frown deepened. She was fairly certain she'd shut them all earlier, to ward off the evening chill. Casting another quick glance over her shoulder, she hurried over to the window, pulled it shut, and snapped the safety bolt into place. She leaned against the window seat and took a few calming breaths, listening intently.

Nothing.

"I must have imagined it." She blew out a breath. "I need a drink."

She pushed away from the window and started across the room, but before she'd made it halfway all the lights went out, and a terrified gasp escaped her lips. She'd never been fond of the dark, and this wasn't just dark: it was pitch. She bit down hard on her lower lip as the realization swept over her that she had no idea where the fuse box might be, not that she'd know what to do with it if she did.

A floorboard creaked again. This time she was certain it came from upstairs.

She felt her way along the corridor back to the den and fumbled in the bottom drawer of the desk for the flashlight she'd seen once before. Her fingers closed over it and she switched it on. It emitted only a very faint glow, but it would be enough to get her safely upstairs and into bed. In the morning she'd find someone to help change the fuses.

And just in case she got unexpected company, she had the .45 in the drawer by her bed . . . Maybe now was a good time to go up and get it.

Marlene made her way slowly up the stairs. A slight rustling as she reached the top landing made her pause. Her head swiveled toward the sound, and she let out a startled gasp as she noticed the door to her office was partially open. Gripping the flashlight, she moved toward the door, paused, listened.

Silence.

Taking a deep breath, Marlene reached out a tentative hand, pushed the door all the way open. She moved slowly into the room, moved the flashlight slowly around in a circle.

The soft glow partially illuminated the features of a tall figure, shrouded in shadow, standing not two feet to her left. The figure moved forward, the face now fully illuminated in the dim light.

She sucked in her breath. "You?" she gasped, staring in surprise at the face before her. "What in hell are you doing sneaking around up here? You're not expected till—" She stopped, peered a bit more closely at the intruder. Her brows drew together. "Wait a second. You aren't—" Her nerveless fingers lost their grip on the flashlight and it dropped and clicked off, plunging the room into darkness and Marlene into self-doubt.

Maybe I should have bought that bulletproof vest. Maybe I should have carried that gun around with me. Maybe I . . .

Bang.

Marlene slid into the darkness forever.

<u>One</u>

"Chérie, I don't know what is getting more attention—the lunch items or that television."

I brushed an auburn curl out of my eyes and cut the speaker, my BFF Chantal Gillard, an eye roll. Although born right here in the little California seaside town of Cruz, my friend loved to affect a French accent (she thought it made her sound more "international"), so the sentence come out sounding more like, "Vat ees getting more atten-shown, ze lunch ah-teems or zat te-lay-viz-see-ahn." I glanced at the throng of customers, all pressed up against my glass display case, eyes glued to Rachel Rae whipping up some sort of yummy pasta dish on my brand-new forty-two-inch flat-screen television that hung suspended from the ceiling.

"Right now," I sighed, "eet looks like 'zee TV' ees winning." I ignored the eye roll she shot at *my* attempt at a French accent and rapped my knuckles sharply on the counter. "Next," I called out. "Who's next in line?"

No response. They might all have been zombies, staring mindlessly at the figures on the wide screen. "Hey, there, is anybody hungry? Who wants lunch?" I called again.

"Oh, sorry. I love Rachel Rae. What a great idea, Nora. Whatever made you decide to do it?" Alvina Wilkins, the assistant librarian, tore her gaze reluctantly from the TV and stepped up to the counter. A woman in her mid-forties, she was reed-thin, with a sunny disposition and a quirky sense of humor. Both excellent qualities, in my opinion, that made her able to get along with head librarian Jemina Slater, who'd always been something of a tyrant (scratch that—make it bully), and even though she was well into her seventies, showed no sign of wanting to vacate the post she'd held ever since I could remember.

"Blame my sister," I said. "When I went to visit her and Aunt Prudence a few weeks ago she dragged me to this little café. Their line was practically out the door, but the customers weren't complaining. They were all gushing about how entertaining it was to watch TV while they waited for their food. The owner happened to be there and he said his business had almost tripled since he'd installed it, so Lacey dared me to give it a try."

"You never could resist a challenge, could you? Especially from your sister." Alvina wiggled her fingers in a careless gesture and glanced at the sign above the counter. "Did I hear you say you added something new to the menu?"

"You did." I beamed and pointed to the sign to the left of the counter, excited as always when I added a new sandwich to my already teeming menu. "The Megan Fox is grilled chicken and cheese dipped into egg batter and sautéed in butter. Your choice of cheese, of course, although I recommend the cheddar. The Brian Austin Green is made identically, except I substitute ham for the chicken."

Alvina flashed her pearly whites at me. "They both sound yummy. I'll try the Megan Fox. I do love my chicken. And a decaf coffee too, please."

"Might as well make that two," said a deep voice. I glanced over at the speaker, a broad-shouldered guy with silky hair, redder than my own, that reached to just above his shoulders. Steel-gray eyes peered at me from under two bushy eyebrows, even as his well-shaped lips split in a grin, revealing teeth so white I was positive he bleached them. Or they were caps. Or both. The ID badge swinging from the black lanyard around his neck had "Paul Jenkins" printed in big black letters. He'd only joined the *Cruz Sun* a few weeks ago but "Jenks," as he liked to be called, had already become a steady customer—and, apparently, one of the few not mesmerized by my new television. "Know what would really go good with that sandwich, though? A strawberry banana smoothie."

"You're not the first customer to tell me that," I admitted, reaching into the glass case for my chicken cutlets and cheese. "I did look into it. I priced a really high-end gourmet ice machine, one that can be used for slushies, smoothies, even frozen cappuccinos. Let's just say unless a winning lottery ticket's in my future, my budget doesn't stretch that far right now."

"It will once you get a few more catering jobs," Alvina said with a toss of her head. "You did such a splendid job with the Cruz Museum gala, it's only a matter of time."

Chantal cocked her head and whispered too low for the others to hear, "Or you could ask Violet Crenshaw. She did promise you a reward, after all."

"Yes, she did," I hissed back, "but I have a feeling the reward has already been decided. Violet said she'd be in touch about it when she and Alexa returned from England."

"Oh, pooh. Well"–Chantal's black cap of curls bobbed as she rubbed her hands together–"it's probably something really unimaginative, too, you know. Money or a gift card to Nordstrom."

"True," I said teasingly. "Not everyone has someone in their life who can give them the perfect birthday gift, like a new set of crystals and tarot card deck."

Chantal blushed right down to the roots of her black hair. She knew I was referring to her sometime beau, Rick Barnes, a DOJ official who worked in nearby Carmel. For Chantal's birthday a few weeks ago, he'd gifted her with just that, and she hadn't stopped talking about his 'thoughtful gift' for days.

Alvina glanced over at Jenks, who appeared to be listening intently to the conversation. "Violet Crenshaw is our museum director. Nora recently reunited her with her missing niece."

"I know. I read some of the stories in the newspaper archives about the exploits of Nora Charles, sandwich shop owner by day, sleuth by night. That one and the Lola Grainger affair." Jenks turned and gave me an appraising glance. "You're quite the amateur sleuth. I've always had a yen to be a Hardy Boy. Someday you've got to let me in on how you do it."

A large black-and-white paw snaked over the edge of the countertop, then disappeared. Jenks drew back, obviously startled. "What the heck," he cried. The paw appeared again, clicked its nails on the Formica, and then vanished.

"Come on up Nicky," Chantal sang out. "Don't be shy."

Jenks frowned. "Nicky?"

"Yes." Chantal's eyes danced with mischief. "Nicky Charles, Nora's partner in crime solving."

A second later a large tuxedo cat lofted onto the rear counter. He held up one paw and flexed it, displaying razor-sharp shivs.

Jenks took a step backward, his eyes wide. "Uck, a cat. I hate cats, especially black ones. Don't you know they're bad luck?"

Nick wrapped his tail around his body and sat erect, his glossy black and white-tipped paws tucked under him, and let his unblinking stare rest first on Jenks, then Alvina and Chantal, before finally settling on me. "Merow," he said, and sniffed.

"Technically, he's not a black cat, he's a tuxedo who gets upset when he's not included," I said. I gave him a light tap on his derrière and he leapt down to the floor, then shuffled over to his favorite spot in front of my double-door refrigerator, where he arranged himself, Sphinx-like, all the while bestowing me with a look of catly disdain. "As for the bad luck part, I can think of a few criminals who'd agree with that observation."

Jenks swallowed and continued to stare at Nick. "You're kidding, right, about him being your partner?"

I shook my head. "Not at all. Nick and I are a team, just like the original Nick and Nora Charles, except this Nick prefers milk to martinis."

Nick blinked again and the corners of his lips tipped up. Then he stretched out his forepaws, laid his head down on them, and closed both eyes.

Jenks continued to eye Nick warily. "So, what does he do exactly? Carry a magnifying glass in his paw at crime scenes? Hiss when he suspects homicide, scratch a murderer's eyes out?"

One eye winked open. Nick's tail bristled, and a loud *grr* rumbled in his throat.

"Believe it or not, Nick's more effective than you'd think when it comes to apprehending the bad guys. He has his own way of communicating clues, pretty successful ways, I might add. His former owner was a PI."

"Former owner? What happened to him?"

Ah, a very good question. I certainly wasn't about to share with Jenks what I'd recently learned: that Nick Atkins might be involved in espionage. I shrugged. "He's . . . been away. On business."

Nick sat up and batted his paw beneath my refrigerator, and a few seconds later three small square tiles came into view.

Jenks looked amused. "So the cat's a Scrabble player, huh? Is he any good?"

"You could say that," I said as Chantal dropped the tiles into my palm. An *s*, a *p* and a *y*. Spy. "He has an uncanny sixth sense about things. Cats are supposed to have psychic abilities, you know."

Jenks backed away from the cat, who'd lofted onto the counter again and was now chewing on the edge of another tile. He turned back to me. "So you and this PI were close, I take it?"

"Ah . . . not really." I hesitated and then added, "I never met the man."

Jenks's jaw dropped. "Never met him? I thought you said he left you his cat to take care of."

"That's not how it happened. Nick just showed up on my doorstep one night."

"Just like that, eh?" Jenks rubbed the stubble on his chin with one long finger. "And I suppose the cat learned how to be a sleuth from that PI."

I wasn't quite sure how to answer that. I couldn't deny the fact feline Nick possessed a decided flair for detective work, ferreting out clues and communicating via the use of Scrabble tiles, another long story. Without his help, though, I'd never have solved three mysteries. Plus, I'd most likely be pushing up daisies. The little fellow had saved me from an untimely demise on more than one occasion. In return, he got a roof over his head, a warm bed (although he preferred to sleep on mine), three square meals a day, plus he got to sample all my specials before the customers. Really, what more could a cat ask?

I lifted my shoulders in a shrug. "I don't think he learned it from anyone. I think it just comes naturally to him."

Nick had apparently decided I'd suffered enough for my oversight on his role in our partnership and now turned his full attention to licking his thick coat into an ebony sheen.

Alvina touched Jenks's arm. "It's all so exciting, isn't it? I think Nora and Nick would make a great human interest story for the Sunday edition. People love cats. They're the most popular house pet, right above hamsters and dogs." She leaned toward me and whispered, "I read it on Google."

Jenks scratched at his head, making the jagged ends of hair above his ears stand out. "As much as I dislike cats, I have to admit an article on you two would probably be a lot more interesting than the interview old Marker's got his heart set on."

A smile touched my lips at that assessment. Henry Marker, editor of the *Cruz Sun*, was a crusty curmudgeon who brought to mind images of Perry White clenching his cigar and screaming "Great Caesar's Ghost" at Clark Kent and Lois Lane. When he had his mind set on a particular article, it practically took a sign from the Man Upstairs himself to make him change his mind.

Alvina tossed Jenks a curious look. "What interview is that?"

"Oh, some romance novelist holed up in the old Porter house off Highway 11." He felt around in his jacket pocket and whipped out a worn notebook, flipped to a back page. "Marlene McCambridge. Ever hear of her?"

"Marlene McCambridge! You're kidding!" Alvina squealed. "She's really here in Cruz?"

Jenks put a finger to his lips. "Shush, not so loud! It's supposed to be a secret," he hissed. "Marker only found out because his cousin Joannie took care of the rental."

"Sorry," Alvina murmured. She gave a quick glance around to make sure no one was listening and then said in a low tone, "Everyone loves the Tiffany Blake books. Their new one comes out Tuesday, *Love's Deepest Desire.* I ordered five copies! I just can't keep them in stock. I'm convinced Maude Applebee confiscated most of 'em for her own personal library."

Jenks swatted at his ear with his hand. "I'm sorry, I think my hearing is going. Did you say *their* new one? Plural?"

"Oh, yes. Two women write those books. As a matter of fact"— Alvina smiled at me—"Nora's mother was friends with the other woman, Desiree Sanders."

Jenks turned to me. "Is that right?"

I nodded. "Desiree was Dora Slater back then. She had some modest success after she changed her name, but she really hit it big when she teamed up with Marlene and invented the persona of Tiffany Blake. I think practically every book in that series has been on the *New York Times* or *USA Today* Bestseller list, or both."

"Yes, it would be quite a coup to get Marlene to make an appearance. Maybe you can put in a good word for me, Jenks, when you do your interview," Alvina said hopefully.

"If I do it," Jenks said with a sigh, reaching for his tray. "She's not exactly the most cooperative person in the world, from what I can gather. I've left several messages but so far no dice." He turned to me and his lips twisted into a half smile. "Think about that article, Nora. I might be back."

As they moved away, Chantal touched my arm. "I forgot to tell you I promised Remy I'd take the afternoon shift at the flower shop. Will you be okay here with Mollie gone?" Mollie Travis was the high school senior who helped out mornings and afternoons, but school was closed this week and she and her parents had gone to Big Sur to visit relatives.

I stared down the line of heads tilted upward, their eyes now glued to a popular talk show. "I don't see why not," I sighed.

"Great. I'll give you a call tonight to find out how long it took for them all to come out of their comas."

"Better make it tomorrow morning. I've got a date with Daniel tonight."

One well-shaped eyebrow rose. "You two haven't been out together since the costume ball. Why is that?"

I pulled a face at her. She knew darn well why.

I'd met FBI Special Agent Daniel Corleone during my investigation of Lola Grainger's death. At six-two, broad-shouldered with burnished blond hair cut a bit on the shaggy side, tanned skin, and clear blue eyes, he was the epitome of the word *hunk*. Sparks had flown between us from the first, but our budding romance was slow to take off, due partly to the demands of Daniel's job and partly to my reluctance to rush into a relationship. As it happens, my reluctance has a name.

When I'd first met Leroy Samms, we were seniors at the University of California, and he'd just been appointed editor of the college paper. From our first encounter there had been a spark of . . . something. I couldn't tell you just what. When we weren't trading insults, we were butting heads over everything from bylines to the use of commas. The night before graduation, though, we'd decided to celebrate the completion of a difficult story with champagne and ended up in each other's arms. The details on just what transpired that night have always remained a bit fuzzy, but suffice it to say we made it through graduation without ever speaking another word to each other. Then, fifteen years later, I ran into him again, under much different circumstances. He was my sister's arresting officer. Was there still a spark between us? Had I wondered through the years what might have happened had Samms and I gotten together? My answer would have to be a definite . . . maybe.

Chantal winked at me and started to hum "Torn Between Two Lovers." I mimed throwing a plate at her as she blew me a kiss and disappeared out the back door. I started to turn back toward the counter and almost tripped over Nick. He squatted at my feet, and I gasped at the object I saw clenched beneath one paw.

My brand-new iPhone. I'd barely had it a week and was still getting used to all the bells and whistles. "No claws," I cried. The last thing I wanted were scratches on its nice, shiny exterior. I bent down and ticked his paw. Nick backed away, shooting me a look of catly disdain. He held up one forepaw, innocent of claw tips, and sneezed.

"Sorry, Nick. Do I even want to know how you manage to get your paws on these things?" Cell phones, journals, Scrabble tiles . . . nothing was sacred to this cat.

"Merow-owww," he warbled, reaching up to bat at the phone with his paw. A second later it rang.

I raised both eyebrows. "I just hate it when you do that. It's so . . . spooky." I glanced at the number, but it was one I didn't recognize. I started to click it into voice mail, but Nick let out a loud meow and raised his paw, pointing at the phone, black tail swishing to and fro like a metronome.

"All right, all right, I'll answer it." I clicked the Accept button and made a face at Nick. "Hello."

"Is this Nora Charles?"

The voice was feminine, but it wasn't familiar. "Yes," I said cautiously.

"The same Nora Charles who used to write for the *Chicago Tribune?* Laura Charles's daughter?"

Now my radar tingled so much I shivered. "Yes. Who am I speaking with, please?"

Ignoring my question she went on, "I simply cannot believe this is how that—that hack repays my loyalty! All those years of dedication—plotting, character creation, the actual writing, not to mention flying all over the globe on those damned personal appearance tours—down the drain! I thought we had something good, something solid, and now it's up in smoke. She's an ingrate, I tell you. A total ingrate, and she must be stopped. I'm sick, I tell you, just sick."

She paused for a breath and I saw my chance. "I'm sorry but I haven't the faintest idea who you are or what you're talking about."

"What?" The voice at the other end sounded incredulous. "This is Desiree Sanders, and isn't it obvious? I'm talking about my partner, that no-talent, good-for-nothing ungrateful hack of a human being." She paused for a breath.

"She's trying to murder me."

Two

For a second I was so stunned I couldn't speak. Finally I managed to croak out, "You said your name is Desiree Sanders?"

"Yes." Her tone softened a bit. "I knew your mother. Laura was one of my dearest friends."

"Yes, she spoke of you often." I blew out a breath. "I assume the partner you mention is Marlene McCambridge?"

"Who else?" Desiree's voice had risen to an ear-splitting shriek. Nick's sensitive ears picked up on the increase in decibels. He stretched out on the floor and put his paws over his ears. I moved farther back into the corner, afraid the sound would carry out to my customers.

"What has she done that's led you to think she wants to kill you?" I asked. "If that's so, then you really should contact the police."

I heard a sharp intake of breath and then Desiree said in a calmer tone, "I'm sorry, I should have clarified my statement. She doesn't want to murder me, she wants to kill my career. Although if she goes through with what she has planned she might as well just take a knife and stab me through the heart. I'll be as good as dead. I'll be ruined!"

I remembered my mother describing Desiree as dramatic, and I thought that assessment accurate. "What exactly is it she's planning to do?"

"Miss Priss wants to dissolve our partnership. Yes, that's right! As of two p.m. tomorrow, the writing team of McCambridge and Sanders, better known as Tiffany Blake, will be no more."

Ah, light was beginning to dawn on the reason Marlene had come to Cruz alone. I dragged my hand through my hair. "Are you certain she's serious? If the two of you had an argument, maybe this is just her idea of payback."

"Arguments are a way of life with us," Desiree spat. "We disagree every other day. And no, this wasn't a spur-of-the-moment, heat-of-the-moment threat. She's hinted at dissolution before, but this time it's different. She's got paperwork all drawn up and she actually expects me to sign it. I'm here in Cruz because I need to try and talk some sense into her, the witch." Desiree grunted softly, and I detected a hint of something besides anger in her tone. Desperation? "This dissolution is just the tip of the iceberg. Your mother always said how cool and levelheaded you were, and those qualities are exactly what I need right now. Look, I know you don't know me from Adam. I wouldn't even ask you, except I was such good friends with your mama and—honestly, I don't know who else I can turn to. Please, just meet with me and let me explain. I promise I'll abide by whatever decision you make after that."

I hesitated. Part of me was yelling: *This is trouble. Cut and run!* But another part of me shot back: *This is your mother's friend. She sounds like she's really in trouble. Maybe she just needs a shoulder to cry on. You know it's what your mother would want you to do.*

I sighed. "I close at three. Where would you like to meet?"

Desiree let out a little squeal. "You'll come then? Wonderful. I'm at the Cruz Inn. Room 523. Just come right on up. I'll be waiting for you."

I disconnected with the distinct feeling I'd just been played, and very well at that. I glanced over at Nick and pointed an accusing finger. "Okay, bud, this is all your fault, you know. You wanted me to answer that call. What have you gotten me into now?"

He stretched out and put his head between his paws.

I rolled my eyes. "Yeah, that's just what I was afraid of. Well, guess what. You're coming with me."

I heard his *grr* of protest as I turned back to the counter. Old Harold Robinson was leaning against it, tapping his cane impatiently on the floor. "About time," he grumbled as I hurried over. "I'll have a Bogart salad, hold the bacon bits. And when are you gonna get a damn smoothie machine?"

• • •

Promptly at three I ushered my last customer out the door. Bennie Hemming went out kicking and screaming because I shut the TV off during the Lightning Round of *Family Feud*. I patiently reminded him that Hot Bread was an eating establishment, not his living room. He not so patiently reminded me that if it weren't for people like him, I'd have an *Out of Business* sign on my door. We finally agreed to disagree, and with a promise of free coffee tomorrow, he left. I leaned against the door and looked over at Nick, sprawled comfortably across the counter, his front paws just grazing the register. He swiveled his head toward my back door and a second later I heard a loud knock.

"Uh-oh," I said, whipping off my apron. "We'll have to ditch whoever that is quick so we can keep our appointment." I hurried over to the door and opened it, prepared to shoo my visitor away . . . and then stopped dead as I saw who stood there. None other than Daniel Corleone, looking decidedly sexy in a black leather jacket, tight-fitting denims, and black alligator boots, a far cry from his usual working attire of staid navy blue suit and white shirt. He looked darn hot and dangerously yummy, maybe because of the serious five o'clock shadow he had going on. "Well. This is a surprise. You look . . . different." I managed.

He cocked a brow. "Different? I was hoping for dashing, maybe sexy."

"Oh, that's a given." I laughed and motioned to his stubble. "What's up? When did you decide to grow a beard?"

He swiped the back of his hand against his cheek. "I've been undercover on a case that went longer than expected. I only just wrapped it up about an hour ago."

I studied his face and said, "Let me guess. You're beat and want a rain check on our dinner tonight, right?"

He did look miserable as he nodded. "I hate to disappoint you again. Heck, I was looking forward to a nice relaxing evening with you myself, but . . . would you mind terribly if we postponed it?" His lips twisted into a lopsided grin. "I'd be a lousy date, worse than usual."

"Oh, stop it. You're a great date. And of course I understand. We can have dinner another time. Actually, I've been quite busy myself today."

"Ah, that's right. Today was new sandwich day, right?"

"That and . . ." I pointed upward. Daniel saw the television and let out a low whistle.

"Whoa. Is that what Violet Crenshaw rewarded you with?"

I laughed. "No, that's still a mystery. The TV was my sister's idea. It's an experiment to see if it would generate more business."

"And," he prodded as I hesitated.

"Jury's still out. Today it seemed to be more of a distraction than an attraction. The general consensus, however, is I should have sunk my money into a smoothie machine instead."

"Well, they are popular. I like a good strawberry banana smoothie myself." He reached out and touched the tip of my nose with his finger. "I'm sorry about tonight. I wouldn't blame you if you wanted to dump me and find some guy who'll appreciate you."

I tamped down my guilty conscience at the mental image of Samms that arose and gave him a sunny smile. "Don't be silly. I wouldn't dump you just because you broke a date or two . . . or three."

"More like ten." He placed his hands on my shoulders and looked deeply into my eyes. "You're the best, Nora. I really hate that we haven't been able to spend quality time together—but don't worry. Things are going to change. I'll make this up to you, and in a big way."

"Well, that sounds very promising."

He leaned into me. "I can even give you a little preview."

He dipped his head toward mine and his lips captured mine in a long, satisfying kiss. His arms slid around my waist and mine roamed up and down his back and then . . .

His cell phone chirped.

He broke away reluctantly, hand dipping into his jeans pocket. He glanced at the screen and sighed. "I'm sorry. Duty calls. I've got to get over to the Field Office right away."

I tightened my grip around his waist. "What are you, the only agent on duty? What about Samms? He is still with the FBI, right?"

"Actually, he's—" Daniel held up a finger as his cell chirped again.

He glanced quickly at the screen. "I'm sorry. I really have to go," he said, slipping the phone back into his pocket. "But first let me finish that preview."

He pulled me to him and pressed me against his rock-hard length. His lips came down on mine in a crushing kiss. And then, with a brisk wave, he was gone. I put a finger against my tingling lips and then let out a gasp as an image of Samms's chiseled features rose before me.

I bit my lip. Here I had a perfectly nice boyfriend, one other girls would kill for, yet it only took seconds for me to fall back into a schoolgirl crush. I saw Nick watching me, head cocked, and sighed. "I know, I know. Kiss one guy and dream of another. My mother would have said I'm fickle."

Nick opened his mouth wide in a yawn.

"So you think my love life is boring, do you? I'd call it more of a puzzle myself." I gave his derrière a swift pat. "Get your rear in gear, bud . . . and let's go see Desiree. Look on the bright side—if you can call it that. With no date to get ready for tonight, at least we don't have to rush back."

• • •

A half hour later I guided my silver SUV down the circular driveway and into the parking lot of the Cruz Inn. The quaint, vine-covered edifice had always reminded me of the inn from the old *Murder, She Wrote* TV series. In fact, each time I passed I half expected to see Jessica Fletcher whiz by on her bicycle or Amos Tupper cruise by in his police car, and I was always oddly disappointed when neither made an appearance (although if they had, I'd have had to be carted off to the nearest mental hospital—immediately!). I parked under a spreading elm, shut off the engine, and stole a glance at my companion curled up in a ball in the passenger seat. Nick lifted his head, and I gave him a quick scratch on the white spot behind his ear.

"So, what do you say? Ready to face the lion known as Desiree in her den?" Nick flicked his ears and gave his long black tail a twitch. I took that as an affirmative.

We entered the lobby, and as always, I paused for a second to admire the cozy setting. Dark paneling set off the thick wall-to-wall raspberry pink shag carpeting. A small berry-colored damask couch and wing chair sat in front of the large bay window. In the center of the room was a tall table with a vase of fresh-cut flowers and a guest registry. A chandelier hung gracefully above it. At one end was a large mahogany reception desk where a redheaded guy in his early twenties sat behind a massive computer, one ear glued to the telephone tucked under his chin. At the other end stood a marble fireplace, flanked by high-backed chairs, clearly the focal point of the lobby. The mantel was a combination of mahogany, walnut and oak, with designs of flowers and leaves carved into it. A beveled mirror hung directly above it in its center, flanked by hand-painted tiles. Embers glowed from its depths, but there was no mistaking the fact the piece generated plenty of heat on its own merits.

I bypassed the front desk and went straight to the bank of elevators at the rear. The clerk glanced up as we sailed past, then returned to his conversation. There was a cage ready and waiting; Nick and I stepped inside and I pressed the button for the fifth floor. We emerged onto thick sky-blue carpeting and walls covered in blue-and-cream-striped wallpaper. A sign right in front of us read *Rooms 501–523*, followed by an arrow pointing to the left, so we headed in that direction, my heels and Nick's paws sinking into the three-inch pile carpeting as we made our way down the hall. Room 523 turned out to be the corner one. I paused and raised my hand to knock on the wood-paneled door, but it was flung open before I ever made contact.

My first thought was her book jacket photo didn't do her justice. Desiree was even more striking in person. Tall and narrow with an angular face and snapping brown eyes, she wore her short dirty-blonde hair cut in an angled bob that curved softly toward her delicate chin. Her skin was smooth and clear. She had to be in her early sixties but she appeared at least ten years younger, maybe even late forties. She was dressed stylishly in a long black-and-white-striped tunic with matching black leggings and ballerina flats. Her chest heaved slightly, almost as though she were straining to catch her breath. She placed one well-manicured hand over her heart and her full, red-glossed lips parted in a wide smile, revealing teeth that resembled wet Chiclets.

"Ah, finally! You have to be Nora," she said in a breathy voice. "I'd know you anywhere. That red hair, those green eyes . . . it's almost as if I'm looking at your mother again." She swung the door wide. "Please, come in."

I stepped over the threshold, Nick at my heels, and gave a quick look around. The room was large, furnished with heavy, ornate furniture that included a queen-sized feather bed set between a dark wood head and footboard. A gas-fired fireplace (definitely *not* as ornate as the lobby's) occupied one end of the room, flanked by two Queen Anne chairs. At the other end was a door I presumed led to the bathroom. It was partially open, so as I crossed to the overstuffed chair by the window I took a quick peek. It boasted a whirlpool tub large enough for two, framed with dark-edged wood, a sink and a shower. Only the pair of khaki-colored pants and turquoise blouse tossed in a careless ball underneath the sink disturbed the apple-pie order of the suite. Desiree saw me looking and glided over to the bathroom and pulled the door all the way shut with an apologetic shrug.

I sat down on the edge of the chair. Nick lofted his tubby self onto the window ledge and arranged himself, paws folded in front of him. I saw Desiree's eyes widen as she noticed him for the first time.

"Yours?" She inclined her head slightly.

I nodded. "This is Nick."

Her eyes clouded for a second, and then her expression cleared and the wide smile was back. "Nick Charles. How clever." She pointed at the cat. "He's a handsome fellow, too. I asked because this hotel allows pets, you know, and they let them roam free. Imagine that! One has to be careful. I've already had to evict a parrot and a Maltese today. The little buggers just seem to sneak in whenever I open the door."

I chuckled. "Yes, they're pretty informal with the rules here. I think it's one of the reasons they're so popular with tourists." I crossed my legs at the ankles. "I'm sorry I'm so late."

"No problem. I appreciate your doing me this favor." She crossed over to the other side of the room, pausing before a small cart with a covered silver tray and coffeepot on top. Desiree lifted the lid with a flourish, revealing a large silver bowl filled with an assortment of cut fruit. "Can I get you something? Coffee, fruit?"

"I'm good, thanks."

She poured herself a cup of coffee and I noticed her hand trembled slightly as she added cream and sugar to the china cup. She took a sip, then perched herself on the edge of the bed. "I can't tell you how nice it is to finally meet you in person, Nora. I've heard quite a bit about you through the years."

"Likewise." I smiled at her. "My mother thought very highly of you, Dora—I'm sorry, Desiree."

Her face took on a wistful expression. "Lord, it's been ages since someone called me that! Forty years, to be exact. I legally changed my name to Desiree Sanders when I was twenty-two and started writing. I haven't been Dora Slater for so long it seems like another lifetime. She let out a deep sigh. "A much simpler lifetime, I must say." She took another sip of coffee and set the cup down. "I grew up here and I've got to tell you, when I graduated high school I couldn't get out of here fast enough. It was the best day of my life when I got that scholarship to Kenyon College. I wrote for the *Kenyon Review*, you know. Won an O. Henry Short Story Award in my sophomore year, and interned in my last two. It gave me an excellent look at the publication process, I can tell you that." She sniffed. "It was just one of the many perks I brought to my partnership with that two-bit, good-for-nothing hack who has the nerve to call herself a writer. Hah! Want to know where she went to school? She didn't! Why, if it weren't for me—"

I decided to stop her before the name-calling got any more intense. "Do you have any idea what might have precipitated all this? I mean, it sounds to me as if all this happened rather . . . suddenly."

"You bet your ass it did—oops, sorry. No need to be a potty mouth." She gave her cheek a light slap and then clasped both hands in her lap. "I guess I should begin at the beginning."

I leaned back in the chair. "That seems logical."

"O-kay then, well—" She rose and started to pace back and forth in front of the bed. "I've sensed the past few months that something was the matter. Marlene contributed less than usual to our latest book, and I was pretty irritable, I must admit, having to do all the work and meet all the deadlines by my lonesome. Then, two weeks ago, she springs it on me that she's not going to be able to do any publicity tours for the book, and then she took it a step further. She's not doing 'em, ever again. Well, I was incensed, I can tell you that. As much as I hate to admit it, Marlene's got all the charisma and she's probably the reason Tiffany Blake got so popular. Anyway, then she tells me that 'thirty-some years is enough, don't you think?' And then she up and says *Love's Deepest Desire* is our last book.

"I was enraged. I told her she couldn't just up and do that, and she says right back, 'Oh yes I can. Remember our original agreement? All one partner has to do is notify the other in writing they want it dissolved and voilà! Thirty days later it's a done deal.'" She jumped up, crossed over to a high bureau, and whipped out a piece of paper, which she shoved right under my nose. "See, here it is. Marlene's official notification to me she wants out."

I took the paper and read it. It was indeed a formal letter, to Desiree from Marlene, on embossed stationery no less, requesting their partnership be dissolved. The date of the letter was twenty-nine days ago, which would make it official tomorrow.

"Certainly seems as if she covered all her bases." I handed Desiree back the paper. "It does seem odd, though. You make a lot of money from your books, and you enjoy a certain amount of fame in the literary world. Why would she suddenly want to give all that up?"

Desiree paused, hands on hips. "She's got something else up her sleeve, I just know it. She's hinted at writing a book on her own. Can you believe that? She told me I've been cramping her style, can you believe the nerve? If anything, I've enhanced it. She couldn't string two sentences together when we met, not that she's any great shakes now. The hints have been flying for a while now about striking out on her own, but I never took her seriously. I tried confronting her about what she had in mind, but all she'd say was 'you'll just have to wait and see.' That's trouble, right there. Wait and see with her means a floodgate of trouble is about to open. Oh, she's got something up her sleeve, all right." Desiree paused in her tirade to kneel in front of me and grab both my hands. "You were a top-notch reporter. You know how to get the truth out of people. That's what I need you to do.

"I need you to get the truth out of Marlene. I need you to find out the *real* reason she wants our partnership *finito*."

<u>Three</u>

I paused, unsure of how to answer Desiree. She must have sensed my uneasiness because she laid her hand on my arm and said, "It's simple, really. All you have to do is tell her you want to do a story on her. That hack glory-hound lives for interviews and publicity. She'll eat it right up." I opened my mouth to protest but she held up her hand. "I know, I know. You're not a reporter anymore. Marlene doesn't know that."

"I don't think I'd be comfortable lying to her," I said. "However, I happen to know there's a local reporter who's been tasked with getting an interview with her. I'm sure if we explain the situation . . ."

"No!" Her eyes held a wild light, and she gripped my arm. "No one else. I-I only trust you."

I studied Desiree for a moment, took in her overbright eyes, her flushed cheeks, and I could hear my mother's voice in my head: *For pity's sakes, Nora, the woman's a wreck. Help her.* I released the breath I'd been holding in a gentle whoosh. "I do write articles part-time for an online magazine. I could say that I heard a rumor regarding the breakup and I'd like to know if she'll tell her side of the story."

Desiree clapped her hands together. "Oh, that'll probably work. You are such an angel to do this for me!"

Angel? More like sucker. "I could make some time tomorrow afternoon . . ."

"Tomorrow!" Her face twisted into an expression of mingled annoyance and dismay. "Couldn't you do it today? Maybe . . . now?" At my raised eyebrow she added with a thin smile, "Sorry. Patience was never my strong suit. This just has me so upset . . . I won't be able to rest until I know exactly what that witch is planning."

I hesitated. I hadn't planned on another side trip, but there was something, an undercurrent in Desiree's voice. Panic? Fear? I glanced quickly at my watch and said, "I am done at the shop for the day so I guess I could make a quick trip out there."

"Perfect," Desiree said. Her gaze roved to Nick. "Do you need me to watch your cat while you're gone?"

Nick had left his post on the window ledge and was comfortably arranged near Desiree's chair, flopped on his back, paws in the air. At Desiree's words he closed his eyes, wiggled his legs, and purred loudly before flopping comfortably over on his side. I walked over and prodded him with the toe of my shoe. His head swiveled around, and he let out an injured "merow."

I tossed him a look that said plainly, *Oh, no, you don't. You got me into this.* I gave him another nudge and he lumbered to his feet, shook himself, and then pranced over to the door, tail held high.

I gave Desiree a grin. "Not necessary. He'll come with me."

• • •

The old Porter house was in actuality a bungalow remodeled into a modest two-story with a compact front yard planted with dark green ivy instead of the more common green grass. Pink, mauve and lavender impatiens bloomed in bright ceramic pots on either side of the door, which was painted a dark purple, almost black. A large rattan welcome mat with a grinning dog on it proclaimed "Welcome" in faded black letters. I wondered what on earth had ever possessed a woman like Marlene McCambridge to rent such a monstrosity of a house, and then decided that possibly that was the reason.

If she was looking for anonymity, what better place? No one would expect a famous author like her to reside in a place like this in a million years. No, wait . . . make that two million.

It was *that* bad.

I turned off the car, and eyed Nick, who was sitting up straight in the passenger seat, his gaze trained on the house. "This is a fine kettle of fish," I murmured.

At the word *fish* Nick's ears flicked forward.

"I knew that would get your attention. No treats for you until we figure out how we're going to broach the partnership topic to Marlene." I sighed. "Too bad she didn't go for letting Jenks in on this. We could have killed two birds with one stone."

At mention of Jenks's name, Nick let out a soft *grr* that turned into a deep, rumbling purr at the word *birds*.

We exited the car and walked up the path to the house and up the short flight of steps to the front door. I rang the bell and stood, my arms folded across my chest. Nick hefted himself up to the porch railing, where he sat, tail extended behind him. Directly across the street stood a large brown stucco house, set back from the road. Farther down was a smaller, light pink bungalow, a twin no doubt of this one before its renovation, all but its sloping roof obscured by a thick patch of trees. I started to turn away, then stopped, certain I'd seen a curtain move ever so slightly in one of the brown stucco house's second-floor windows. Hmm, I'd have to take back that thought about nosy neighbors. Still, what could they see? The house was a good seventy, eighty yards away, unless they had a pair of binoculars at the ready. I waited a few minutes, but the movement wasn't repeated.

"Guess my imagination's on overdrive again," I murmured. I squared my shoulders and pressed the bell beside the doorframe.

I could hear the chimes echo eerily through the house, but no one came to the door. Nick suddenly let out a sharp meow. Next thing I knew, he'd hopped down from the railing and started to trot around the house. I hesitated only briefly and then hurried after him. Around the side of the house was a wall comprised of glass doors. Nick paused before it, his tail sticking straight out in back of him. I walked over to the doors and saw that one was slightly ajar. Nick turned and looked at me expectantly.

"Oh, no." I shook my head. "That's breaking and entering, buddy. We can't just barge in here."

Nick turned his back on me, and before I could do more than blink, he'd miraculously managed to squeeze his plump body through the opening.

"Great," I muttered. Well, I couldn't just abandon him. I walked over to the door and gave it a tentative push. It swung back, and I stepped inside.

The house was deceptive. It was definitely larger than it appeared, which might have been part of its charm and could account for Marlene's decision to acquire the rental. As I moved cautiously around, poking my head into rooms filled with antique trappings and silk-covered sofas definitely too fragile to sit on, I realized why most people had been loath to rent it. Who wanted to live in a museum? I kept on meandering, calling out Marlene's name, but only a thick silence answered me.

Nick was sitting in front of the circular staircase, tail wrapped around his paws. "Come on," I said. "She's not here. We'll come back another time."

"Er-owl!"

With that, he uncurled his tail and scooted up the staircase. At the top landing he paused and looked back at me as if to say: *What's keeping you, human?*

"I should leave you here," I muttered, but my niggling sense of curiosity won out over my better judgment and I climbed the staircase, the sound of my heels muffled by the expensive carpeting that covered the stairs. A wide hallway extended itself on either side of me, and no sign of my tubby tuxedo. "Nick," I hissed. "Where are you, you devil?"

No response, so I moved over toward the right side and opened the first door, which appeared to be a bedroom, and a holy mess. The bedclothes had been stripped from the massive canopied king-sized bed and thrown in a ball in its center. Drawers were pulled out of the cherrywood highboy and dresser and hung limply, their contents strewn helter-skelter around the room. A high-backed chair was overturned in the middle of the floor, and the closet door was half open. I could see dresses hanging half off hangers, and a half-open suitcase was propped up against the interior.

"Oh my God," I cried. It certainly looked as if someone had been searching for something. A thief, perhaps? A chill ran down my spine at my next thought: Could he still be here? Had Marlene possibly caught him in the act? I stepped back into the hallway, uncertain what my next move should be.

"Ar-owl."

The cry came from the left, so I moved in that direction. I saw Nick, squatting before a door at the end of the hallway; he looked up, saw me, and ducked inside. I hurried down the hall and peered into the darkened room. It was set up as an office, boasting a small cherrywood desk, file cabinet, and a laptop square in the desk's center. "Nick," I hissed. "Where are you?"

"Er-rup."

"I hear you, Nick, but I can't see you. This room is too dark to spot a cat that's mostly black."

I felt along the wall and finally my fingers touched a light switch. I flicked it on, illuminating a table lamp that cast a rosy glow through the room—and highlighted the colorless face of the woman slumped on the floor just to the left of the desk. I sucked in my breath.

Even though I'd never met her in person, I'd seen enough pictures on the inside covers of her books to know the woman framed in the circle of dim light was Marlene McCambridge, and she looked to be stone-cold dead.

Four

I made my way carefully over to the body. I took in its waxy pallor, the face frozen in a rictus of surprise, and the large red stain that spread across the front of the expensive silk blouse onto the carpet. Oh, yeah, she was dead all right. Still, I knelt down and touched the side of her neck with two fingers just to be sure. I winced; the flesh was cold and hard to the touch, and I couldn't feel the barest thrum of a heartbeat.

Behind me, Nick let out a sharp yowl.

She'd been dead a while. I was no expert, but I was betting twelve hours, maybe more. I glanced over at Nick, who'd hopped up on the desk. "We'd better notify the police."

One ear twitched, the only sign he'd heard me. He padded over to the laptop and leaned over, his paw touching the partially opened middle drawer. He extended his nails and tapped at the wood. "Oowww."

"What did you find?"

I moved over to take a look. Nestled in the drawer was what looked like an appointment book. I could see it was open to yesterday's date. There were two names scrawled there, but I couldn't make them out. I whipped a Kleenex out of my pocket and opened the drawer all the way to get a better look. I still couldn't tell who the names were, so I turned the page to today's date. Next to ten a.m. was a slightly smudged set of initials. *DS*, for Desiree, no doubt. Five p.m. had *Morley Carruthers* printed in neat letters. I glanced at my watch, thinking it wouldn't be long before Morley showed up. I pulled my phone out of my pocket and flipped it into camera mode, then snapped pictures of both pages. Then I carefully pushed the drawer in, being careful to leave it open about a quarter inch, as it had been.

Nick stared at me with wide eyes. "Don't give me that look," I said. "Technically, it's not disturbing evidence. Everything's still in the same place. All I did was open the drawer a bit." I waved the Kleenex in the air. "See, no extra prints."

Nick gave a yodel of approval.

I examined the photos on my camera. They'd come out a bit dark but would have to do. I slid the phone back into my pocket and noticed Nick had moved his rotund body back onto the floor and was sniffing alongside the body. As I put out my hand to shoo him away, I heard a loud pounding on the front door, followed by the clanging of chimes as someone with a heavy finger pressed on the doorbell. This was rapidly followed by a gruff voice calling out, "Police. Open up."

Good grief. What were the police doing here?

I took the stairs two at a time, Nick at my heels, reached the bottom landing, and flung the front door open. My jaw dropped as I met the startled gaze of the person on the other side.

"What are *you* doing here?" Leroy Samms and I both chorused.

I took a step backward and Samms pushed past me into the foyer. "Responding to an anonymous 911 call. The person said they saw a suspicious character lurking around here." He cocked his brow at me, intimating he thought he knew just who that suspicious person was.

I drew myself up to my full height. Even so, I still fell a bit short of Samms's impressive six-three frame. "Sorry to disappoint you, but I came in through the door." I inclined my head toward the sliding glass door, visible through the parlor door. "It was open. I did ring the bell first, but no one answered." I paused. "I was going to call 911 myself. I wanted to report the dead body." I said the last in a calm tone I knew would infuriate him.

I wasn't disappointed. Samms froze in his tracks. Slowly, very slowly, he turned around to face me.

"What!"

"I wanted to report the dead body," I repeated. "It's proper procedure, correct? I know what a stickler you are for procedure."

"A dead body." He sucked in a sharp breath. "And here I thought you found your quota for the year."

I resisted the impulse to stick my tongue out at him. "Sorry, I guess I've still got a few to go."

His lips set in a grim line and then his gaze fell upon Nick. "I see your body-sniffing cat is here, too. I should have expected that." He shifted his gaze to me. "Where is it?"

I ignored his barb about Nick, but I was hard-pressed to stifle a grin as a soft growl reached my ears. "Upstairs. End of the hall."

He trudged up the stairs. After a second I followed, Nick close behind me. Samms went into the office and I watched from the doorway as he knelt down beside Marlene, put his fingers to her neck, as I'd done only scant moments before. He straightened, whipped out his cell phone, and I heard him say, "I need backup. Porter house. 10-45D. Pronto."

He pocketed his phone, turned and caught my eye. "You found her like this?"

"I've already said yes."

"I suppose you know the identity of the corpse, too?"

I squared my shoulders and said with a curl of my lip, "As a matter of fact, I do. Marlene McCambridge. She's an author." I paused. "A romance author."

He grunted softly and pulled a notebook from his pocket. "Yeah. Tiffany Blake, right? Pretty racy stuff." He laughed outright at my raised eyebrows. "What! I don't live in a cave, you know. Not that I'm a fan," he added quickly, "but I may have glanced at a chapter or two somewhere along the line. What's so funny?"

I chuckled. "Sorry. It's just I can't picture you as a fan of romance novels."

His lips twitched upward. "I didn't say that I was, or that it was my book I might have glanced at." He ducked his head and started to flip through his notebook. "Wonder why such a celebrity would choose to stay here, in an out-of-the-way rental property and not a luxury suite at the Hilton?"

"Maybe she needed some R&R, or some alone time. She might have wanted to go somewhere, you know, where nobody knew her or would think to look for her."

"Someone found her," he said dryly.

"The bedroom's a mess," I volunteered. "Looks as if someone might have been hunting for something. Jewelry, maybe, or cash."

"Robbery?"

"Maybe." I glanced around the room. "I'm no expert, of course, but it appears the shot was fired at close range, which could be an indication she knew her assailant."

He made a motion of doffing his cap. "Thank you, Dr. Watson. I'll be sure to take your observations under advisement in my investigation." He scribbled something in his notebook, snapped it shut. "So. You never answered my original question. What are you doing here?"

"What do you think? I came to see Ms. McCambridge."

"I figured that. Why?"

I swallowed. I certainly wasn't going to say anything about Desiree, or my mission of mercy concerning their partnership dissolution, at least not until I'd spoken with her. I decided playing it cool was my only option. "Like you, I was in the neighborhood."

The annoyed look morphed into a full-out glare.

"Fine." I held up both hands in a gesture of surrender and said the first thing that popped into my head. "I came out here to try and get an exclusive interview."

"An interview? Really?" He rubbed his forehead with the back of his hand. "Since when does *Noir* publish interviews from schlocky romance authors?"

Schlocky. Hm. I glanced quickly at the corpse, half expecting Marlene to rise up and smite Samms for that remark. "It's not for *Noir*," I said quickly. "I was going to freelance it. Marlene was quite a hot ticket in certain literary circles. I'm sure there are plenty of romance magazines, traditional and online, who would jump for an in-depth interview from half of Tiffany Blake. The pay's pretty good, and I could use the extra cash. I've been thinking of buying a smoothie machine."

"Well, that certainly sounds logical." He leaned in a bit closer to me and leaned over so his lips were level with my ear. "But I'm not buying it."

"Too bad, because it's the truth."

"No, it's not. I can tell. You do a funny thing with your face when you lie."

"I do not!" I cried, and my hands flew instinctively to my face. "What funny thing?"

"Your nose kind of squinches up, and your eyes get really, really wide and bright."

"They do not."

"Do too." He aimed an accusing finger at my nose. "You did it in college, and you're doing it now."

Darn, where was a mirror when I needed it! I rubbed at my nose, then scrubbed the back of my hand across my face. "Don't be silly. I'm just tired. It was a very busy afternoon at Hot Bread."

"So I heard. That new television might end up being more of a nuisance than a magnet for new business."

My eyebrows drew together. "How on earth did you hear about that? Wait, don't tell me. Did you talk to Lacey?"

He ignored my question and made a shooing motion with his hands. "It's time for you to fly away, little bird. Take Buster here and go back to Hot Bread, where you belong."

Nick looked at Samms and let out a low growl.

"What's with him?" Samms asked.

"For one thing, his name is Nick. For another, I don't think he likes you," I said.

"Ah." Samms looked from Nick to me. "Something the two of you have in common, eh? Now run along. I can't have the two of you contaminating the area any more than you already have." His hand cupped my elbow and started to push me toward the door, but I dug in my heels.

"One second. Why are you *here?*"

"I told you. Someone called in an anonymous tip. I heard the 10-66 come over the radio—that's suspicious person, by the way—and since I was in the area I said I'd check it out. Little did I dream it would turn into a murder investigation with the Queen of Finding Dead Bodies right in the thick of it. Take my advice, Red. Get yourself another hobby."

Ignoring his sarcasm, I jerked my hand from his arm and waved it impatiently. "I don't need another hobby. And you're missing my point. Why are *you* answering police calls? You're FBI now, aren't you? Do they investigate local crime now? I knew the Cruz PD was shorthanded, but—"

He cut me off with an impatient gesture. "That's what I like about you, Red. The way you jump to conclusions. You take a button and you don't just sew a vest around it. You go for the whole dress."

My redhead temper started to flare, but luckily for Samms, the jangling of the doorbell cut off further conversation. We went downstairs in stony silence, and Samms opened the front door to admit two more policemen. I knew both of them. One was David Dougherty, who I knew was also studying law in his spare time, and the other was Stephen Kellett. Kellett had been a staple on the Cruz force for years. Both men's eyes widened a bit at seeing me, and then Kellett looked at Samms.

"Where's the body?"

"Upstairs. Did you call the coroner?"

"Yep," Kellett nodded. "He's on his way."

"See if you can pull any prints out of the office and the upstairs bedroom, for starters." He flicked his thumb at me. "Okay, Nora, thank you for your cooperation. You're done here."

"Are you sure you don't need me to hang around? I might be of some help."

"Yes, your crime scene experience is invaluable but I've got this." He pointed again toward the front door. "I might have some more questions for you later."

"Fine. *I* have nothing to hide. You know where to reach me."

"Indeed I do. Oh, and not a word to anyone. I don't want even a

whisper of this getting out until I'm ready to make an announcement."
He rubbed at his chin. "You know how the media gets, especially when
a celebrity's involved."

I really couldn't take offense at that, because I had once been a part
of that very media, and I did know how they could sensationalize a
story. "You can trust my discretion. Mum's the word. By the way, a
reporter from the *Cruz Sun* might show up here. Paul Jenkins. His editor
wanted him to do a story on Marlene."

Samms gave me a brief nod. "Thanks for the heads-up." He made a
shooing motion with his hand. "Run along now."

"Oh, and if you find you need some help with the investigation,
don't hesitate to call—"

He swung the door shut right in my face.

"I guess he doesn't want my help," I blustered. "Some nerve, right,
Nick?"

I looked down at the cat. Nick gave a sharp yowl and raised one paw.
I could see he had something caught on his nails.

"What's that you've got?" I reached down and disengaged the object,
held it up. It was a strand of hair, dark blonde in color. I slid Nick a
glance. "Where'd you get this, Nick? Not the crime scene, I hope?"

If a cat could look innocent, Nick had mastered the art. He widened
his eyes, and his pink tongue darted out, licked at his lips.

"Well." I turned the hair over in my hand, then slid it into my
pocket. "Since I can't prove just where you got it, there's no use telling
Samms about it. He'd only make fun of us anyway." I looked again at
Nick, who'd turned away from me and now had his gaze fixed on the
stucco house across the street. I followed his gaze and saw the curtain on
the second floor move back, very slightly, as if someone had been
peering around the edge.

So I hadn't imagined seeing movement over there earlier. More than
that, I had a pretty good idea who'd called 911. Either they had vision
like a cat or a good pair of binoculars. And if they'd seen me, who
knows what else they might have noticed?

Nick rubbed against my ankles. "What do you think, Nick? Worth looking into?"

His yowl of assent was all the encouragement I needed.

"Right on. Maybe we'll get lucky and find out just who phoned in that anonymous tip."

Five

We hurried across the street and up the short flight of steps to the front door of the stone and stucco house. Like most homes built in the French Country style, the house had a square, symmetrical shape with windows balanced on either side of the entrance and a steep-hipped roof. The front door was a smooth mahogany, with a stained glass mosaic inlay. I pressed the intricately carved doorbell, and instead of the usual *ding dong* or *brrring* heard instead several different animal sounds. I recognized a duck, a loon and a lion reverberate through the building. Well, that was different. I waited a few minutes, then pressed the bell again. This time I heard a dove cooing, as well as the sounds of a sheep and even the snort of a pig. Any minute now I expected to hear the strains of "Old Macdonald had a Farm."

"Hello," I called loudly. "Anyone home?"

Still no answer. Either their hearing wasn't as good as their vision or they wanted to stay under the radar. I glanced at my watch. Nearly five o'clock. I pulled my phone out of my pocket and flicked it on. Desiree's number was there, all right, but she hadn't left any messages. No doubt she'd worked herself into a nervous snit by now, a snit that would no doubt get worse once I delivered my news. I slid the phone back into my pocket and motioned to Nick, who squatted at my feet. "Come on, Nick. Whoever's in there apparently doesn't want company. We'll come back another time."

Nick looked up, almost seemed to shrug, and then turned and started down the steps. When I opened the door of the SUV he hopped right onto the passenger seat, turned around twice, and then curled up in a tight ball, paws tucked in, head resting gently against the leather seat. A second later I heard the sound of light snoring.

Yes, I had to agree. Detective work could be very tiring. Too bad not all of us had the luxury of taking a catnap.

I started the car and then felt in my pocket and pulled out the strand of hair. Nope, definitely not the same shade as Marlene's. Her hair had been dyed a brassy blonde. This was a much darker shade, more like Desiree's.

I slid the hair back into my pocket and put the car into Drive. As I pulled away, I glanced in my rearview mirror and saw the upstairs curtain of the stucco house was pulled back about a half inch. I slammed on my brakes, and the curtain slid back into place.

Nick sat up and blinked twice, annoyed at being jostled out of his catnap. He reared up, put both paws on the window and yowled. Loudly.

"Sorry to disturb you, pal. I was performing a little experiment. We'll have to do a little research on just who might be staying there when we get home."

I slowed to a crawl as I approached the stop sign on the corner just as an expensive tan colored Cadillac El Dorado whipped around the other side and sped down the road, coming to an abrupt stop in front of the Porter house. I pulled over to the curb, slid the car into Park and craned my neck out the window. A thin, stoop-shouldered man dressed in a neatly pressed suit exited the car, a bulging briefcase clutched in one hand. I was betting this was Morley Carruthers, Esquire, no doubt. He started up the drive and then paused, his gaze riveted on the police car parked there.

I turned my head toward the stucco house and saw the curtains on the second floor part again for a fraction of a second, then fall back into place.

I put the car back into Drive and turned the corner. Yep, that house and its tenant definitely merited a return visit.

• • •

Desiree listened wide-eyed as I recounted the afternoon's events. When I finished, she sat quietly for a few moments, hands folded in her lap, eyes cast downward, examining the pattern in the rug. "Murdered," she finally murmured. "Really?"

I regarded her through slitted eyes. For someone who'd just learned her partner of over twenty years had been murdered, she seemed unusually calm. I'd expected some show of emotion. Crying hysterically, throwing things, maybe even a little foot pounding, but . . . nothing. She must have sensed my unease because she put a hand dramatically to her forehead and leaned back in the chair. "I'm sorry. I must be in shock. It's been quite a week."

Nick looked up at me, his eyes going from my face over to Desiree's and then back to mine. He reared his head back and gave an emphatic "meow." I looked at him and nodded. "My thoughts exactly, Nick." I turned to Desiree, folded my arms across my chest. "You're a much better writer than you are an actress."

Her eyes widened and her tongue made little clucking sounds. "Nora, whatever do you mean?"

"I can get a sense of when someone's not being absolutely truthful with me, like you are right now." I rose and took a step toward her. "You knew Marlene was dead when you asked me to go out there, didn't you?"

She looked away, and one hand fiddled with the chain around her neck, twisting it around her fingers. She was spared from answering by a preemptory rap on the door. "Cleaning," came a loud voice.

Desiree hurried to the door and opened it. A freckle-faced bellboy thrust what appeared to be a pair of light-colored slacks and a blue blouse at her. "We managed to get them done in an hour. ma'am. No problem." He smiled.

Desiree stood uncertainly, holding the cleaning in her hand. I stepped forward for a closer look. The freshly laundered clothes looked a lot like the ones I'd seen bundled under the sink earlier. Desiree caught me looking and thrust the clothes to the side, looking aimlessly around the room. "Dear me. I seem to have misplaced my purse. Nora, would you mind?"

I pulled out my wallet and pressed a five-dollar bill into the boy's hand. He tipped his cap and strutted off down the hall. I shut the door and looked over my shoulder, but by then Desiree had ditched the clothes and had returned to the chair. I walked over and stood, my hands on my hips.

"You didn't answer my question, Desiree."

Her head jerked up and her gaze bored into mine. "Yes," she whispered, so low I had to strain to hear it. "Yes, I did."

I'd half expected her to deny it, so I took a step backward. "Why did you do that? Why would you put me in a position like that?"

"I don't know. I panicked, I guess." She removed her hands from the chair arms and started to twist them in her lap. "I did go out there, but I didn't kill her, you have to believe me. She was dead when I got there."

Now she did start to cry, very softly. Even Nick was moved. He went over, plopped his plump body down and rubbed his head against her ankles. She stroked him absently as I plucked a Kleenex from a box on the nightstand and handed it to her. She took it, blew her nose. I sat back down on the edge of the bed. "Desiree, what were you wearing when you went to see Marlene?"

She raised her tear-stained face to mine. "What?"

I nodded toward the closet. "I couldn't help but notice your recently cleaned clothes. When I first came in, the bathroom door was ajar and I saw a pair of slacks and blouse just like those thrown under the sink. Did you get them cleaned because Marlene's blood was on them?"

She turned away from me. "Yes," she mumbled.

Oy. Sending bloody clothes down to the inn cleaner was not the best idea in the world. "Can you tell me what happened?"

"Sure." She blew her nose again. "Marlene called me yesterday, said she was dissolving the partnership according to the terms of our agreement, but she'd appreciate it if I'd come out around ten or ten thirty to sign paperwork. It was just a formality, but it would make things easier for *her*." Desiree sniffed. "I told her she could rot in hell before I'd make anything easier for her, and she just laughed at me.

"We hung up and I sat here, stewing. I confess, I'd also had a bit to drink. It made me a bit bolder than I'd usually be. I decided I wasn't going to wait, I was going to confront that witch right then and there.

"I got in my rental car and drove out there. It was late. Maybe one, two in the morning? The street was dark and deserted when I approached. I parked my car up the block and walked back and right up to the front door. I rang the bell, and there was no answer. I walked around to the side of the house, and that sliding door was wide open, which I thought odd. Marlene's always a stickler about making sure everything's locked, like she thought somebody would break in and drag her off somewhere. Anyway, it was open, so I went in. The house was dark, still as a tomb. I called her name several times, and I thought I heard a floorboard creak above me, so I found the staircase and went upstairs. I saw the light on in her office . . ."

"The light was on?" I interrupted again. "Not off?"

Desiree shook her head. "It was on. I remember that distinctly, because I stumbled over a flashlight on the rug and wondered what the heck it was doing there when the light was on. I bent to pick it up, and that's when I saw her, lying on the floor." Her lower lip started to tremble and she put both hands up over her face. "I could tell she'd been shot. The front of her blouse was all red. And her eyes, oh, I'll never forget them! Wide, glassy, sightless. Ooh." She hiccupped and blew her nose again. "I knelt down and I turned her on her side, and then back again. I saw I'd gotten some of her blood on my hands. Not a lot, but I didn't want to touch anything with bloody hands, so I wiped it off on my clothes."

She started to cry again, and in spite of the fact she'd acted foolishly, I felt a wave of pity for her. "You're going to have to pull yourself together. The police are probably going to want to question you, particularly when they realize you paid a nocturnal visit in advance of your scheduled appointment."

Her head snapped up, and she blinked, swiping at her wet cheeks with the back of one hand. "Why? Do you think they know I was there? They couldn't! No one saw me."

I was tempted to tell her about my experience with the house across the way but didn't want to further upset her. Instead I rubbed her back in a comforting circular motion. "You didn't want to touch anything with bloody fingers, but you'd already touched the sliding door, the stair rail, the office door?" At her nod I said gently, "So when they dust for prints . . ."

A small cry like that of a wounded animal escaped her lips. "Drat. I forgot about that. But how would they know I was there in the first place?"

"Her appointment book was in the drawer. Your initials were in it. If I found it, you can bet they will too." I let out a breath. "There's more. Carruthers was just arriving when I left. No doubt he's already told the police about the partnership termination. My advice to you is not to hold anything back. It'll only come back to bite you."

She slumped down lower in the chair. "I should have looked at that book and scratched my name out when I had the chance."

I shook my head. "It's a good thing you didn't. Tampering with evidence is a crime, which the U.S. government takes very seriously. A person convicted of evidence tampering under federal law could face a prison sentence of twenty years, a fine, or both."

Desiree's eyes still gleamed with unshed tears. "But don't they have to prove that you did so willingly? Doesn't a prosecutor have to prove the person knew the item with which they allegedly tampered was evidence in an ongoing investigation?"

"That's true," I admitted, "but—"

"He'd also have to prove," Desiree went on, "that the person charged with evidence tampering intended to interfere in the investigation when the alleged evidence was destroyed. So, if it was done accidentally, then no crime was committed." Desiree spread her hands wide, palms up. "It was just an unfortunate accident."

"That's also true," I admitted. I gave her a sharp look. "I didn't realize you knew so much about the law."

A sly smile teased the corners of her lips. "The character in our last book was a law student. You'd be surprised at the wealth of legal information one can find on the Internet. Who knows, someday maybe attorneys will be obsolete."

I laid my hand on her arm. "You said she was dead when you got there. If you're telling the truth then you've got nothing to worry about." I thought about the strand of hair in my pocket, the one so close to Desiree's own shade. "Did the two of you fight, or have any physical contact?"

She tossed me a puzzled glance. "We had words, but get physical? You mean slap or something? Lord, no. When Marlene and I fought, we fought with words, barbs."

She sounded sincere, and yet . . . I studied her a minute, taking in the flushed face, the shallow breathing. "You aren't hiding anything, right? You've told me everything?"

She averted her gaze downward and mumbled, "Yes."

Oh, no, I thought as my gut twisted. *I knew it. She's lying.*

What else is she hiding?

Six

I tamped down my reservations, pulled out my phone and put it in camera mode. I called up the picture I'd taken of Marlene's appointment book and showed it to Desiree. "Those are names of other people Marlene had appointments scheduled with. Are any of them familiar to you?"

Desiree took the phone and squinted at the image. "It's not a very clear picture." She pointed with the edge of her nail at the first name. "I recognize Morley Carruthers but . . ." She squinted at the other names.

I leaned over to peer at the screen. "That one the day before at ten a.m. Looks like Sheila . . . Susan, no . . . Scarlett something?"

"Oh, it must be Scarlett Vandevere. She writes the Shelby Daye romance series. We met her at a RomCon five years ago."

"RomCon?"

"Romance convention. Scarlett had just gotten her first book contract, and Marlene took her under her wing." Desiree sniffed. "It's a wonder Scarlett became a best-selling author after that, because everything Marlene could have possibly taught her would fit on the head of a pin."

"Is Scarlett from around here?"

"Pebble Beach, I think. She's old money. That was her selling point, you know. Rich girl makes good career-wise. Now this next name . . ." Desiree held the phone at an angle and squinted. "Dudley? Damon? Oh, wait, I know. It's Dooley. Dooley Franks." Desiree's lips twitched. "Ever hear of Sable St. John?"

I let out a low whistle. "Who hasn't? She wrote that soft-porn book that sold almost a million copies, right?"

"Yep. Only Sable isn't a she."

My eyes widened. "You mean . . ."

"Yep." She tapped the screen with one long nail. "Hard to believe a guy could write so . . . eloquently about sex, isn't it? And seeing Dooley Franks on the cover would hardly have the same impact."

"Could that have been what Marlene was holding over his head? That Sable St. John is actually a man?"

"It might have been, if he and his publisher hadn't revealed that little fact two months ago at Book Expo America. Apparently people found it fascinating America's beloved smut author was a man. His sales doubled. So it's got to be something else."

"Does he live around here too?"

Desiree shook her head. "Nope. He still lives in his family home in Indiana. He raised chickens before he hit it big, can you believe it? He wrote that first book in his spare time and hit it big. His first convention Marlene latched right on to him. She introduced him to his agent, one of the biggest scumbags around—oh, wait!" She snapped her fingers. "I did read somewhere he was making a series of appearances here on the West Coast, to publicize his new book. If I'm not mistaken, this week and next he's in Carmel and Monterey."

Both of which were minutes away from Cruz, as was Pebble Beach. "So it's likely these were in-person meetings. You have no idea why she'd have wanted to meet with them?"

Desiree's spine went ramrod straight, and once again her gaze dropped to study the rug. "No," she mumbled. "None."

I didn't want to flat out accuse her of lying, but it was all I could do to keep from grabbing her by the shoulders and shaking her until those capped teeth rattled. I brushed a stray lock of hair out of my eyes and stood up.

"Okay, then. I'm going to go back home and see if I can worm anything out of the man in charge of the investigation, and then I'm going to check out the whereabouts of Scarlett and Dooley. My advice to you is to lay low. Don't speak to anyone. If the police get in touch with you, don't refuse them, but you might want to have a lawyer present, as a cautionary measure."

"I don't have a lawyer right now. Could you possibly recommend someone?"

My mind instantly flew to the young attorney who'd represented my sister when she'd been accused of murder. I nodded. "Yes, I could. His name is Peter Dobbs. He practices in Saint Leo, which isn't far from here. If you'd like, I could give him a call and explain the situation. If he can't help out, I'm sure he can recommend someone."

"Would you? That would certainly be a load off my mind." Desiree let out a giant sigh, then suddenly swept me into her arms and crushed me against her ample bosom. "Thank you, Nora. Your mother was right. You are cool and competent in a crisis. I couldn't ask for a better person on my side."

I nodded. Actually, I had another reason for wanting to enlist Peter's help. The young man had a winning way about him, an easy manner that made people want to confide in him. Lord knew he'd managed to break through my sister's barricade, and not many people could claim that honor. Maybe he could get Desiree to admit whatever it was she was hiding. At any rate, it was worth a try.

I rose, slung my purse over my shoulder. "Try to get some rest in the meantime," I advised Desiree. I glanced around, looking for Nick, and spied him by the bathroom door. When I took a step toward him, he ducked inside. I threw Desiree an apologetic look and hurried after him. "Nick, come on. No exploring. We have to go."

"Merow."

He was seated atop the toilet, his paw jabbing at an overhead shelf. I looked and saw a brush and comb lying there. The brush was clean, but there were a few stray hairs clinging to the comb. I plucked them out, wrapped them in a square of toilet paper, and slipped them into my pocket. "Good work, Nick," I whispered.

If any cat could manage a shit-eating grin, it was him.

• • •

Back in the SUV, I dialed Peter's number and got his voice mail. I left a message asking him to call me regarding a possible case and drove back into town, where I pulled up in front of our local bar and grill. The

Poker Face was owned and operated by my former high school sweetheart, Lance Reynolds, and his brother Phil. Lance had, at one time, aspired to a nine-to-five job but he'd decided he wasn't cut out for that life at around the same time his brother decided he wasn't cut out to be an accountant. Since Lance liked to mix drinks and his brother loved to, well, drink, it seemed a match made in heaven. Lance and his brother had made a lot of improvements since buying the bar a dozen years ago from its former owner. Petey's Bar and Grill had once been a thriving business, but thanks to mismanagement on the part of the owner, who'd hit on some hard times, they were able to get it at a greatly reduced price. Renaming it the Poker Face had been Phil's idea. What can I say? He loves Lady Gaga.

The bar was housed in a narrow, high-ceilinged building on Main Street, not far from Poppies, the flower shop owned by Chantal and her brother Remy. The centerpiece of the establishment was the polished wooden bar that ran long and deep along one entire wall. Directly across from the bar was a row of booths that had been newly upholstered. Two rows of tables ran parallel to the big plate-glass window that read *The Poker Face*, etched in gold lettering. A copy of their limited menu was also on display in the window. Lance knew he couldn't compete with me, or any other restaurant in town for that matter, and didn't even try. His menu consisted of a hamburger, a cheeseburger, a club sandwich, fries and potato skins—and whatever sludge his cook Jose passed off as coffee that week. But the real attraction was the drinks Lance took such care in making. If I were the Michelangelo of sandwiches, he was the Raphael of mixology.

Opening the door, Nick and I slid inside the bar. Happy hour had just begun, and the bar was knee-deep with customers. I caught a glimpse of Lance behind the bar, serving a draft to Ed Levey, the local dentist. Ed raised his mug in greeting as I slid onto an empty stool at the far end. I slapped a ten down on the rich mahogany surface and crooked a finger. "Service, please."

Lance's light brown head swiveled in my direction and his eyes lit up as he recognized me. "Well, well." He grinned, slinging a towel over one broad shoulder as he approached. "Look who's paying me a visit! I hear you got a TV in your store now." He flicked a finger toward the one over the bar, tuned to a popular sports channel. "How's that workin' out?"

"News travels fast, huh. It's too soon to tell, but . . . let's just say I still have the receipt."

Lance chuckled. "I can imagine. So what'll it be? The usual Michelob Light on tap? Or are you in an adventurous mood to try Jose's hazelnut caramel coffee?"

"I could never be that adventurous," I said, wrinkling my nose. "I'll pass on both. Right now I could do with a whiskey. After the day I've had, I'm in the mood to get a bit tipsy."

Lance's eyebrows rose, but he made no comment. "Tipsy, eh? Okay, what's your pleasure? Jim Beam? Knob Creek? Old Crow?"

"You're the pro bartender. Whichever will give me the best buzz."

"Jim Beam it is." He poured two fingers of the pale liquid into a glass and handed it to me. I downed it in one gulp, and then started to cough. Lance slapped me on the back . . . hard . . . but it didn't stop. Then my eyes started to tear.

"Water," I finally managed to get out.

He handed me a tall glass filled with ice water, and when I'd downed that, put his hands on his hips and clucked his tongue. "Now do you want that Michelob Light?"

I brushed a remaining tear from the corner of one eye, clasped my hands in front of me and tried to look humble. "Yes, please."

"You should know better. You can't drink the hard stuff. Neither can your sister. By the way, how is Lacey?"

"Doing good. The TV was her idea."

"Wow, and you listened to her?" He slung the rag over one shoulder. "She still studying at that art school?"

"Yep. She'll be graduating soon, and then we'll see what happens with her career. Right now she's working part-time for the St. Leo police as a sketch artist, courtesy of Samms. Whether or not she'll want to continue is anyone's guess." I wrapped my hands around the frosty mug and took a sip, then licked the white foam from my upper lip. "I'm surprised you still care."

Now his eyebrow shot all the way up. "What does that mean?"

"Nothing." I shrugged. "It's just that a few weeks ago, you were all gaga over Alexa Martin."

"Was not."

"Was too."

He laughed. "Well, okay, but in my defense, Alexa also seemed to be just a little gaga over me too." He swiped at a ring on the counter with the edge of the towel. "She said she'd give me a call when she and Violet got back from London. She, ah, wants to get together and do something."

I arched a brow. "Something? That sounds . . . promising."

"It could be." He stopped wiping down the counter to pin me with his gaze. "Look, I know that my interest in Lacey has never really been reciprocated. Maybe I'm tired of carrying this torch when there are other fish in the sea, and interested fish at that. Besides, you're a fine one to talk, juggling feelings for two men yourself."

Was there anyone in Cruz who *didn't* want to weigh in on my love life? I made a face at him and took another sip of beer so I didn't have to answer. At my feet, Nick let out a plaintive meow.

Lance peered over the edge of the bar. "Hey, little fellow, I didn't see you there. Thirsty?"

Nick let his tongue hang out and panted slightly. Can you say *ham*?

"Want a nice bowl of water? Or maybe some milk?"

The tongue went back in his mouth, and Nick snapped to attention. He looked straight at Lance and reared up on his haunches, his forepaws extended. "Er-ewl. Ar-owl."

"You said the magic *m*-word." I waggled my finger at Lance. "Now you've got to follow through."

"Not a problem. Oh, and by the way," Lance said, pointing toward the rear of the bar, "there's two friends of yours over there you might want to say hello to."

I looked in the direction he'd pointed out and saw Louis Blondell and Ollie Sampson crowded into a back booth. As Nick trotted happily after Lance toward the kitchen, I picked up my beer and wended my way toward their booth. They both looked up as I approached. "Well, well, Nora Charles," said Louis. "Fancy meeting you here."

I grinned. "I might say the same." I nodded at the empty space next to Louis. "Mind if I join you?"

"Not at all." Louis Blondell runs *Noir*, the online true crime magazine for which I freelance. He was a studious type of guy, a self-proclaimed computer geek (and not a bad hacker, either, as he proved on one occasion). Louis was fortyish, overweight and balding. The little hair he had left was a light blond, as was the stunted growth of hair he was sporting above his upper lip. I rubbed the top of my own lip and grinned at him.

"New look?"

"I heard somewhere women go wild for men with mustaches." Louis had recently started to foray into the world of online dating, and so far each of the dozen or so dates he'd had ended in disaster. He gave me a wry look. "Don't believe it."

I turned my attention to the other occupant of the booth. Oliver J. Sampson, or Ollie, as he prefers to be called, is a hulk of a man in his early fifties. Six-three and well over two hundred twenty pounds, he's a man of color, with springy gray hair, a slightly crooked nose, a firm jaw and a slight overbite. His skin has a sort of leathery cast, from all his years of alcohol abuse following the attempted suicide of his only son. His eyes are a pale shade of blue, what some would call a washed-out gray. He's a PI and the former partner of Nick's former owner, Nick Atkins. Ollie's made no bones about the fact he's ripe to take on a new partner: me. However, I'm not quite ready to add professional PI to my résumé just yet. "It's good to see you, Ollie. What brings you to Cruz?"

He flashed his perfectly white teeth in a brief smile. "A consult with a potential client. Unfortunately, it didn't pan out as well as I'd hoped, so I came here for a soda and ran into Louis." He tapped the large glass of Coke in front of him. "What about you? You look a bit frazzled."

I ran my finger around the rim of my mug. "Frazzled is one way of putting it. You might be, too, if you'd had the afternoon Nick and I had."

Louis raised an eyebrow. "That sounds rather ominous."

"It does, doesn't it?" Ollie agreed, looking me straight in the eye. "Don't tell me you and Nick found another body?"

I bit my lip and glanced quickly around the bar. "As a matter of fact, we did."

Both men gasped and then Louis said, "Okay, spill! And don't forget, *Noir* has dibs on the story."

"If I tell you, you have to swear not to breathe a word. Samms specifically said to keep details under wraps, and if he found out I blabbed, well, let's just say I don't feel like listening to one of his lectures." I sniffed. "I don't know what he was doing there anyway. The FBI must be slow on crime these days."

"You haven't heard?" Louis began, but Ollie made a slicing motion with his hand at Louis and leaned forward.

"We're getting off track," Ollie said smoothly. "You were going to tell us about the body. Don't worry, Louis and I won't breathe a word."

I pushed my beer mug back. "Okay, fine. The victim's name is Marlene McCambridge and it looks like she was murdered."

Ollie let out a low whistle, but Louis looked puzzled. "Marlene McCambridge?" he asked. "I don't believe I know that name."

"She's a romance author," Ollie supplied. "She's one half of a duo who writes under the nom de plume of Tiffany Blake."

I stared at Ollie. "Don't tell me you're a closet romance reader too?"

Ollie quirked a brow. "Too? Who else reads these books? Not that I'm admitting I do," he added hastily. "I had a client once who wanted me to track down her husband. He was having an affair with a romance writer."

"Not Marlene McCambridge?"

"No. But I can't say I'm surprised someone finally did her in, though. Marlene's a real bee-yatch. She's made her fair share of enemies over the years." He drummed his fingertips on the scarred tabletop. "How did she die?"

I tapped my breastbone. "She was shot at point-blank range."

"Hm, so it was quick. Her killer was merciful. That probably eliminates lots of suspects. I imagine most of them would prefer she have died a slow, torturous death." One corner of his lip drooped downward. "Might I ask how you got involved in all this?"

"The same way I always do. I poked my nose in where it doesn't belong. I was doing a favor for an old friend of my mother's, Desiree Sanders."

"Ah, the other, and better, half of Tiffany Blake." Both of Ollie's heavy gray eyebrows shot upward. "And she knew your mother. Now that is interesting."

"You don't know the half of it," I said. "I have the feeling she's hiding something from me. Any tips on how I can pry more info out of her?"

"Depends on what it is, and how badly she wants to keep it a secret."

At that precise instant the front door opened, and in strode Leroy Samms, his face darker than a thundercloud. He stood in the entryway, his eyes darting around the crowded room and then they settled on . . . me. His lips compressed into a thin line, and eyes blazing, he made a beeline straight for our table.

"Uh-oh," muttered Louis. "He's loaded for bear. Something has pissed off our new head of Homicide, all right."

My head rocketed up. "Our new what?"

Louis didn't answer, because the next instant a shadow fell across the table. Samms pointed a long finger directly at me and spoke, his words falling like chips of ice.

"Nora Charles, we have to talk. Now."

Seven

Samms crooked his finger and motioned for me to follow him. Reluctantly, I got up from the booth and trailed him to a table for two across the room, directly in front of the entrance to the men's room. He pulled out a chair and made a sweeping gesture with his arm. I eased myself into it, and he settled himself across from me, staring me in the eye with that stern, unreadable expression of his. "You left out a little detail when we spoke earlier."

I deliberately widened my eyes. "I did?"

"Yes. Your visit to Desiree Sanders at the Cruz Inn." He passed his hand along his chin, letting his fingers graze the slight stubble. "Why didn't you mention you were chummy with the deceased's writing partner."

"I wasn't aware you were interested in whom I visit. I'll be sure to let you know in the future, though." I put a finger to my lips. "Let's see, after work tomorrow I thought I'd stop over and see Isobel Sharpe, make an appointment for a haircut, then I'll probably drop in on Chantal . . ."

"Very funny."

"Oh, for pity's sake." I waved my hand in the air. "I didn't mention anything because I didn't think it was relevant. And FYI, we're not 'chummy.'" I drew little air quotes at the last word. "She was my mother's friend, not mine. Before today, I'd never laid eyes on either her or Marlene."

Samms's eyebrows winged upward. "So you wouldn't know why she registered at the inn under an alias?"

"An alias?"

He whipped out his notebook, flipped a few pages. "Dora Slater."

I waved my hand in a careless circle. "That's not an alias. Dora Slater was her name before she changed it. She probably just wanted a break from reporters and fans and didn't want to advertise the fact she was in town."

He cut me an eye roll and leaned back in the chair. "So, why were you visiting her?"

"She called me. She said she wanted to connect with the daughter of her old friend."

"Suddenly, after all these years?"

I shrugged. "Maybe she got hit with a bout of nostalgia."

We were both silent for a moment, and then Samms said quietly, "I find it interesting. You pay a call on your mother's childhood friend and next thing you're off and visiting this McCambridge woman."

I shrugged. "Not so very interesting. I told you, I wanted to do an article on them. It was a happy coincidence Desiree got in touch with me."

He picked up a napkin, toyed absently with its edge. "So she didn't mention anything to you, any concerns she might have regarding her partner?"

"Are you driving at something in particular, or is this just a fishing expedition?" I snapped.

"What do you think?"

"I think you're fishing. I'm not even sure who you're working for right now!" I burst out, throwing both hands up in the air. "What do I call you, anyway? Detective? Special Agent? Head of Homicide?"

He leaned forward, a light in his eyes. "You could be adventurous and call me . . . Lee. You know, like you used to."

My heart did a flip-flop and I felt little beads of perspiration start to break out on my forehead. I swallowed and leaned back in my chair. "I'll stick with Samms," I growled. "And you didn't answer my question."

"I know."

I bit back a sharp retort. "You have some sort of theory about the murder?"

"It's a bit early." He laced his hands in front of him. "I do have an idea I'm toying with, though."

Aha. "Well?" I demanded as he fell silent. "Care to share it?"

He shot me a lopsided grin, more of a grimace. "Not at the moment."

A bulb suddenly went off above my head and I scooted to the edge of my seat. "Fine. She was upset because of an announcement Marlene was going to make concerning their partnership. But you already knew that, didn't you?"

One corner of his lips twitched upward. "Is that your famous gut talking?"

"I saw Morley Carruthers arrive as I was leaving. You don't have to be a genius to figure out he told you about Marlene's plans to dissolve the partnership."

"So Desiree did know what Marlene planned to do?"

I clamped my lips together. "You'll have to ask her. Anything I'd tell you would only be considered hearsay anyway."

"I intend to do just that once I find her."

My head jerked upward. "Isn't she at the inn?"

He shook his head. "She checked out. Seemed to be in rather a hurry, too, according to the desk clerk."

I spread my hands. "Honest, Samms. She said nothing to me about leaving. I got quite the opposite impression. I thought she'd be staying there for a while."

He scraped back his chair and stood up. "If you should hear from her, you might tell her to get in touch with me. I've a few questions for her." He paused and then added, "You might also mention that flight is quite often considered evidence of guilt."

"Desiree didn't kill her," I murmured.

He stopped dead in his tracks and turned around slowly to glare at me. "And just how do you know that? Got a crystal ball? Female intuition? Chantal pick up on a vibe? Or . . ." He shook his finger in the air. "Did Desiree Sanders tell you that?"

I looked him square in the eye. "You're familiar with the Fifth Amendment?" I asked sweetly.

Samms shook his head and pulled a card from his pocket. "Here's my number. If you hear from her, well, you know what to do."

He turned on his heel and walked out the side door. A second later

Louis and Ollie appeared at the table, carrying their drinks and mine. Ollie slid into the chair Samms had just vacated and studied me, a concerned look in his eyes.

"Everything okay?"

I bit down on my lower lip. "I'm not quite sure. According to Samms, Desiree has flown the coop. He was annoyed I didn't tell him I'd been to see her before I went to Marlene's."

Ollie shot me a quick glance. "Why did you go to Marlene's? Did Desiree ask you to?"

I nodded, running my fingers through my auburn curls. "Marlene was set to dissolve their partnership. She was going to make an announcement tomorrow at two o'clock. Desiree was convinced she had an ulterior motive and she thought I might be able to pry it out of her."

"Ah." Louis raised his mug and took a sip. "Knowing you, you probably would have, too."

"Samms learned something that makes Desiree Suspect Numero Uno in his eyes," I muttered. "Maybe he discovered those bloody clothes she had cleaned."

"What!" both men chorused.

Ollie frowned. "Does that mean what I think it does?"

I sighed. "Yes. They had an argument, and she went over there and found the body. She claims she was in shock and just couldn't wrap her mind around the fact Marlene was really dead. When she got back to her hotel, she removed her bloody clothes and tossed them in the bathroom. Later on, she got to thinking about it and realized it would look strange for her to have bloodstained clothing in her suite, so she called the inn cleaning service."

Louis let out a snort. "That was a pretty dumb move on her part. They've written mysteries as well as romances. She should have known better."

Ollie laced his hands in front of him. "Is it possible her naïveté and nervousness could be an act?"

"I don't think she's that good an actress. She does have a heightened sense of drama, though. I do believe she did panic, and panicked people do strange things, things they wouldn't ordinarily do."

"Don't let the fact the woman was friends with your mother cloud your judgment, Nora. There might be a lot more to all this than you know. After all, she has, apparently, flown the coop."

"Marlene had appointments with two other people the day before. Scarlett Vandevere and Dooley Franks, aka Sable St. John. Maybe one of them had a reason for wanting Marlene dead." I sighed. "I need to find out if either or both of them were anywhere near Cruz last night. They both have had books released recently, and they might have had signings in the area."

"Easy enough to check out," Louis said. "I'll be glad to help you out, Nora, but in return . . ."

"Yes, I know. *Noir* will get the exclusive when all is said and done. Thanks."

Lance bustled over to the table, accompanied by Nick. The tuxedo reached up, put a paw on my lap, and started to purr.

I scratched the top of his head. "Well, you look happy."

"Polished off a whole bowl of milk along with some cheese." Lance eyed me. "Don't you feed him?"

I made a gesture at the cat. "Look at him. What do you think?"

Nick shook his portly bottom, removed his paw from my leg and sidled closer to Lance.

"Turncoat," I muttered.

Lance put a hand on my shoulder. "I saw Samms over here. What did he want?"

"Oh, the usual. He claims I've seen more than my share of dead bodies, none of which died of natural causes, and he considers me a pariah. Nick too."

Lance clucked his tongue. "You should make nice with him, Nora. I hear he's going to be the head of our Homicide unit permanently any day now."

I almost choked on my sip of beer. "Yeah," I gasped, "Louis

mentioned something along those lines before. What happened? I thought Samms was all set to join the FBI?"

"He was, but apparently the guy they wanted to take Broncelli's place took ill, and now he's going on early retirement. They don't have anyone qualified, so they asked the FBI if they could 'borrow' Samms for a while, seeing as he used to work Homicide in Saint Leo. He's the acting head until they find a replacement, but . . . I heard from a reliable source that the mayor is so pleased with Samms's track record, he put a request in to the FBI to make the appointment permanent."

"Per-permanent? As if forever and ever?"

"You got it."

I grabbed what was left of my beer and downed it in one large gulp. Nick lifted his head, cocked it to one side, then let out a yowl so loud several patrons turned to stare.

Ollie chuckled. "Nick doesn't like that idea."

I sighed. "He's not the only one."

My cell phone beeped. I fished it out of my pocket, glanced at the number, and answered. "Hey, Chantal. What's up?"

"Where are you?" Chantal's voice sounded tense. "Are you near my shop?"

"Not too far away. I'm at the Poker Face. Why?"

"There is someone here who needs to speak with you."

I heard muffled voices, and then another voice came over the wire.

"Nora?" Desiree's voice sounded reedy. "Can you come here immediately. I've got to see you. I think I might be in real trouble."

Eight

I saw Ollie, Lance and Louis all looking at me curiously. I smiled, mouthed "Chantal," rose and turned toward the bar area. "That's putting it mildly. Why did you leave the inn? The police are looking for you," I hissed.

"I know," she hissed back. "I came here hoping to find you. I really need to speak with you."

Now I couldn't ignore Desiree even if I wanted to, not after she'd dragged Chantal into this. I glanced casually over one shoulder. The boys were engaged in conversation, not paying any attention to me. "Give me ten minutes," I said, and disconnected. I slid the phone back into my pocket and walked back to the table. Ollie glanced up as I approached.

"Everything all right?"

I nodded. "Chantal needs my opinion on one of her displays. Nick and I should get going anyway."

Ollie scraped his chair back. "I'll come with you. There are a few things I want to talk to you about."

Swell. I was trying to think of a good excuse to ditch Ollie when his cell phone chirped. He glanced at the screen and then waved me on.

"Never mind. I'll catch up with you tomorrow, Nora. Some information has come up on a new case I'm working on. Duty calls."

Ah, there is a God. I breathed a silent prayer of thanks as Nick and I hurried out the front door.

• • •

Ten minutes later I pulled up in front of the charming flower store co-owned by my friend Chantal and her brother Remy. Poppies is actually three stores in one. One side is the flower shop, whose window was always filled with colorful and inviting blooms and floral

60

arrangements, and the right side is divided into two equal parts. One is Chantal's New Age Store, where she sells crystals, tarot cards, incense, and the like, and where she also gives (upon appointment) psychic readings; and the last section is devoted to her line of homemade jewelry, Lady C Creations, for which Nick is an unwilling model of pet collars.

The bell tinkled as I pushed open the front door, and I quickly glanced around the shop. Two women were looking at a display of silk floral arrangements, pausing every now and then to ask a question of the tall, thin blond man behind the counter. Remy Gillard wasn't handsome in the conventional sense, but he did exude a certain amount of charm. Like his sister, he spoke with a French accent, but his wasn't a bit put on. Quite the contrary, he'd acquired it from years of living abroad studying in Paris. He glanced up, caught my eye, and motioned ever so slightly toward the curtain that separated the flower shop from his sister's portion. I smiled my thanks, crossed the room, and parted the beaded curtain. Chantal was bent over one of the glass counters, straightening a deck of tarot cards. She looked up quickly at my approach and breathed a heavy sigh of relief, placing her hand over her heart.

"*Chérie!* And Nick! Thank goodness."

"Where is she?"

Chantal rolled her eyes and jerked her thumb toward a door in the far corner. "In the bathroom. She felt ill."

I bit down hard on my lower lip. "There's not an exit to the street from that bathroom, is there?"

My friend shook her head. "She is not going to run away from you, *chérie*. She came here about an hour ago, all worked up and most insistent to speak with you." She moved closer to me and whispered, "I gave her a hug, and the fear rolled off her in waves. It overwhelmed me. She is deathly afraid of something. I tried to get a read on her, but . . . I kept coming up blank. Her fear is so intense, it shuts every other emotion out."

"Do you . . . do you think she could have . . ."

"No." Chantal shook her head emphatically. "I did not get that sort of vibe from her at all, and as you well know, my impressions are usually spot-on. She did not kill anyone."

"I didn't think so," I murmured. "As for the fear, it's probably that she'll be arrested on a murder charge, and right now that fear seems pretty well founded. How did she know to come here, I wonder."

"She remembered your mother telling her what good friends we were," Chantal said, just as the bathroom door opened and Desiree, looking decidedly pale, emerged. Her eyes lit up, though, as she caught sight of me. She ran toward me, arms outstretched.

"Nora. Thank God."

She enveloped me in a bear hug, and clung to me for several minutes before I gently pushed her away. I wasn't even psychic, and I could pick up on the fear that seemed to ooze out of her. She was shaking like a leaf. "Desiree, would you like to tell me why you found it necessary to check out of the Cruz Inn? Leroy Samms is looking for you."

Her brows drew together. "Leroy Samms? Who's he?"

"He's our acting head of Homicide. You remember. I told you about him. He came to the house shortly after I discovered Marlene's body."

"Oh, yes." She pressed a hand to her head. "It's been a most upsetting day. Most."

"I'm afraid it's going to get worse before it gets better," I said grimly. "Your leaving like that makes it look as if you're fleeing the scene, and flight is often considered evidence of guilt. Why did you check out?"

"I just couldn't stay there another minute. I drove around for a while, and then . . ." Her eyes widened. "Evidence of guilt, you said? Am I a suspect?"

"I don't know," I said honestly. "Samms isn't in the habit of sharing who's on his suspect list with me. I do know he has a few questions for you."

"Oh." She sank into a nearby chair and put her head in her hands. "I'm sure he does."

I knelt down and gently put my arm around her shoulders. "Desiree, I think you should be honest about how you went out to the house and found her body. Samms seems pretty anxious to talk to you, which makes me think he's found out some more information."

Desiree twisted her hands in her lap. "I haven't been completely honest with you, Nora."

Well, hey, there was a news flash. I crossed my arms over my chest and gave her a stern look. "Oh?"

"Yes." Her fingers plucked at the hem of her tunic. "When I said that I thought there was more to Marlene's announcement than just dissolving our partnership. I knew there was. I knew she had something else planned."

"How did you know that?"

"Because"—she expelled a long breath—"she told me when she called me to set up the meeting. She said she was tired of keeping everyone's secrets and it was time to speak up."

"Secrets? What sort of secrets?"

"The usual," she said, with just a ghost of a grin. "Infidelity, dishonesty, crimes of passion."

"It sounds like you're describing a soap opera."

"In a way I am." She let her hands fall limply to her sides and leaned forward. "Marlene did write a book on her own. Not fiction, and that's a good thing, because she stunk at crafting it anyway. Nope, the little ditty she was penning was a memoir. What they call a tell-all."

"She was murdered over a book?" I tried hard, but I couldn't keep the skepticism out of my voice.

"Not just any book. This was going to be a bloodbath. Marlene had something, a sort of charisma that made one want to pour out their heart to her. Only problem was, in addition to the so-called sympathetic ear, their troubles were recorded for future use. And these weren't little secrets, either. These were big, jaw-dropping ones. Ones that could ruin a career, a life." Desiree got up and started to pace. "It was years ago, when we first started out. I got a bit tipsy one night and my tongue got just a wee bit loose. I confided something to her. An old secret that, if it ever came out, would ruin me. Utterly ruin me." She paused and looked straight at me. "The only other person who knew, up until my moment of weakness, was your mother. She was such a good, loyal friend. She stuck by someone no matter what. I can see those same qualities in you. If the others' secrets were as devastating as mine, well . . . I know I shouldn't say this, considering the circumstances, but we're all better off now she's dead."

Her fingers brushed through her ash-blonde bob. "I drove out there last night. She'd mentioned it in passing when she called to set up the meeting, and I wanted to talk about it right then and there, but she brushed me off. So I went to that house to ask her to reconsider. She laughed at me. Said that this was her golden opportunity, and she wasn't going to waste it. Then she told me it was my own fault for confiding in her. That after all our years together, I should have known she wasn't a person to be trusted. Besides, my chapter was going to be one of the high points of her book. That, along with what she had on Dooley and Scarlett would make it jump to number one on the *New York Times* list for sure. I begged with her, pleaded with her to leave me out of it. She just turned her back on me and told me to get out, that she'd see me the next day. I told her I'd get my own attorney and she just laughed and told me to go ahead, for all the good it would do."

"And then what happened?" I asked, fearful I already knew the answer.

Desiree shrugged. "Nothing."

I felt a pent-up breath whoosh out of me. "Nothing?"

She stopped pacing and looked at me, and her eyes went wide. "No, Nora. I didn't kill her. I wanted to, believe me. But I didn't. I couldn't." The pacing resumed. "I left and drove around for a while, I couldn't say how long, and then I went back to the house. I decided to pay her as much as I had to in order to get her to leave the chapter about me out of the book, even if it drained my life's savings. I found the sliding door open, and I went in and found her dead. God help me, I went through her desk, looking for the manuscript. Nothing. Then I"—she squeezed her eyes shut—"I turned her on her side, went through her pockets. I thought maybe she'd locked it away, and had a key on her, and maybe I could figure out from that where she'd put it—oh, I wasn't thinking, I know. It was foolish, but I was desperate. Then I kept hearing sounds, all sorts of creaks and groans, and I just left and came straight back to the hotel. The feeling of shock started to wear off, and I knew I had to get out of my clothes. I didn't know what I should do, and then I remembered you, and reading about those mysteries you'd solved. I thought, maybe if you found the body, your interest would get piqued enough that you might get involved in the investigation and maybe *you* could find the manuscript."

Anger flowed through me for just a split second; then, as I looked at Desiree's woebegone expression, it slowly faded. The woman truly had no idea just how selfish her little brainstorm had been. "Are you certain there *is* a manuscript?"

She nodded. "Oh, yes. She showed me a few of the pages she'd written about me. She had it all down, every grisly detail."

"Well, assuming there actually is a book and she didn't just type up a few pages to scare you, how do you know she didn't turn it over to her agent, or her publisher?"

"Marlene wouldn't waste her time just typing up a few pages, trust me. As for the agent, she doesn't have a new one yet. That was another thing that made me see red. She showed me a letter she'd written, dated three weeks ago, terminating her part of the relationship with Anabel Leedson as of two p.m. tomorrow. She made Anabel promise to keep it mum from everyone, including me, until after the announcement. See what a witch she was? And I'm being kind."

"But without an agent, how could she sell the book?"

"Easy. On her rep, excuse me, Tiffany Blake's rep. She sold it, all right, and was to deliver the completed manuscript to her publisher next week."

"Who is the publisher? Do you know?"

She shrugged. "No. She didn't share that with me."

"What about her computer? There must be some information on her hard drive."

"What computer?" The corners of Desiree's mouth turned down in a scowl. "Marlene didn't have a clue how to work one. I typed all our manuscripts on my computer."

"In this electronic age, I find that hard to believe. She didn't type at all?"

"Once in a blue moon. She didn't like to. She claimed it chipped her expensive manicures."

I frowned. "But I saw a laptop in her office."

"Then it must have already been there when she rented the house." Desiree barked out a nervous laugh. "When she did type she used an old electric typewriter she'd had since the Dark Ages. She always said she felt like Jessica Fletcher when she used it. Hah, like Jessica Fletcher would have done anything like she planned to!"

"And you're certain she never used a computer?"

"Well, I'm not one hundred percent certain. She knew how to use the Internet, so she might have rented one on occasion, but trust me, any manuscript she delivered would have been typed on her typewriter."

I still had my doubts, but decided to abandon that line of questioning for now. Remembering the mess the master bedroom had been in, I asked, "Did you ransack her bedroom looking for it?"

Desiree shook her head. "No. Just the desk, I told you. I kept hearing strange sounds. Silly, I know."

"Maybe not so silly. You might have just missed the murderer."

Desiree's rosy cheeks paled and she put both palms up against them. "Ooh! I never thought of that!"

"Your presence probably interrupted his search for the manuscript. When I got there I saw the master bedroom had been upended." I nibbled at my bottom lip, my thoughts whirling. "Unfortunately, taking into consideration the partnership dissolution, the fact your prints are all over the place, throw in those bloody clothes you had cleaned . . . you're in a position to be their prime suspect. It's just fortunate you don't own a gun."

I saw the look on her face and thought I'd never seen anyone look so miserable.

"Like I told you. I'm in real trouble, right?"

Nine

"Here's the kicker. Desiree does own a gun. Marlene asked to borrow it a few weeks before. She told her she'd decided to take shooting lessons and of course conveniently never returned it. How much do you want to bet it's going to turn up as the murder weapon, if it hasn't already?"

It was nine o'clock the next morning. Even though the shop was crowded, most of my clientele had taken seats at tables facing the television. Their eyes were glued to *Good Morning America* and they'd yet to place an order. Chantal, fortunately, had come in early and manned the counter while Ollie and I brainstormed at the table in the back.

Ollie added cream to his coffee and took a sip. "She spent the night with you?"

I nodded. "She really was in no condition to go anywhere last night, let alone be grilled by Samms."

"It would look better if she turned herself in, rather than have Samms arrest her."

I nodded. "I know. I called Peter Dobbs, but so far he hasn't called me back. If I don't hear from him by lunch I'll take her down to the station myself." I rubbed at my eyes. "I didn't get much sleep myself, between wondering what Samms has on Desiree and what else she's hiding."

Ollie set down his mug. "What is your gut telling you? Do you think she did it?"

I considered that a moment, then shook my head. "No. Honestly, I don't."

Chantal suddenly whirled around and started fiddling in my middle drawer. "I almost forgot. A courier came with a delivery this morning, right when you were busy making those fried egg sandwiches for you and Ollie." She whipped out a Special Delivery envelope, which she waved wildly in the air. "It's from Violet Crenshaw." She closed her eyes and ran her finger over the envelope before handing it to me. "It is not a check," she said with finality. "I cannot get a clear picture of what it is, but I get the sense it is something you will get much use out of." As I eyed the envelope Chantal touched my arm. "Just open it and take a peek. You know you want to."

I hesitated, then shook my head. "No. I can't get distracted with this just now. First I've got to clear Desiree. I should wait until Violet returns next week anyway. She wanted me to." I took the envelope and slid it back in the drawer just as the bell above the shop door tinkled. My lips split in a wide smile as Daniel entered.

"Hey, good-lookin'," he greeted me.

"Hey, yourself. A paying customer at last," I said, with a pointed glance at the first table, where two construction workers who were regulars, Otto Klemens and his partner, Harvey Swaggert, sat looking very relaxed, laughing at something Robert Downey Jr. was saying on-screen. If they heard my little dig, they ignored me.

"Got a bagel with cream cheese and some coffee with my name on it?"

"Coming up in a jiff," I said, reaching into the case for the cinnamon-raisin bagel I knew he liked. "What brings you by so early?"

"Breakfast conference," he answered. "You don't mind if we have it here, at one of your back tables, do you?"

"We?" The bell tinkled again and my smile faded as Samms strode in. I pointed the tip of my bagel knife at him and said to Daniel, "Is he who you're conferring with? Just who is he working for? The Cruz PD or the FBI?"

"Lee's officially on loan to the Cruz PD for an indefinite period," Daniel responded. "So I guess you could say he's working for both."

Samms leaned across my counter, an infuriating grin on his handsome face. "Yeah, I'm so talented, both departments can't do without me. Oh, and I'll have an American cheese and egg on an everything bagel. Coffee too, please."

I gritted my teeth and pointed to the lower shelf in my case. "Fresh out of everythings."

"Onion or garlic then, I'm not fussy. You pick." He bounced his eyebrows as he looked at me. "I have no plans to kiss anyone. At least not at the moment, anyway."

I turned my head before either could notice the two bright spots on my cheeks. "Why don't you two sit down, and Chantal will serve you shortly?"

"Great. Put it all on my tab," Daniel said, and the two men headed for the back of the store.

I slapped two slices of yellow American cheese and an egg on my griddle, and out of the corner of my eye saw Daniel and Samms pull out chairs at the table in the far corner, near the rear exit and across from the billboard I'd set up displaying various community flyers. I pulled a plain bagel out for Daniel and then grabbed the stinkiest garlic bagel I could find out of the bin, jabbed the knife in, and sliced it right down the middle.

Chantal came up behind me and glanced significantly toward the rear of the store. "I see both your boyfriends are here."

"I said you'd serve them breakfast," I muttered, ignoring her boyfriend remark. I slathered Daniel's bagel with cream cheese. "See if you can overhear anything they're saying. They're consulting on a case, and I'm betting it's Marlene's murder."

Chantal's smooth brow puckered. "Why would Daniel get involved in that? He is FBI. They don't bother with local homicide cases, do they?"

"He might be doing Samms a favor, seeing as Samms is head of Cruz Homicide and the two of them have gotten pretty chummy." I filled two mugs with coffee and set them on the counter. "It would be too obvious for me to eavesdrop. They'd be sure to clam up."

"And it won't be obvious if I do it?" Chantal's eyebrows shot skyward. "They know we are friends, chérie."

"Look, if Mollie were here I'd make her do it, but she isn't and you are. I have faith in your ability." I thrust the tray with the coffee and Daniel's bagel at her. "You'll think of something. Tell Samms his Howard Stern Breakfast Special will be right out."

"Fine." She took the tray and shot me a hurt look. "Just don't expect miracles."

I flipped over the egg and cheese, and out of the corner of my eye saw Chantal approach the table. The phone rang just then. I saw Babs Bakery on my caller ID, and since I needed to place an order, took the call. I had just hung up when Chantal bustled back. "You will not believe what they are talking about," she said.

I glanced over my shoulder. The two men were engaged in earnest conversation, not paying attention to anyone else. I slid the cheese and egg onto the bagel. "Well, don't keep me in suspense. What?"

Chantal hopped up on one of my stools. "Well, they were talking very low when I approached, and Samms looked up and saw me. He mumbled something about being served last on purpose, but he'd forgive you because you make great coffee. And Daniel chimed in and said, 'She makes a mean tuna melt too,' and then the two of them laughed."

"That's it?" I could barely contain my disappointment. "That's all you overheard?"

"No, of course not." My friend looked offended. "They were talking very low, but I caught a snitch of what they were saying before Samms saw me. Samms said something about prints and then Daniel said if he's in the book maybe he has something to do with it."

I put the plate with Samms's breakfast special on a tray and made shooing motions. "See if you can hear any more."

She made a face, but picked up the tray and moved toward their table. I decided it might be best to keep out of sight, so I ducked back into the kitchen, where I caught a glimpse of a black tail waving in the air next to Ollie's chair. As I approached I saw Nick happily lapping up crumbs from the floor, and I knew just who had put them there. Ollie's attempt at an innocent expression failed miserably, and I shook my head. "He's going to weigh a thousand pounds soon."

"Nah." Ollie looked down fondly at Nick. "It's just baby fat. It'll wear off."

"Not if he doesn't get some exercise other than walking up and down the stairs."

Nick stopped eating and looked straight at me. Then he rolled over on his back and wiggled his hind legs in the air. I tried to keep my expression stern, but I knew I was failing miserably. "Honestly, Nick. You need more exercise than that."

The cat flopped back onto his belly and blinked twice at me.

Ollie laughed. "He gets plenty helping you track down criminals. So, how'd Chantal make out?"

I flopped into the chair next to Ollie and repeated what Chantal overheard. "I think the *he* Daniel referred to might be Dooley Franks, aka Sable St. John. He'd certainly have a lot to lose, depending on what secret of his Marlene was hell-bent on revealing." I huffed a strand of hair out of my eyes. "I just hope they haven't found Desiree's gun."

"Even if they find it, that doesn't mean it's the murder weapon."

"But on the chance it is, it gives Desiree means, motive and opportunity. Don't think they'll look any further when she fits all the necessary criteria."

"Well, if Desiree loaned the gun to Marlene, and it does turn out to be the murder weapon, it begs the question of how the gun got in the killer's possession."

"Darned if I know."

"Of course, it's possible the murderer was someone acquainted with both women, and who knew Marlene had borrowed Desiree's gun. Killer wears gloves, Desiree doesn't, Desiree leaves her prints all over, argues with Marlene about the partnership dissolution, and bingo! You've got the perfect frame." Ollie laced his hands in front of him. "I think the first order of business is to determine that there actually is a book."

"Desiree seems to think Marlene would have considered it a gigantic waste of time to whip up a few chapters just to make people sweat."

Ollie raised his coffee cup. "Of course I didn't know the woman, but from what I've read about her it sounds like just the sort of thing she would have enjoyed."

Chantal came hurrying over to where we sat, her eyes bright, her cheeks flushed. "I brought the sandwich over just as Samms hung up his phone. He said he had to get back to the station, that a very important 'person of interest' had just arrived, and he needed to be there."

I jumped up and peered into the main part of the store. Sure enough, the table where they had been sitting was now empty.

Chantal touched my arm. "Daniel said to tell you he would call you later."

"And Samms?"

Chantal's expression was perfectly serious as she answered, "He did not say anything about calling you."

I made a face at her. "Very funny."

She laughed. "*Chérie*, Samms didn't say a word. He just picked up his sandwich and took off." She paused. "He seemed pretty jubilant, though, when he mentioned that person of interest."

"I'll bet," I murmured. Ignoring the sinking feeling in my stomach, I bolted for the door that led upstairs to my apartment and took the steps two at a time. I burst into the den and stopped.

The roll-out bed had been made, the room straightened. Desiree was nowhere to be seen. I saw a piece of paper fluttering from beneath one of the throw pillows and reached for it. The hastily scrawled note read:

> Nora: *Thanks for your support, it means the world to me. I've been enough of a bother to you. Thanks for the shoulder to lean on. Your mother would be proud.*
> *Desiree.*

"Desiree, Desiree," I sighed. "You picked a honey of a time to get noble." I whipped my phone out of my apron pocket and punched in Peter Dobbs's number. Once again it went straight to voice mail.

"Hey, Peter, this is Nora Charles. A friend of mine is in trouble. No, that's an understatement. She's up to her neck and sinking fast, just like the *Titanic*. How quickly can you get here?"

Ten

After a few more pleading sentences stressing the gravity of the situation using words like *desperate* and *last hope*, I disconnected and went back downstairs. Chantal was waiting on a customer; Ollie was sipping his coffee and throwing more bagel crumbs to Nick, who purred at his feet.

"I left an urgent message," I said. "The only problem is, I have no idea where Peter is or how fast he can get here, and who knows what Desiree will say before he arrives. She just might blurt out everything."

"Of course, it will depend on what Samms hits her with, and you know darn well Samms wouldn't let you be present while he interrogates her, so in the meantime perhaps you can pursue another angle of the investigation."

"Good idea. Any suggestions?"

"I think it's prudent to confirm the existence of this tell-all book. Do you know the name of their agent? You could say it's part of your article, and you just want to confirm."

"Not a bad idea, except Marlene is agent-less at the moment. Desiree told me that she severed ties with the one they shared, and she hadn't signed with a new one yet."

"Well, then, you could always contact the publisher directly. You can use the same excuse. The news of her death hasn't been made public yet, has it?"

"Not yet, which strikes me as odd. You'd think some reporter would have gotten wind—" I stopped speaking and snapped my fingers. "That reporter from the *Sun*, Paul Jenkins. He was supposed to try and get an interview with Marlene for the Sunday edition. He might have stopped by yesterday too."

"I doubt that," Ollie said. "It would be in the paper already if he had."

"Maybe not if Samms used his charm on him like he did me." I used my fingers to draw air quotes around the word *charm*.

I whipped out my phone, looked up the number of the *Cruz Sun*, and when I was connected asked to speak with Paul Jenkins. A few seconds later a bored-sounding voice muttered a terse "Hello."

"Jenks? Hey, it's Nora Charles, from Hot Bread."

"Oh, hi." A pause and then, "Does this call mean you've changed your mind about that Sunday article?"

"No, sorry. I was just wondering if you ever got to interview Marlene McCambridge."

There was a slight hesitation and then, "No, I didn't. And I won't get a chance, now. That feature's dead in the water. Literally."

"I know," I said. "I'm the one who found her body."

"You?" He gave a low chuckle. "I guess I should have figured as much. And let me guess. Your body-sniffing cat was with you, right?"

I ignored his comment and said, "Samms swore me to secrecy, and since nothing's appeared in the media, I'm guessing he did the same with you?"

"Yep. He made me swear to hold off on reporting her demise for at least forty-eight hours. I argued with him—I mean, it's not like she was a big movie star, or anything like that, but he wouldn't budge. Said he didn't need to deal with the press hounding him for details and messing up his crime scene. So I gave in. I figure who knows, if I scratch his back, maybe one day he'll do the same for me, ya know."

"Sounds like you have something in mind."

"Oh, yeah." He clucked his tongue. "An exclusive on the arrest of the murderer."

I sucked in my breath. "They have a suspect?"

"Not officially, but I hear her writing partner was in town and checked out of the Cruz Inn with lightning speed. It makes her look guilty as sin, you know." He paused and then added, "I must say, I'm shocked. I mean, Marlene was half of the goose that laid the golden egg, the more public half, the money generator. You don't shoot it in cold blood without a very good reason. So, any idea what the motive might be?"

"Why would I know? I'm not investigating the crime," I protested.

"Yeah, but the prime suspect was your mother's close friend. Makes it kind of personal for you, doesn't it? Oh, wait, I'm getting another call. I've got to take this, but we'll talk again."

Jenks disconnected and I turned a troubled gaze to Ollie. "Samms made him agree to wait forty-eight hours. So by this time tomorrow Marlene's death will be public knowledge. We've got no time to waste. With all the cyber gossip sites out there, there has to be some sort of clue somewhere, I hope."

Ollie pushed his chair back. "If there's anything out there, we'll find it, trust me, or my name isn't Oliver J. Sampson." He went over to my laptop on the rear counter and booted it up, then clicked on Internet Explorer. He pulled up Bing and then typed in "Marlene McCambridge—recent gossip."

Twelve pages of sites came up.

Ollie typed in: "Marlene McCambridge—unsubstantiated rumors."

Three pages of sites came up.

I pointed to the first hit. "Look at this. Literary Gossip dot com has an article on her from last month."

He clicked on it and the site came up, right on the article. The title screamed at us in large blue letters: *Marlene McCambridge—A Force to be Reckoned With.*

"Ah." He rubbed his hands together in an anticipatory fashion. "This looks like a good place to start."

I leaned over Ollie's shoulder and scanned the article. Basically it was a rehash of Marlene's (and Desiree's by omission) literary career, how tough it was to maintain the persona of Tiffany Blake, and some awards received.

The last part of the interview, however, was interesting:

Reporter: Marlene, what's in store for Tiffany Blake? What's your and Desiree's next venture?

Marlene: Well, I can't speak for either Tiffany or Desiree, but I can tell you that something interesting is in the offing for moi.

Reporter: Can't you give us a little hint?

Marlene: (winks) Now that wouldn't be fair, would it? You'll just have to wait and see, like the rest of America—but I promise you, it will be well worth waiting for.

Reporter: Rumor has it that you were seen down at Peachtree Press a few weeks ago. They're a nonfiction house. Can you confirm you met with an editor there?

Marlene: I confirm or deny nothing. As I said—you'll have to wait and see.

There was a little more, but I'd seen enough. "Peachtree Press, eh? Sounds like a start."

"Of course, that might have been a red herring supplied by Marlene, but it's worth a shot," said Ollie. "Peachtree Press is primarily a nonfiction house, after all. They're known for their large advances."

Ollie got up and I sat down. I plugged Peachtree Press into the search engine and the site came up. I clicked on the About Us tab and found a list of editors. Twenty, to be exact. I combed through the list and narrowed it down to eight who specialized in celebrity nonfiction. I picked up my cell phone and dialed the first New York City number, putting it on speaker so Ollie could hear. The first two editors were at a conference; the third was out on medical leave. I had to wade through about three layers of assistants before finally connecting with the fourth.

"Jendine Blair," she answered with a brisk New York accent.

I introduced myself and went through a quick spiel: I was in the midst of writing an article on selling nonfiction and I'd been referred to her by several experts in the field. Jendine seemed pretty flattered and agreed to give me a few minutes of her precious time.

"Can one get a contract on a book that's not written?" I asked.

She laughed. "Of course. We sell books all the time that way. Nonfiction is easier to sell than fiction in that regard. Usually it requires no more than a chapter outline, sometimes a sample chapter or two, and a marketing plan." A pause and then, "It's all about the *platform*."

"Platform?"

A long, drawn-out sigh, and then, spoken in a tone one might reserve for either a first-grader or a mentally challenged person, "It's all about the author, and their credentials. His or her fame, or, in some cases, their notoriety. How savvy are they with social media? Do they Facebook? Tweet? What's their topic? How hot is it? How likely is it to garner media attention? Things like that." She gave a throaty chuckle. "And the juicier the topic, the better."

"I see. And do you have any books on tap right now that meet that criteria?"

She hesitated. "Possibly."

I plunged ahead. "I researched an article on Marlene McCambridge on the Internet. They alluded to her visiting your offices."

Jendine let out a ginormous sigh. "Damn net. Can't hide anything anymore. I really shouldn't say anything, but . . . after today it'll be public knowledge, so what the hell."

I glanced at Ollie out of the corner of my eye and returned his thumbs-up sign, thinking that the book deal wouldn't be all that was public knowledge. "I'm all ears."

"I've got a book lined up with her for next fall . . . it's going to be hot, hot, hotter than hot."

"Really?" I tried to keep the mounting excitement out of my voice. Not only had I gotten an editor to speak with me, I'd gotten *the* editor. Talk about a stroke of luck! "So, is this another book she's writing with her partner?"

"Nope." Jendine's voice dropped to a whisper. "As of two p.m. Pacific Standard Time today, that partnership is his-to-ree!"

"You're kidding."

"No, it's true. She didn't want to feel encumbered." She fairly crowed into the phone. "Marlene is one of the hottest romance authors out there, and man, does she have stories to tell. This book is going to let quite a few skeletons out of their closets, I can tell you that." She let out a throaty chuckle. "If I were one of those who'd confided in her over the years, I'd be afraid. Very afraid. This tome is going to set the literary world on fire!"

"Well, that does sound interesting. I take it you've read the book?"

"Um . . . no, not yet."

I eyed Ollie. "Really? Because if it were me, I'd have sunk my teeth right into that puppy and devoured it in one sitting."

"I plan to, once the book is delivered."

"You mean she hasn't written it yet?"

"Oh, yes, it's complete. Marlene's just giving it a final once-over. She sold that with just her outline, and it was some outline, let me tell you. The words were steaming off the pages. We have a major deal in place. Mark my words, that book is going to make millions. It'll easily earn back that six-figure advance Marlene insisted on."

"It does sound exciting," I stammered. "You know, getting a look at that outline would certainly help me spice up my article. I don't suppose you could email me a copy, in strictest confidence, of course."

"I'm afraid not." Jendine's voice turned cagey. "We don't want any details leaking before publication."

"But you said that's still a year off."

"True, but the contents are so hot, we don't want to give anyone any advance notice. This book is destined for the *New York Times* and *USA Today* bestseller lists, trust me. I have an instinct for these things. I can't take any chances, sorry."

"But she's definitely written it," I said doggedly. "You know this for a fact."

"Yes, yes, of course," Jendine snapped. "Now, if you'll excuse me, I'm late for a meeting. I'll switch you back to my admin. Just let her know the name of the article and the magazine so we can look for it."

Jendine hung up and I disconnected before admin number three could get back on the line to grill me for info about my nonexistent article. "Well," I said, placing my phone down in the middle of the table, "at least we know there definitely is a book, and a detailed outline too. Hopefully it's still somewhere in that house, unless the killer found it."

"If that's the case, you can bet it's been destroyed." Ollie drummed his fingertips on the table. "Perhaps you should share this information with Samms."

"Are you crazy?" I gave him a wide-eyed stare. "Telling him this would surely put another nail in Desiree's coffin, if not the final one."

"Or it might also open up other avenues of investigation."

"You know how the police work." I sighed. "Once they find a suspect who fits their criteria, they stop looking. And while I grant you Samms is more broad-minded than most police detectives, it still boils down to the fact Desiree had motive and opportunity. And if they find the murder weapon, and if it is Desiree's gun . . ."

I didn't have to say any more.

My cell chirped. I glanced at the screen, saw Cruz Police Headquarters, and snatched it up. "Desiree, is that you?"

"Yes, Nora. I'm using my one phone call for you." She sounded calm but I detected a twinge of tension, like a finely tuned piano wire, humming through it.

"I do sincerely hope you've managed to secure me a lawyer, because I'm definitely going to need one. A good one." A pause. "They're charging me with Marlene's murder."

Eleven

After assuring Desiree that her lawyer would be there soon, I dialed Peter's number again. This time he answered on the second ring.

"Thank God," I said. "Did you get my messages?"

"I only just got back from a conference in LA about five minutes ago," he answered. "What's up? Is something wrong? Is Lacey okay?"

Peter had developed a ginormous crush on my sister when he was defending her on a murder charge a few months ago. I was pretty sure the feeling was mutual, and that part of the reason Lacey stayed with Aunt Prudence was to be near him. I assured him that my sister was in fine shape, completely law-abiding (at least I hoped she was), still working part-time for the St. Leo force, and then hit the highlights concerning Desiree's situation.

He was silent for a few minutes after I'd finished, and I could picture him running his fingers through his already unruly sandy hair, making it stick up even more. "Do you have any idea what they have to make an arrest so quickly?"

"Well, as I said, Desiree originally discovered the body, and in the process left her prints all over the place. I don't know this for a fact, but there's a good chance they've recovered the murder weapon, and it's Desiree's gun."

There was dead silence for a few seconds and then he said briskly, "I'll call the station. Who's the officer in charge?"

"Our old friend Leroy Samms."

"Samms? He's on Cruz Homicide now?" He tried but couldn't keep the surprise out of his voice. "I thought he joined the FBI."

"Yeah, we thought so too. Lucky us, he's filling in here. You heard about the Curtis Broncelli fiasco, right?"

He let out a short grunt then took the number of the Cruz station, promised to keep me posted, then ended the call. I turned a troubled gaze to Ollie. "Someone's framing her but good. I need to do something, and fast."

"Well, I'll help in any way I can. What did you have in mind?"

"Well, Louis is working on finding out the whereabouts of Scarlett and Dooley. In the meantime, how'd you like to take a trip with me to the house across the way from the crime scene?"

I explained about the anonymous phone calls to 911, and about seeing the curtain part during my own visit there. I pulled up the Yellow Pages on my phone. A few seconds later I had the Cruz Realty office on the phone, and none other than Ms. Joannie Adams.

"Hey, Nora, I didn't expect a call from you," she said and laughed. "Are you finally interested in unloading Hot Bread? If so, your timing is good. There's been a lot of interest in commercial properties in Cruz."

"Not at the present time, Joannie. I called for a little information. You rented the Porter house to Marlene McCambridge, right?"

"Yes, and it was a ginormous relief. That woman was a real pain in the you know where. We must have seen at least two dozen properties before she settled on something. My feet are still sore. I didn't rest easy until she finally signed the lease agreement." Joannie's voice lowered. "I was biting my nails the whole time. She really wanted that brown stucco house, the one across from the Porters', but it was already rented. I thought for sure she was going to hem and haw and ask me to try and talk the renter out of it, but I lucked out." She chuckled. "Rita would have had my head if I'd lost that commission."

That I could believe. "I don't suppose you have the name of the person who rented that stucco house, do you? I was out there the other day and I think I might have lost one of my earrings near that property. I'd like to get in touch with the tenant, see if they might have found it."

"Wait a minute, I can check. I didn't rent out the property, but it should be in the computer. Ah, here it is. Got a pad and pen? Okay, it's Anne—A-n-n-e. Last name: Onymus. O-n-y-m-u-s. Weird, right? I've been trying to figure out what nationality it might be."

Weird didn't begin to describe it. The country of Phony came to mind. I thanked Joannie, then passed the paper over to Ollie. He looked at it, then did a double take.

"That tip might not have been so friendly after all," Ollie agreed.

"I can't believe Joannie actually thinks Onymus is a real name." I whipped off my apron. "Let me ask Chantal if she can watch Hot Bread for the lunch crush. We need to find out who's really renting that house." I shot him a grin. "I'll put ten bucks on Scarlett Vandevere."

He grinned back. "You're on."

• • •

We made the trip out in Ollie's new car, or rather, his new vintage car, a 1967 canary yellow Ford Mustang convertible, probably one of the last cars on earth anyone would expect a six-foot-three man built like a 49ers linebacker to drive.

"Aren't you afraid of getting noticed in this?" I asked. It was a beautiful balmy fall afternoon in California, low humidity, the temperature in the mid-seventies. Ollie had the top down, and a gentle breeze riffled my auburn curls. "Should a low-key PI be driving such a stand-out car?"

"That's exactly what does make it so low-key," he said and grinned. "But this baby can really fly! Sports cars was one of the few interests Nick and I shared. Someday I'll take you out on the interstate and show you all the horses she's got under that hood. But right now, we've arrived."

Ollie pulled up across the street and I peered over at the house. It looked even more desolate today than it had yesterday. My gaze flew instinctively to the second-floor window. The curtains remained tightly drawn; no unseen hand parted them as we got out of the car and hurried up the stone steps. I rang the bell and this time we were treated to the braying of a donkey, the cooing of a dove, and the bleating of a lamb before the sounds faded away into nothingness.

Ollie shot me a look. "Interesting acoustics."

"To say the least."

We stood there for ten minutes cooling our heels; no one came to the door. I leaned over the porch railing and glanced up at the second floor, but the drapes remained intact. Ollie and I walked all around the house, even checked out the garage, which was empty.

The place was silent as a tomb.

"Looks like no one's at home, for real this time," I said finally.

"So what now? A little B&E, perhaps?" He flexed his fingers and patted his rear pants pocket. "I've got brand-new credit cards in my wallet."

I chuckled, remembering our last attempt at a felony. "You've been practicing?"

"All part of being a PI. You should be taking notes. You still want to get a license someday, right?"

I offered him a thin smile. "It's on my bucket list."

"Well, then. Consider this a part of your education, sort of an apprenticeship." He made a sweeping bow. "Shall we?"

He started for the front door but I laid a hand on his arm. "If we're going to commit a felony, I can think of a better place to start." I gestured across the road. "After all, we still aren't sure if there is a manuscript. If there is, it might still be in there somewhere."

We hurried down the long winding drive and approached the Porter house. I noted the absence of crime scene tape from the door. In my experience, crime scene barrier tape was only removed when crime scene protection was terminated. And crime scene protection was only terminated after the detective, forensic investigator or other authorized personnel completed their crime scene investigation and processing.

Ollie removed a shiny American Express Platinum card from his wallet and wiggled it in the air. "Here goes."

He knelt before the door, positioned the card . . . and then the door swung wide open. Ollie rocked back on his knees and bumped into me, sending me crashing against the side rail. I regained my balance and stared straight into the eyes of a handsome young man, his blond brows arching upward and an expression of mingled shock and surprise marring his chiseled features. He wore a pale blue T-shirt and dark denim jeans, and the blue of the shirt complemented his deep blue eyes. When he spoke, I detected the merest trace of an accent I couldn't quite place. British? Australian?

"So sorry, old chap. Might I ask what in hell you're doing, kneeling at the front door like that?"

I stepped forward quickly. "He was helping me. I thought I dropped my contact lens."

"Oh, no." The stranger's eyes moved over me in swift appraisal, taking in my own white denim jeans, freshly laundered, and pink cotton shirt with matching tank. He ran appreciative eyes over my figure, lingering just a tad too long for my taste on the swell of my breasts before raising his gaze all the way back to my face. "Can you see all right?"

"False alarm, actually." I managed a weak laugh. "It just floated to the side of my eye. It does that sometimes."

"Wouldn't know. I've got twenty-twenty vision, myself." He tapped below one eye with the tip of his forefinger. "What are you doing here? Are you with the police?"

I started to shake my head but Ollie straightened, reached in his pocket and flashed his PI license. "Oliver Sampson, private investigator. This is Miss Charles, my assistant. Might I ask who you are?"

The man examined Ollie's license, handed it back. "Sure. I'm Simon Gladstone."

Ollie slipped his license back into his jacket pocket, then stood, legs apart, arms folded across his chest. He glowered at the man and said, "And just what are you doing here, inside a crime scene, Simon Gladstone?"

Geez, he had me shaking. Ollie glowering isn't a pretty sight. Simon, however, seemed unaffected by the fact a six-foot-three-inch man built like a sumo wrestler was practically breathing down his neck.

"I have a perfect right to be here," he said, a bit haughtily I thought.

"Marlene McCambridge is, or I guess I should say was, my aunt."

Whoa, talk about being knocked over with a feather! "Your aunt?"

He nodded and brushed a tear from the corner of his eye. "Yes."

"I'm very sorry for your loss," I finally got out. "Were you and she close?"

"Not particularly. I mean, she was a loner. Kept to herself quite a bit. They tell me writers are like that." He managed a lopsided grin. "Anyway, she told me she'd be in Cruz for an indefinite amount of time. I only wished we could have had longer together. I was just getting to know her."

Ollie had been standing quietly by, his arms still folded over his chest. "You from around here?"

He cleared his throat, and looked at me when he answered. "Heavens, no. I'm from the Boston area originally, but I've been studying theatre arts in England the past two years. Aunt Marlene said she was going to try and help me get a foothold in the theatre. That's what I really want to do. I trained for the stage. But in the meantime, got to pay the bills, you know. I work three days a week over in Brisberry as a consultant."

"Do tell," Ollie said. "I know quite a few businessmen over there. What firm do you consult for?"

Once again, Gladstone looked at me when he answered. "Fallon Industries. You can check with the owner if you want. Ned Fallon."

"Why are you here today?" I asked.

Simon gave a light laugh. "When I was notified of her death I was in shock. I couldn't believe it. I had to come, see for myself."

"Did they call you to identify the body?"

He shook his head. "That had already been done. No, I just needed to see the place where it happened for myself. Get it real in my own head."

"I see," said Ollie. "And this was the only reason you came here? To see the spot where your aunt was murdered?"

Simon fidgeted, then took a step backward so he was standing inside the doorway. "Of course. Why else would I be here? I needed to look the place over, because I'll have to get a service to remove my aunt's things."

"Samms gave you the okay to do that?"

"Samms?"

My antenna was starting to rise. "Yes, Leroy Samms. He's the detective in charge of your aunt's murder investigation."

"Oh, him." He shifted uneasily and shook his head. "No, he hasn't given permission yet. It's only a matter of time, though, and I want to be prepared. So, if you'll excuse me . . ."

The next instant the door slammed in our faces.

"Well," I said after a second. "Talk about rude!"

"Never mind that," Ollie growled. "We've got to get in there at once. I happen to know that Marlene McCambridge was an only child, and she never married. That guy is no more her nephew than I am."

Twelve

As Ollie hurled his entire 225-pound frame against the door. I sprinted down the steps and around the side of the house, just in time to see a shadowy form emerge from the sliding doors and take off in a sprint across the lawn.

"Stop. Stop, thief," I yelled at the top of my lungs, although I was fairly certain there was no one around to hear me except Ollie. However, Simon Gladstone–if that was even his name–might not know that.

I'm no slouch when it comes to running, but apparently Simon wasn't either. I caught a quick glimpse of him before he disappeared into the thicket of trees that lined the property. I thought I saw something white clenched in one hand, but I couldn't be sure. In any event, what I'd seen was certainly not big enough to be an entire book manuscript. As I approached the edge, I heard the faint sound of a car engine starting, and a few seconds later he gunned it. I paused, leaned against a shady elm for a few minutes to regroup, and then trudged back to the house.

I let myself in through the sliding glass doors and hurried to the front entrance. I swung the door wide just as Ollie advanced, shoulder to the ready. I sidestepped and Ollie went sailing past me, crashing into the stair bannister. "You could have warned me you were opening the door," he admonished.

"Sorry. I didn't think. Why didn't you follow me?"

"I didn't think that door would be so tough to break down," he grumbled, rubbing his shoulder. "I've broken down sturdier ones than that."

"Maybe you're just out of practice. Anyway, I saw him cut through the woods, but he was too fast for me."

"Probably a good thing," Ollie said, dusting himself off. "What would you have done if you'd caught up to him? He might have had a gun."

"Oops, you're right. Like I said, I didn't think." I started to turn away when a flash of black under the hall table caught my eye. I knelt down and pulled out a black leather book.

Ollie, recovered now, towered over me. "What's that?"

I flipped the book open. "It's Marlene's appointment book."

His eyes widened as he stared at it. "The one you wanted to take a look at?"

"The very same. What is it doing here? I would have thought Samms would have bagged it as evidence, seeing as his prime suspect's initials were in it." I flipped the pages until I came to the spot where this week's appointments should be, and frowned. "There are pages missing."

He leaned in to peer over my shoulder. "Are you sure?"

I nodded. "Someone made a pretty clean tear, but there is still a slight ridge here where pages should be." I nibbled at my bottom lip. "The pages I photographed, the ones with all the names, are gone." I glanced grimly out the wide picture window at the thick tangle of trees. "And I've got a pretty good idea who took them." I quickly explained about seeing a white object clenched in Simon's fist.

Ollie rubbed at his jaw. "Now why would Simon Gladstone take such a risk coming here to swipe a few pages out of an appointment book? Those pages must be more important than we figured."

"They'd only mean something, though, if someone perhaps wanted to try and hide the fact he'd been here," I mused. "Ollie, do you know what Dooley Franks, or Sable St. John, looks like?"

"No, but it's easy enough to find out."

Ollie reached into his pocket for his phone and called up Google Images. He typed in "Sable St. John" and "Dooley Franks," and a few seconds later thumbnail images started to appear on the screen. He clicked on one to enlarge it. I took in the olive complexion, the dark, almost black eyes, the chocolate-colored hair that fell carelessly across the high forehead, and the word *swarthy* came to mind.

"The guy looks more like a Mafia hit man than a romance novelist," observed Ollie. "He's definitely not our intruder."

"But he might have hired him."

"Just to get those pages out of the appointment book?"

I frowned, thinking how closely the shade of Simon's hair had matched the strand Nick had found near Marlene's body. "Maybe that and more. He might have come after the manuscript."

We raced up the stairs, peering into first the office, then the master bedroom. Both rooms looked pretty much as I'd seen them yesterday; as a matter of fact, it would be pretty darn near impossible to tell if either one had been ransacked further.

The other three rooms, however, were a different story. Throw rugs were thrown carelessly around, and sheets had been ripped from the beds. Closet doors stood open and drawers hung out at odd angles. The place looked as if a cyclone had ripped through it.

I dragged my hand through my hair. "These rooms could have been like this yesterday. I didn't get a chance to look in them. I'd have to check with Samms. Here's the thing, though. I saw Simon Gladstone disappear into the woods, and I'm pretty sure he wasn't carrying anything with him."

Ollie pondered this for a moment. "A manuscript would definitely have stood out," he agreed. "It's bulky, unless, perhaps, he only needed to remove a few pages."

"A chapter? Ten, fifteen pages at most? He could have had that on him, tucked inside his jacket, maybe. But then what did he do with the rest of the book?"

"Hid it somewhere else, or burned it. That's what I'd do," Ollie said.

"There's a fireplace in the living room," I said. "We can check it on the way out." I tapped the appointment book, which I still held with my other hand. Something still rankled me, some little detail I couldn't quite put my finger on . . .

"Initials!" I cried.

Ollie looked at me as if I'd lost my mind. "Come again?"

"Initials," I repeated. "In that book, on those pages . . . Marlene had everyone's name written out next to the time of their appointment, except for Desiree. Next to ten a.m., she had *DS* printed in large caps, and the caps looked smudged, I remember that much. Damn!" I pushed my hand through my unruly curls. "Why is it that Desiree's name was the only one in initials?"

Ollie shrugged. "Maybe she just didn't feel like writing out the name?"

"Or maybe the appointment was for another *DS*. Those initials might not stand for Desiree Sanders at all!"

"It has to be her, though." Ollie frowned. "Didn't she say she was supposed to meet Marlene at ten a.m.?"

"She said around ten or ten-thirty. *DS* was written next to ten, so maybe Marlene figured she'd be done with whomever it was in a half hour."

Ollie coughed lightly. "Assuming your theory's right . . . if *DS* isn't Desiree Sanders, then who is it?"

"A good question. *D* could stand for Dooley, I suppose. And the *S?* Scarlett? Maybe she saw both of them together?"

"That doesn't make sense. She had Scarlett down for ten a.m. the day before. Why would she see her again with Franks?"

"You're right," I sighed. "Unless there's some reason she wanted to see the two of them together, I imagine it's more likely that *DS* stands for Desiree. And speaking of Desiree . . ."

I reached into my purse and pulled out the two squares of paper. "Think your pal down at the lab could run a match on these strands of hair for me? Tell me if they came from the same person?"

Ollie took the squares. "Do I want to know where you got these?"

I returned his grim stare with one of my own. "Probably not." Depending on the test results, I had a decision to make, but like Scarlett O'Hara, I'd think about that tomorrow or whenever.

• • •

The main fireplace was untouched, so Ollie and I drove back to Cruz. He had an appointment with a prospective client, so he dropped me off in front of the police station. Lenny Barker was on duty at the desk. He'd been in Lacey's class and had had an enormous crush on her as well—when you got right down to it, who in our high school hadn't had a crush on my sister? He gave me a big smile as I approached.

"Hey, Nora. Come to see Detective Samms?"

Oh, so they were calling him Detective Samms, not Agent Samms. Made me think of the first time I'd met Daniel. It had been in this very police station, and he'd been Detective Corleone at the time, but only because he was undercover. It was only later . . . much, much later . . . I'd learned he was actually Special Agent Corleone for the FBI.

Well, now Samms was in charge, not Daniel. And he wasn't undercover.

I shoved both hands in my pockets and smiled at Lenny. "Yeah. He in?"

"Yep. He's in the back, doing paperwork. We got a ton of paperwork around here. He told me to bring you on back when you came in."

"Which office? The last one on the left?" The office Daniel had occupied. Lenny nodded, and I waved my hand as he started to get up. "No need. I know the way."

I walked down the long corridor and didn't knock, just pushed open the frosted glass door that, right now, had no name emblazoned on it. Samms was seated behind the wide oak desk, a mountain of paper littering its top. He was hunched over, a frown on his face and a coffee cup clenched in one hand. I took a quick look around. Same scarred, beat-up file cabinets, same black Keurig coffeemaker perched atop the tallest one.

Some things never changed.

I cleared my throat and he looked up. The frown didn't leave his face as he gestured with his free hand for me to sit. I walked over, eased myself into the familiar hard-backed chair.

"Nice digs," I said. "Kind of a comedown for you, though, isn't it? I bet that office at FBI headquarters in Carmel would be a heck of a lot nicer, or at least that's what I hear from Daniel."

"It's all what you get used to. Fancy trappings aren't my style. You do remember my office in Saint Leo, right?"

"I remember a lot about Saint Leo," I mumbled. "You were a hard-ass then, and you haven't changed much." I slid him a glance and I could swear the corners of his lips tipped in a brief smile; however, it was gone as soon as it appeared, the frown firmly in place. "You know, your face might freeze that way." When I got no reaction I leaned back in the chair, shifting a bit against the hard wood. "So, where's Peter? I'm assuming you've got Desiree in one of your cozy cells?"

"Actually, they're probably at Hot Bread, waiting for you. They left about a half hour ago."

I almost fell off the chair. "What? Desiree said you were arresting her for Marlene's murder."

"I did." He took a long sip of coffee–deliberately, I was certain–before he set the mug down and looked back at me. "But our friend Peter Dobbs was on it even before he got here. He has friends in high places, as you know. His uncle phoned Judge Black and arranged for him to come here for an impromptu hearing. Black agreed to release her on bail."

I knew Peter's uncle, Helmut Dobbs, had enjoyed a long and successful career as a DA before retiring. I'd also hoped Peter might call upon him for help. "What's she charged with?"

"Second degree. The DA's inclined to think it might have been a crime of passion."

"What do you think?"

He eyed me. "Honestly? I can't see that woman as a cold-blooded murderer. I could see her offing someone in the heat of the moment, though. She's strung tighter than a violin."

We were silent a few minutes, and then I asked, "I imagine the fact you arrested her in the first place means you found the murder weapon."

"Out in the bushes, near the garage. It wasn't hidden very well." He rubbed a hand across his eyes. "Her prints were the only ones on it. Oh, and the dead woman's too. It looks to be the same caliber as the bullet we took out of the body. I'm just waiting for the ballistics test to confirm."

"Did you do a gun residue test?"

He shook his head. "Too much time elapsed. Residue only sticks around for about three hours, you know that."

I did know that. I also knew that, contrary to what shows like *CSI* and *Law & Order* wanted you to believe, gunshot residue test results were often misleading. A positive GSR test did not always mean the individual fired a gun, much less the gun in question. Then again, a negative test result didn't necessarily mean the person didn't fire the gun, either. It all boiled down to too many variables: time, activity, the condition of the testing surface.

I leaned forward to rest my elbows on the edge of his desk. "Does it really seem likely to you that she'd kill her partner and then put the gun where the police would be certain to find it?"

He shrugged. "She's an excitable person. Excitable people sometimes do irrational things."

"Like kill their partners?"

Samms leaned back in his big chair, laced his hands behind his neck. "For one thing, she was afraid of the secret her partner was planning to reveal in her new book."

"There were lots of others afraid of the same thing, Carruthers included."

"True, but their prints weren't found on the murder weapon."

We sat in stony silence for a few minutes before I asked, "So what else do you have on her, other than the gun?"

"I'm not at liberty to discuss that, and you know it, Nora."

"Well, then can you discuss the crime scene? What about the other rooms in the house?"

"The first floor appears not to have been disturbed. Can't say as much for the upstairs rooms. All of 'em look like a tornado passed through."

Which could mean Simon Gladstone might or might not have done some snooping. "You're slipping, Samms. You left a key piece of evidence in the house and now it's ruined."

His eyes narrowed. "What are you talking about?"

"Marlene's appointment book. You didn't remove it from the premises, and now it's been tampered with. The page with Desiree's initials is now missing, as well as a few other pages."

He shot me a puzzled look, then picked up the telephone. When the person at the other end answered he barked, "Bring me 1076, right now." He slammed down the receiver and glared at me, his brows cutting a deep V in the center of his forehead. "Just how do you know pages are missing? You were in that house, weren't you!"

I squirmed a bit in the chair. "Maybe."

He let out a deep sigh. "Nora, Nora. Didn't you learn anything from your last little adventure about tampering with evidence?"

"I didn't tamper with anything by entering. The crime tape is down. That's an indicator the scene's been cleared."

"The place was locked, and there was supposed to be a guard out there."

"Really?" Now it was my turn to frown. "We didn't see a guard."

"We?" A long sigh came out of those gorgeously shaped lips. "Ah, don't tell me. You and the body-sniffing cat decided to do a little exploring?"

"Not this time. I went with Ollie."

"Ollie? Oh, yes, Atkins's partner. You like to hang around PIs, it seems."

"Well, I for one am glad he was with me, because he kind of intimidated Simon Gladstone. If he hadn't . . ."

The V cut even deeper into the forehead. "Simon Gladstone?"

"Yes. Marlene's nephew—only he's not. Marlene was an only child, and she never married, so he couldn't be her nephew. He wanted us to think he was, though, but Ollie was on to him. I chased after him but he got away through the woods, and when we went inside, we found the appointment book tossed under the hall table, and those pages were ripped out."

A knock sounded at Samms's door, and Lenny shuffled in, carrying a plastic bag, which he handed to Samms. I glanced at it, then did a double take. My eyes widened. My jaw dropped.

"You mean this book?" Samms asked, as he dangled the bag in front of me.

Sure enough, the black appointment book was clearly visible. I didn't know what to say. My mouth moved, but no words came out. Finally I squeaked, "But that's impossible! The appointment book was in the house. Ollie and I both saw it. And we both saw where the pages had been ripped out."

Samms put the bag on the desk in front of him and eased the book out. He flipped the pages until he came to the section he wanted, and then pushed the book in front of me. "That what you saw yesterday?"

I leaned over. Sure enough, there were the pages I thought had been taken, right in *this* book. There was the *DS* right next to ten thirty, and Morley Carruthers's name scrawled beside five p.m. On the opposite side, the previous day's appointments had Scarlett Vandevere and Dooley Franks, just as I'd seen them.

I frowned and looked closely at the book again. Something didn't hit me right, but I couldn't put my finger on it. "Something's wrong," I muttered.

Samms closed the book abruptly and slid it back into the plastic bag. "Tell me more about this Simon Gladstone."

I leaned back in my chair, drummed my fingers on the scarred arm. "Sure. What do you want to know?"

"A description might be nice."

"Around five-ten or eleven, slight build, pale complexion, blond, blue-eyed. Good runner."

Samms stared off into space, eyes slitted. "Uh-huh. Anything else? How was he dressed?"

"Pale blue T-shirt, pressed jeans. The blue of the shirt was a nice complement for his eyes—oh, and he spoke with an accent."

He jerked forward in his chair, his eyes alight with interest. "An accent? What kind?"

"I found it kind of hard to place. He said he'd been studying theatre in London but was originally from Boston, so I guess that could account for it."

"Boston?" Samms leaned forward a little more. I thought he might actually tip the chair over.

"Yes. Ask Ollie if you don't believe me. And why is that so interesting to you?"

He shrugged and picked up the phone again. "Lenny? Send a squad car out to the Porter place. Nora here tells me the guard we had on duty wasn't around when she was out there about a half hour ago. Thanks." He replaced the phone and pushed his chair back. "I think that's all. Like I said, Desiree and Dobbs are most likely waiting for you over at Hot Bread. I'm sure you'll want to talk to them."

"I'm not finished talking to you."

"Yeah, you are."

He stood, took my elbow, gently raised me from the chair and propelled me toward the door. As he opened it, clarity suddenly washed over me and I snapped my gaze to his. "There are two books," I said.

He stared at me. "What?"

"I remember now. The book I saw had the initials *DS* written next to ten a.m., not ten thirty. What's more, they weren't neatly printed; rather, they looked slightly smudged, almost as if they'd been written over an erasure. There were two books, and you got the wrong one."

His face darkened for just a fraction of a second, and then it cleared. He gave me a gentle nudge outside the door. "You've been following that darn cat of yours to too many crime scenes. Now you're seeing things that aren't there."

"I'm not—I have . . ." I started to say, *I have proof*, but stopped. All I needed was for Samms to confiscate my phone as evidence. "I have a gut feeling," I finished lamely.

"I know you're not good at taking advice, Nora, but please stay away from this one. It's not a safe place to be."

"Why not? You've supposedly apprehended the murderer, right? Or is this your way of telling me you have doubts about that?"

"Just steer clear of that crime scene. I don't want to feel responsible, or worse yet, answer to Daniel if something should happen to you."

"What might happen? And why would you have to answer to Dan—" I got no further as the door swung shut, very firmly, in my face. I started to walk away, then turned back. I stood in front of the door, hand raised to knock, and then I heard Samms's deep rumble.

"Daniel Corleone, please. No? Well, tell him to call Lee Samms. It's urgent." He let out a deep sigh. "We've got a problem."

A problem? I was darn curious as to this problem's nature, but then I heard his chair scrape back and heavy feet making their way toward the door. I turned and ran down that hallway, as fast as one can run in four-inch heels. As I approached the front desk I caught a glimpse of a man in a three-piece suit talking to Lenny. He had a thin slash for a mouth, beady eyes behind wire-rimmed glasses, a cruel set to his jaw. As I passed I heard him say, "Detective Samms is expecting me." I knew sure as anything this was Morley Carruthers. I debated sticking around for a few minutes and trying to eavesdrop, but before I could make up my mind yea or nay my cell chirped. I glanced at the screen and saw it was Louis Blondell, then quickly pushed my way outside and answered.

"I hope this call is good news, Louis."

"Nora, I have information for you." Louis sounded jubilant. "Sable and Scarlett are both on tours, and the last few days they've been in this vicinity. I've got their schedules."

"Great. You're in the office? I'll be right down."

I hung up and hurried over to my car. As I slid behind the wheel, I saw Samms and another policeman hurry out the side door of the station, jump into a cruiser, and take off. For a second I was tempted to follow them. I had a gut feeling they were headed for the Porter house—but then I turned my SUV in the direction of Louis's office. I wasn't in the mood for more verbal sparring with Samms, and besides, Louis was waiting for me. As I made a left onto Main, I felt a familiar tightening in my belly. It told me there was more going on here than just Marlene's murder. Hopefully very soon I'd find out just exactly what that might be.

Thirteen

Noir's office was in the downtown section of Cruz, in a big rambling building with vaulted ceilings and wooden floors. It had originally been a firehouse back in the day, and when a more modern one had been built, someone had made the decision to chop the original structure up to make lots of small offices and generate rental income. Louis Blondell had always maintained he'd gotten the smallest office, most likely because that was what he could afford.

He'd started out with his own consulting business but had grown tired of it after a year and decided to sink his life's savings into doing something he'd always wanted to do: publish a true crime/pulp magazine. A favorite aunt of his had died around the time he'd made this decision, and the tidy stipend she'd bequeathed him had gone a long way toward making his lifelong dream come true. Still, he wasn't foolish with the money. He'd invested most of it, in order to have capital for the magazine, and he'd flatly refused to move to larger quarters. No one could claim he was extravagant with his office space; in fact, his office was rather Spartan. Desk. Chair. Guest Chair. The walls that didn't have framed *Noir* covers hanging from them were lined with bookcases filled to overflowing with magazines and true crime books; I thought Louis must have every Anne Rule book ever published. A few scarred file cabinets were scattered around, and on top of one sat an ancient Mr. Coffee. He had a girl who came in three days a week to help out with arranging the magazine and typing; otherwise, it was pure, vintage Louis.

I pushed open the door and walked inside, my heels clicking on his hardwood floor. Louis sat, shoulders hunched, behind his desk, his head partially obscured by the thirty-inch-plus Dell flat-screen monitor in its center. Louis had once bragged he could type one hundred twenty words a minute, and as I watched his fingers fly across his ergonomic keyboard, I could believe it. He glanced up, saw me, then lifted one hand to motion me into the lone guest chair; with the other he pawed through the mound of papers next to his keyboard. He yanked a lined sheet of paper out of the myriad and passed it across to me. The paper was divided into two sections: the top half read *Scarlett*, and had a listing of cities and times; the bottom read *Sable*, with another list of cities and times.

"Those are the appearances they're slated to make at some indy bookstores." He tapped the paper with his nail. "See where both of 'em are gonna be tomorrow?"

I did indeed. Both of them were at the bookstore in Saint Leo. Scarlett's appearance was scheduled for four, Sable's at seven. I looked over the entire list. On the date of the murder, Scarlett had been in Carmel, and Sable in Castillo. The time of their appearances had been early evening. Both towns were less than twenty minutes from Cruz.

I folded the paper and slipped it into my pocket. "You're amazing. I don't know how to thank you."

"Just write up one heck of a story when this is all over."

"You got it."

"Oh, and by the way," he called after me as I started for the door, "I hope you're still interested in taking some PI courses. I haven't forgotten about that column. We'll have to carve out some time to talk about it."

• • •

I let myself in the back door of Hot Bread about twenty minutes later. Nick was sprawled across the braided carpet near the storeroom door; he rose from his post to amble over, sniff at my shoes, and give me an injured "merow." (Translation: *Where have you been, puny human, and why did you not take me with you?*) I bent over, gave him a swift pat on the head, and then the murmur of voices beckoned me toward the kitchen area. I pushed open the door and saw Chantal, Peter and Desiree huddled around the table, large mugs of steaming coffee in front of them. Peter was speaking to Desiree and I could tell by the expression on his face it was something serious. Desiree looked nervous, her head lowered, eyes slitted, tongue darting out at intervals to swipe across her lower lip. Chantal was leaning forward, her elbows on the table, listening intently to what was being said, but as the door swung back it let out a soft creak that caused all three heads to swivel in my direction. Chantal jumped up, nearly upsetting her mug, and hurried over to me.

"*Chérie*, you look exhausted! Come, sit down. I'll pour you a cup of coffee."

"I could use one, thanks."

I followed her back to the table and sat down while she went to get me a cup of coffee. Peter smiled at me across the table. "Hey, there," he said. "It's a shame we only get to meet under these circumstances."

"Right. Next time we should double date, dinner and a movie."

He chuckled. Desiree reached out and her fingers closed over my hand. "You did an excellent job, Nora. Peter is very competent. He had me out on bail in no time flat. I don't even have to wear an ankle monitor, or anything."

Peter shrugged. "What can I say? I can be pretty persuasive. Thank the Lord for our 'innocent till proven guilty' system." He threw me an apologetic look. "There was a condition though. I had to promise that Desiree would stay here under your watchful eye. I hope that's all right."

"Of course it is." I took the mug Chantal pushed over to me and took a long sip before I continued, "After Samms and I were done reminiscing about the good old days, he told me the DA's going for second degree, they found the murder weapon with only Desiree's and Marlene's prints on it, and he's convinced himself it was a crime of passion."

"Well, they found a .45 all right, but when I left they were still waiting for ballistics to confirm." Peter scratched at his ear. "Crime of passion, eh?"

"Passion my rear," snorted Desiree. "Although if I had killed her, I would have been pretty passionate about making sure she suffered as much as possible."

"I'd be careful about making any remarks like that in public," Peter cautioned her.

"It's true, though. She must be laughing from wherever she is. Down there, most likely." She pointed a finger at the floor. "She's probably enjoying the mess I'm in. Honest, if she weren't dead already, I'd kill her myself for putting me through this."

Peter and I exchanged a look, and then I laid a hand on her arm. "Desiree, did Marlene have any family? Anyone she was close to?"

"Family? Let me see. Her parents are dead, she had one maiden aunt who must be almost a hundred, in some nursing home in Akron. No husbands, no in-laws. So, nope. There's no one."

"Are you certain? She had no siblings, no nieces, no nephews?"

"No aunts, uncles or cousins that I know of, anyway. When you think of it, except for me, and all those Latin boyfriends of hers, she was pretty much alone in the world. Kinda sad, really." Her eyes narrowed. "Why do you ask?"

"Because Ollie and I ran into a young man who said he was her nephew. Simon Gladstone."

"Simon Gladstone? Really! Well, ain't that a hoot." She gave me a reproachful look. "Simon Gladstone is a recurring character in our Ada Spencer series. He's a former cat burglar—a jewel thief to be exact—by night, a British playboy by day. He likes kinky sex and fast women with glittery diamonds." She clucked her tongue. "That series was the only one Marlene ever contributed more than her PR skills to. It was her idea from the get-go. She outlined all the characters—Gladstone, Ada—even Ada's shady sort of boyfriend, wealthy industrialist Nathan Eberhardt. I always thought she modeled Ada after herself ,and Nathan after Bruce Wayne."

"Well, I guess this guy was a fan. No wonder he picked that alias. This Simon Gladstone turned out to be a thief as well."

"Oh, no!" Desiree's face paled and she gripped the table with both hands. "Don't tell me he took . . ."

"I don't know," I admitted. "I chased after him but he got away.

Ransacked the upper floor pretty good though." I stretched my legs out in front of me, bumping Nick in the rear. He cast me an affronted look before rearranging himself next to Chantal's chair. "Do you happen to know if Marlene had two appointment books?"

She cut me an eye roll. "What would she need two for? She didn't have that many meetings, and to be honest, she didn't keep up with the one she had."

"That does seem to be the general consensus. However, when I was down at the station, Samms showed me another appointment book, exactly like the one back at the house—only this one had the pages intact." I reached into my bag, pulled out my phone. "I had a hunch and checked the pictures I took. In the book Samms has, your initials are printed very clearly next to ten thirty a.m. In this photo"—I held it out so the others could see—"they're written sort of cramped, next to ten a.m. Notice anything else?"

Peter squinted at the screen. "The initials look kinda smudged, like maybe they were written over an erasure."

"My thoughts exactly." I flicked on the keyboard option and started to type. "I'm going to send this photo to my pal Hank Prince." Hank was a PI who'd been my confidential informant when I'd done the crime beat in Chicago. If there was information to be found, he and his stable of contacts could usually ferret it out. "Maybe one of his cronies can enhance that photo to tell what's really written there."

"Good idea," said Peter.

I typed a quick text message to Hank, attached the photos and hit Send. Then I turned to Desiree. "There's something else I wanted to ask you. Was Marlene McCambridge her real name, or did she change it?"

"A good question. I don't know," Desiree said. "She's always been Marlene McCambridge to me."

"Did you ever tell her you changed your name?"

"Of course. I was always completely honest with her, much to my detriment."

"But she never alluded to having done the same?"

"No."

I nibbled at my lower lip. "If she did, would Morley Carruthers have known about it?"

Desiree frowned. "Maybe, but only if she wanted him to know. She was a past master at keeping secrets, and her own the best of all." Suddenly she scraped her chair back and stood up. "Wait a second. One day I saw her with a necklace. It was a pretty thing, a silver initial surrounded by a few diamonds. She kept it in a pouch in her purse. She saw me looking and put it away faster than you could blink your eye. Funny thing, though. You'd have thought it'd be an M, right? For Marlene or McCambridge? Nope. It was an E."

"An E? Did you ask her about it?"

Desiree clucked her tongue. "You really didn't know Marlene. If she wanted to avoid a subject, it was avoided. And she definitely didn't want to talk about that. As a matter of fact, she seemed very upset I'd seen the necklace. I never saw hide nor hair of it again, I can tell you that."

"In her purse, you say? I wonder if it might still be there, with her things, or if Simon Gladstone got that too. Speaking of her things, what's going to happen to them?"

"Good question. I imagine they'll just leave everything as it is until after her will is read. If you ask me, the real mystery is who she left her money to, if there is any. She's been a bit strapped for cash the last few years, thanks to her taste in men. Another reason for her writing that tell-all book."

"There's something somewhere," I said. "When Ollie and I called the publisher, she alluded to Marlene having gotten a large advance. Very large."

"Really?" Desiree frowned. "Another thing she kept from me. She complained right up until the end how strapped she was for cash." Suddenly her eyes went wide, and she clapped a hand over her heart. "Oh my God," she breathed. Her other hand reached out and gripped mine so hard I nearly cried out. "I know who killed her."

She released my hand and pushed her chair back with such force it nearly toppled over. Nick, startled, hopped up on the back counter and stood, back arched, tail twitching.

"It had to be Anabel," she murmured. "Anabel Leedson, our agent. Or should I say my agent and Marlene's former one." She raised a hand, passed it across her eyes in a dramatic gesture. "If she did murder Marlene, I suppose I should look for a new one, especially if she's trying to frame me for *her* crime!"

"What makes you think it's Anabel?" Peter asked

"Marlene borrowed money from her, quite a tidy sum, too. The week before Marlene fired her, I happened to be in Marlene's apartment. She had a pretty extensive library, and I needed to look up something. I heard her let Anabel in. They had quite a disagreement over the money. I heard Marlene tell Anabel she couldn't scrape up anything to repay her, not at this time, and Anabel said that she had a few tax problems and needed the money to make a payment to the IRS." Desiree let out a bitter laugh. "Marlene told her in no uncertain terms that wasn't her problem. I caught a glimpse of Anabel's face. It was beet red, and she looked as if she'd like to hit Marlene over the head with something. The next week Marlene fired her."

Peter looked over at me. "Sounds like a pretty good motive."

"If Marlene got that advance, she sure could have paid Anabel back," Desiree continued. "What she said to her makes sense, now."

"What did she say?"

"Anabel told Marlene that she knew she had money, that she'd lied to her, and she owed it to her to return what she'd borrowed. She said that she'd worked hard for us all these years, and she never had a peep of trouble out of me, but Marlene was another story." Desiree nibbled at her lower lip. "She told Marlene she was an ungrateful . . . witch."

"Anabel knew Marlene had gotten the advance?" I asked. "How?"

"She didn't come right out and say it, but it was implied. I believe her exact words were . . . now let me think a minute." Desiree closed her eyes. "Oh, yes. She said, 'You're lying, Marlene. I know you've come into a good sum of money, and that you've been lying to me and to Desiree these last few weeks. I've been nothing but loyal to the two of you, and I've always defended you, even when you were wrong. You owe it to me to return the money I lent you.' And then Marlene drew herself up and says back, 'I don't owe you anything, Anabel. If Desiree feels that way that's her business. Myself, I'm an independent spirit. Tiffany Blake made you the agent you are today, and don't you forget it! Without us, you'd be nothing! You should have lent me that money—no, you should have *given* it to me. Now, I've told you the truth. When I get some money together, I'll repay you. Until then I don't want to hear another word. I can make plenty of trouble for you if you keep pestering me, and don't think I won't do it.' Then Anabel muttered something I couldn't hear, and Marlene laughed—just like Margaret Hamilton did, you know, when she played the Wicked Witch—and she said, 'Honey, that's nothing compared to what I've got on you.' And that's when Anabel called her a lying witch, and stormed out."

"From that conversation it sounds as if Anabel had a secret as well, and Marlene knew it. Was she in that book too?" I asked.

Desiree shrugged. "It's possible. Like I said, Marlene was very adept at getting people to talk to her. Spill their guts."

Peter rubbed his chin thoughtfully. "I wonder where Anabel was at the time of the murder?"

"It's easy enough to check out," said Desiree. "I can just call her."

I handed Desiree my phone, and she punched in a number. A few seconds later she mouthed, "Voice mail." Then she said, "Hey, Anabel, it's Des. Can you call me back. It's kinda important, thanks." She disconnected and then punched in another number. "Hey, Becky. Hi, it's Desiree. Very well, thanks. I'm in California. Thought I'd do some R&R before the new book comes out. No, I haven't heard a word about a tour . . . really? I just called her and it went to voice mail . . . great. Do you know where I can get hold of her? No, huh? Well, when she calls you, tell her to call this number." She repeated my cell number and then hung up. Her gaze was troubled as she looked at us. "I called her admin,

Becky Blount. Becky said that Anabel left a week ago to come out here to California to set up a book tour for me."

"Is that a usual procedure?" Peter asked as Desiree hesitated.

Desiree shook her head. "No, it isn't. This tour was different. Our publisher usually arranged our tours, but when Marlene said she wasn't going to do publicity for the new book, our publisher canceled their plans. That's when Anabel stepped in and took over." Desiree brushed her hand through her neatly coiffed hair. "What is unusual was the fact she flew here to do it in person. Such things are normally handled via the phone or email. Which might mean . . ."

"She had another reason for wanting to come to California," I finished. I thought of the mysterious Anne Onymous. Was it possible she could be Anabel Leedson? "Did Becky happen to mention where Anabel was staying?"

"She didn't have her book a hotel like she usually does. Told her that her accommodations were taken care of, and she'd be in touch. She didn't give her a hotel name or number." Desiree chewed at her bottom lip.

Maybe not so odd, I thought, not if you were renting a house and wanted to keep your identity a secret. Maybe the nosy neighbor in the stucco house wasn't just a random neighbor after all. I needed to get out there and get some answers.

And I knew just the person who could help me.

Fourteen

I was in the middle of the breakfast rush the next morning when Jenks ambled in the front door. He took his place in line behind Henry and Lauretta Trimble, a retired couple who came in every morning for bear claws and coffee before starting their customary three-mile walk. Lately, though, they'd been skipping the walk and sitting at one of the front tables to watch the morning news, like most of my other customers. Right now the story of the hour was Marlene's murder, and everyone's eyes were glued to the screen. I gave Henry and Lauretta their donuts and coffee and greeted Jenks with a smile as he approached the counter.

"I see you got my message," I said. "Your voice mail wasn't on, so I had to leave it at the switchboard."

"Technical troubles." He chuckled, brushing an errant strand of hair out of his eyes with the flick of a finger. "I've never been one to turn away a free breakfast. Or, as you put it, 'the scoop of the century.' What exactly did you mean by that?"

I leaned across the counter so my nose was level with his, and I whispered, "How'd you like to possibly catch Marlene McCambridge's killer?"

His eyes widened slightly and then he coughed. "Well, it would certainly put me back in Marker's good graces. He wasn't happy that we had to share the news of her murder with every other newspaper and TV station in the vicinity, especially since I'd had prior knowledge. I'm lucky he didn't demote me to reporting on local news, like that pet show over in Castillo." He let out a small groan. "I hate pet shows. I had to practically grovel for him to let me stay on features. That detective really owes me for keeping quiet like he asked."

I was relatively certain Samms wouldn't care in the least about Jenks's career problems, but I refrained from making any comment. I set some eggs frying on the griddle before I turned back to him. "So you're in, then?"

"Heck, yeah." He stroked his chin thoughtfully. "You know who killed her?"

"I have a pretty good idea."

His eyes widened. "You do?"

"Well, it's nothing definite. It's a gut feeling. But as gut feelings go, it's a good one."

He seemed to relax a bit. "Oh."

I transferred the fried eggs to a fluffy roll, topped them with a thick slice of cheddar cheese, some crumbled bacon bits, and a slice of tomato, filled a mug with steaming coffee and placed it on a tray in front of Jenks. "Here you go, one Jimmy Fallon Special. Now, do you recall the house across from the one where Marlene was killed?"

He shook his head. "Not really, no."

"It's a brown stucco one. I saw the curtains move on several different occasions. At first I thought it might be a nosy neighbor, you know, like *Rear Window*? But certain things have come to light that make me think the person in that house might have had a more vested interest in recent events."

He added cream and sugar to the coffee. "So you think whoever's in that house is the killer?"

"Either that, or they might have seen who did do it." I glanced around to make sure no one was listening and then continued, "I've gone out there a couple of times and tried to get in by conventional means, but either they weren't home or they didn't want visitors."

"And now you want to use unconventional means? To try and confront a person who may or may not be a murderer?" He bit down on his lower lip. "Have you thought about what might happen if this person you want to confront *is* the murderer?"

"We're not going to accuse her of anything outright. I just need to ask her a few questions."

One shaggy eyebrow rocketed skyward. "The murderer is a woman?"

I splayed both my palms on the counter. "Were you listening when I used the words *possibly* and *might?* And do I look like I'm the type to stand in front of a possible killer and accuse her outright of murder?" I took my hands off the counter and turned back to the griddle. "If you don't want to help, I'll do it on my own. I just thought . . ."

He held up his hand. "Hey, no need to get so touchy. I was just pointing out a few flaws in your plan."

"You do know what they say about plans, right?"

"Say no more. I'm in. Just tell me the time and place."

I did a quick calculation in my mind. Scarlett's book signing was at four, and I wanted to approach her before it started. Chantal had already agreed to close for me, so twenty minutes to drive there and back, maybe a half hour with Scarlett at the most . . . "Can you meet me out there at five?"

He picked up his tray. "You got it."

Jenks ambled off to a table in the back and I poured myself a cup of coffee. Nick rose from his favorite spot by the refrigerator, walked over to me, rubbed against my ankles, and then looked up at me with his unblinking golden stare.

"Sorry, bud. You're not coming with me."

Nick made grumbly noises in his throat.

I opened the glass case, took out a slice of ham, put it on a paper plate and set it on the floor in front of Nick. "Peace offering," I said.

He walked over to the plate, sniffed at the ham, and then began to eat it. Midway through his feast, he raised his head and fixed me with a baleful glare. "Merrrow," he warbled.

Apparently my peace offering was not enough.

"Too bad," I told him. "I've got a lot of ground to cover in a short period of time. I don't want to have to worry about you while I'm doing it."

"Er-ewl." His look plainly said, *You? Worry about me? Who's saved whose life more than once, hmm?*

I bent down to pat him but he ducked his head. "It's not that I'm not grateful. You know I am. But I can't afford to take any chances. If Ollie, or Samms, or Daniel knew what I was planning, why, they'd all skin me alive."

"Who's skinning who?"

I glanced up sharply. Daniel, looking particularly handsome in his usual navy blue suit, white shirt and maroon tie, smiled at me across the counter.

I flushed guiltily. "I was—ah—just having a little conversation with Nick. Disciplining him, actually."

"Really?" Daniel looked across the counter at the cat, who had lofted up to the counter and sat, back straight, his eyes fixed on me. "He does look a little angry."

I turned and shook my finger at Nick. "Bad cat. I told you not to jump on the counter during work hours."

Nick blinked twice, then calmly raised his left front paw and began to lick it.

Daniel eyed him. "You can't discipline a cat, Nora. They have minds of their own."

"Tell me about it. Still, every now and then I have to lay down the law. After all, I am the human." I walked over and gave Nick a swift pat on his bottom.

"Merow," he said, and then jumped down, ambled over to the ham, and began to slurp it down.

Daniel laughed. "The two of you are more alike than you realize." He sobered, stuffed his hands into his pockets. "Can we talk?"

"Sure. Do you want anything? Coffee, an egg sandwich—"

"Actually, I need a little information." He nodded toward my back room. "Can we talk privately?"

I waited as Daniel walked around my wide front counter into the kitchen area. I motioned for him to follow me into my storeroom; I figured I could spare a few minutes, since no one was waiting on line. Once I'd closed the door, he said, "I understand you and Ollie found an intruder at the Porter house yesterday."

I shifted from one foot to the other. "Good news travels fast, I see. You've spoken to Samms."

"What were you doing out there, Nora?"

In two seconds flat Daniel had made the transition from hunky male customer to cool, detached FBI agent. When he had that steely look on his face, I knew I'd better not try to duck any of his questions. "I wanted to question the person who's renting the house across from the Porter house—her name is Anne Onymous. I kid you not," I added as I caught the steely glint in his eyes. "Ask Joannie Adams if you don't believe me. Ollie and I both figure it's an alias."

"Why did you want to question her?"

"When I was out there and found Marlene's body, I saw the curtain move twice. But no one answered the door. Samms said he'd gotten an anonymous tip there was a prowler. I thought maybe whoever it was in that house might have seen something."

He was silent a minute then asked, "How did you end up back at the Porter house?"

"When no one answered, we thought we'd just check it out."

"You wanted to hunt for that missing manuscript."

"The thought did cross my mind."

"And that's when you ran into the intruder?"

"Yes. He said his name was Simon Gladstone and that he was Marlene's nephew. Ollie realized that he couldn't be Marlene's nephew, and he realized we were onto him, that's when he slammed the door in our faces. I chased him around the side but he was too fast. He got away through the woods."

"Did you see him take anything from the house?"

I shook my head. "I'm not sure. I saw a flash of something white in his hand, but it didn't look big enough to be a book manuscript. I think he ripped some pages out of Marlene's appointment book."

"Yes, Lee told me about that."

I raised one eyebrow. "Did he tell you there must be two books? Because the one he's got in evidence is *not* the same one I saw."

"Lee mentioned your opinion on the subject."

"It's a lot more than my opinion," I huffed. "It's a fact."

I went back into the kitchen and returned a few minutes later with my phone. I clicked it into picture mode and called up the two I'd taken of the appointment book and showed them to Daniel. "See this one?" I pointed. "The initials—DS—look smudged, like they've been written over something else that's been erased. And in this one, *DS* is by ten a.m. In the book Samms has, they're written clear as a bell, and next to ten thirty."

Daniel frowned. "Where did you take these pictures?"

"Right after I found Marlene's body. The book was lying in a half-open drawer under the laptop."

Daniel pursed his lips and stared at the pictures. "Um-hum."

"Listen, if I found the book, there's no way Samms could have missed it. He's too good of a cop, unless . . ." I paused as a sudden thought struck me.

"Unless what?" Daniel prompted as I remained silent.

I shook my head. "No, sorry. It was a crazy idea. Forget it." I huffed a strand of hair out of my eyes as Daniel shut off my phone and handed it back. "Samms said there was a guard at the house, but we didn't see anyone."

"That's because the guy was knocked unconscious and dragged onto the back porch."

My eyes widened. "Gladstone's work, I assume?"

"Most likely. It's a good thing Ollie was with you, Nora. If you had been alone . . ." He let that thought hang in the air for a moment, and then asked, "Can I show you something?"

I nodded and he reached into his jacket pocket and pulled out a photograph, which he laid on the counter in front of me. "Does that man look familiar?"

I stared at the man in the photo. He was dressed in a three-piece suit, and his hair was shorter and combed in a slightly different style, but there was no mistaking those blue eyes. I tapped the photo with my finger. "That's him. That's Simon Gladstone."

Daniel nodded and slipped the photo back in his jacket pocket. I looked at him. "Well? Aren't you going to tell me who that is? I already know Simon Gladstone isn't a real name."

He shook his head. "Sorry, I can't. At least not at this time."

My eyes widened. "So that man is somehow involved with the FBI? With a case you're working on? And Samms knew this?"

Not an eyelash flickered. His expression didn't change one iota.

I brushed at a piece of lint on my apron. "You know, sometimes you can be incredibly frustrating."

He leaned both elbows on my counter. "How about incredibly cute?"

"You can't blame me for being curious, Daniel. After all, what would a guy wanted by the FBI be doing pillaging a murder scene?"

He gave me a bland look. I wondered if he practiced it in front of the mirror. "Did I say he was wanted by the FBI?"

"You don't have to. It's obvious."

He clucked his tongue. "Now you're making an assumption."

"Okay, then. He's not wanted by the FBI."

"Another assumption."

I sighed. "Okay. He was hired by someone who's wanted by the FBI."

I saw one of his eyebrows twitch, ever so slightly.

"Oh my gosh, I guessed it. Someone wanted by the FBI hired him to do what?" I sucked in a breath. "You think Marlene's death was a hit?"

"At this point, I'm not ruling out the possibility," he said. "But nothing's cast in stone."

My brain was already whirling with possibilities. Who would have hired a hit man? Scarlett Vandevere? Dooley Franks, aka Sable St. John? Morley Carruthers? Anabel Leedson? Could any of them possibly be wanted by the FBI, and was that the secret Marlene had held over their head?

Or was it someone else entirely?

"The initials," I suddenly cried, and my fingers dug into Daniel's arm. "Marlene erased someone's initials and wrote *DS* over it because she didn't want anyone to know about that appointment. Marlene was meeting with someone wanted by the FBI?"

Silence greeted me.

I decided now was as good a time as any to test the theory I'd worked out in my head. "I think Samms knew all along there were two appointment books, because he planted one there. You two are working together, aren't you? And you set a trap for . . . someone. Simon Gladstone? You were hoping he'd show up!" I gave a little cry. "Except it didn't go the way you planned. Somehow the books got switched, and he made off with the pages from the right one."

"That's a very nice theory you've worked up," Daniel said. "However, at this point, it's all supposition."

"But on a scale from one to ten," I persisted. "How good is it?"

"Nora, Nora." Daniel shook his head. "Why do you keep backing me into corners? You know I can't answer you. I've already told you more than I should."

Which was damn little, in my estimation. "Can't? Or won't?"

He studied my face for a moment, then reached out and tucked a loose tendril of hair behind one ear. "What do you think?"

I sighed. "I think you would if you could."

"Precisely. You have to trust me, Nora. This is nothing to fool around with. Both Samms and I are trying to keep that pretty head of yours intact."

"Samms said almost the same thing. Actually, he said he didn't want to have to answer to you if anything should happen to me."

"He's right." His thumb made circular motions on the back of my hand. "I want you to be around for a while, Nora Charles. There are lots of things I would like to do with you and we haven't even scratched the surface."

I looked deeply into his eyes. "There are?"

"Yes. Many, many things."

We stood there, gazing into each other's eyes, and the moment stretched between us, pregnant with possibility . . . and then Nick let out a loud yowl from the other side of the door, at the precise instant Daniel's cell phone chirped.

I opened the door a crack and eyed the cat, who was sitting in front of the refrigerator. "Nick, that's just damn spooky. Cut it out."

Daniel was reading a text message. He shut his phone off, slid it back into his pocket. "I've got to go. I was thinking about dinner and a movie this weekend? I've got Sunday off. We can stay out late—paint the town."

"That sounds great."

"Try to stay out of trouble until then, eh?"

The corners of my lips twitched upward. "I hate to make promises I'm not sure I can keep."

He gave me a look then leaned over and touched his lips briefly to mine. "Try your best, okay? I kinda like you in one piece." He motioned toward my back door. "I'll go out this way. My car's in the alley."

I caught his hand, gave it a quick squeeze. "I know you're trying to keep me safe, Daniel, and you have my best interests at heart, but you know me well enough to know I'm not backing down until I get answers."

He nodded. "I know." He started toward the door, then abruptly turned. "I'll tell you this much. That scale you asked about? For your theory?"

A tingle crept along my spine. "Yeah?"

"Try eleven."

Wow.

Fifteen

Chantal came at two thirty to take over closing duties, and after leaving her some last-minute instructions on what to do with the few straggling customers who were more interested in watching *General Hospital* than in ordering more coffee, I attempted a quick goodbye to Nick (who turned his back on me and wiggled under the rear table). After wheedling and coaxing for about five minutes I gave up. "Goodbye, Nick. I'm sure you'll make certain that I make this up to you."

"Oh, do not worry about Nicky," Chantal said and laughed as I started out the door. "I have some new collars to try on him. We will have fun on my break, right, handsome?"

Nick stuck his head out from under the tablecloth, fixed me with a baleful stare, and let out a low *grr* as I shut the door. Boy, was I gonna pay for this.

I arrived in Saint Leo a few minutes before three thirty. The area was crowded, and I saw a long line of people standing around the entrance to the Book Haven; apparently Scarlett was more of a draw than I'd figured. I ended up having to park on a side street near the St. Leo library, about four blocks away. The good news was, by the time I reached the bookstore, most of the waiting people had disappeared inside. There was a big sign set up right in the entryway:

Appearing today, 4 p.m.
Author of My Ravaged Love
Scarlett Vandevere

Underneath the printed words was a picture of the book's dust jacket, which depicted a girl with flowing black hair, wearing a white blouse that came all the way off her shoulders, displaying a generous amount of cleavage, swooning in the arms of a muscular man with flowing black hair, his white shirt all the way open, displaying yards and yards of tanned, muscular chest. The man's hands were locked around the woman's waist in a death grip; her hand was caressing his cheek. It made me warm just to look at them.

Below the cover art was a headshot of a pretty girl with light colored hair and a wide, even smile. It was impossible to discern her exact hair or eye color because the photograph was black-and-white, but I was guessing Scarlett was the quintessential blonde-haired, blue-eyed maiden. I pushed through the double doors into the store itself and took a deep breath. I've always loved bookstores; there's just something about them, maybe it's the smell of the books, I don't know. Nowadays, though, that smell is less and less prevalent, probably due to the popularity of electronic reading devices like the Nook. I noticed practically half of the first floor was devoted to the reader.

Off to my left there were racks of hardcover books marked "Clearance," a wide table covered with Daily Calendars, and another rack off to the back that boasted a selection of greeting cards and tote bags. More tote bags lined the walkway to the bank of registers lining the far wall—off in the rear of the store was a small section devoted to CDs and DVDs. Right next to that was an escalator leading to the second floor and a large sign: *Book Signing Upstairs*

There was a small throng of people, both men and women, heading for the escalator, so I joined them. Once upstairs, I followed the crowd past the Mystery and Romance section to a large corner that had been set up with about four dozen folding chairs. Two love seats flanked the chairs, and in the front near the railing was a large podium with another folding table. I saw two teenaged boys pass wheeling a cart laden with boxes and deposit them near the folding table; Scarlett's books, no doubt. I glanced quickly around the area. It was filling up quickly, but there were still a few seats left. The air was abuzz with the sound of people chattering.

No sign, however, of the author.

A young girl with long dark hair, wearing jeans and a black T-shirt with a name tag pinned above her right breast, passed me, and I reached out and touched her arm. She swung me an inquisitive gaze, and I noted the name on the tag read *Bonnie*. I gave her a wide smile.

"Hello, Bonnie, is it? I assume you work here."

She nodded, still regarding me warily. "Yes, ma'am."

"I was wondering if you could help me. I need to speak to Scarlett Vandevere before the signing starts."

Her eyes widened slightly, but her expression was one of clear boredom. "I'm sorry, ma'am. No fans are allowed to see Ms. Vandevere before the event. You'll get a chance to speak with her when she signs your book." She glanced pointedly down at my empty hands.

I brushed some hair out of my eyes and gave her a wide-eyed stare. "Oh! You think I'm here to have her sign a book? You think I'm a *fan?*"

The bored look morphed into a puzzled one. "Aren't you?"

I gave a light laugh and stuck my hand into my tote. I pulled out my old press pass (thank God there was no expiration dates on these babies!) and dangled it under her nose. "Gosh, no! I'm a reporter. I'm here to interview Ms. Vandevere."

Her well-shaped brows drew together, cutting a deep V in her otherwise smooth forehead. "Interview? Really?" Her lips puckered into an O shape. "Gee, we've never had reporters come to a book signing before, at least not as long as I've worked here. Three months now." She said the last with a certain amount of pride.

"No? Well, then." I widened my smile. "This can be a first."

She took my pass in her hands and studied it a few seconds before passing it back to me. "I'm sorry, but I wouldn't be able to give you permission. I'll have to run this by Milton," she said at last. "He's the store manager and the one in charge of this event. If you'd like to wait here . . ."

"Oh, I have another interview in about a half hour. Would it be all right if I went with you? To save time?"

She hesitated, then nodded. "I guess so."

I followed her down the aisle to a small door behind the Self-

Improvement section. She pushed it open and motioned for me to follow her. I did, and found myself in another small room, with two doors branching off from it. In the center of the room was a metal desk. The nameplate on it read M. *Fennwick*. A navy suit jacket was thrown over the metal chair behind the desk, but there was no one in sight.

Bonnie stood a trifle uncertainly, hands on hips. "Can you just wait here a minute? He's around somewhere." She muttered something about taking fifty breaks a day under her breath and disappeared through the door on the left.

Once she'd gone, I immediately crossed to the door on the right and flung it open. A narrow hallway greeted me, with a closed door at the end. I walked boldly over to the door and rapped on it.

"Scarlett? Are you in there?"

No answer. I was just about to retrace my steps when I heard a soft click. I turned around and stared straight into the eyes of the woman on the poster. Her eyes were blue, a real, vivid, sky blue. I noted her hair was a dull ash-blonde, the same color as Desiree's . . . and the strand of hair I'd given Ollie. I cleared my throat.

"Scarlett Vandevere?"

She nodded, her hands running down the sides of her lime green linen skirt. "Who are you? Are you with the store? Is it time for the signing?" She held up a bare wrist. "Sorry, I forgot my watch."

I looked at mine: three forty-five. "You've got a little time. My name is Nora Charles, Ms. Vandevere." I waved my press pass under her nose. "I was wondering if you could spare a few minutes." I glanced quickly over my shoulder. No sign yet of Bonnie or Milton. "You'll be done in plenty of time for your signing."

Her eyes widened a bit as she looked at the pass, and the hard lines around her mouth softened. "You want to do a story on me?" I nodded, and she swung the door wide. "Why didn't you say so in the first place? Come on in."

The room was little bigger than a broom closet. There was a tiny table in one corner, makeup strewn over its top, flanked by a large mirror and a chair, and another small wooden chair folded up in the far corner. Scarlett went over, unfolded the wooden chair, and motioned for me to sit. She eased her slender frame into the other chair, her back facing the mirror. She crossed her legs and laced her hands over her knee. "So? What do you want to know? The usual? How I got my start? What advice I have for aspiring writers? What my next project is?"

"Actually, I was hoping you'd answer a few questions about your relationship with Marlene McCambridge."

The light faded from her eyes and her jaw thrust forward aggressively. "Marlene and I don't have a relationship. She's dead, in case you haven't heard—although if you haven't, then you must live under a rock. That's all they've talked about on the TV all day."

"I was told that you were a sort of protégée of hers."

She laughed, a short bitter sound. "Cripes, who told you that? Sable St. John?" She rose and gestured toward the door. "If that's the story you're after, you can forget it. I've got nothing to say about Marlene, or at least nothing you'd want to print, believe me."

"Not even about that tell-all book she was writing, and your chapter in it?"

Her eyes narrowed into mere slits, and her nails, painted the same lime green as her skirt, fiddled with its hem. "You're not really a reporter, are you?"

As her gaze narrowed, I tapped the pass and said, "As you can see, my name is Nora Charles. I covered the true crime beat in Chicago, but I moved back here to take over the family business."

"Family business?"

"I run a specialty sandwich shop in Cruz. Hot Bread. Feel free to Google me."

She cocked her head, studying me. "So let me get this straight. You said you're a reporter but you're not, not anymore. Yet you're asking me all these questions about Marlene. If you're not with the police, then you're a PI, and I don't have to answer anything without a lawyer."

"That's true, you don't." I set down the pad and pen. "I'll be straight with you, Scarlett. I'm not with the police and I'm not a PI, but I have an interest in this case. My mother was friends with Desiree Sanders, Marlene's writing partner. The way things stand now, it looks as if someone's framing her for Marlene's murder."

"Ah, so you're trying to find someone else to pin it on." She jumped up. "Well, look somewhere else. I didn't kill her."

"I'm not here to judge, Ms. Vandevere. I'm just trying to cover all the bases, get all the facts. Marlene told Desiree she was writing a tell-all, and your name was in her appointment book. You met with her the day of her death."

"I see."

"Was that why she called the meeting? To tell you that she was publishing the secret you'd told her in confidence in her tell-all?"

Scarlett blew out a breath. "Well, I don't know what Desiree told you about Marlene, but she wasn't a nice person, not at all. There are plenty of people who are glad she's dead, trust me."

"Including you."

"I won't deny that." She was silent for several minutes, and I saw her bottom lip tremble. At last she met my gaze. "Have you ever done something you've regretted, Ms. Charles? Something so supremely stupid, but it didn't seem so at the time? And have you ever made the mistake of confiding in the wrong person about it?"

Oh yeah, I could identify. Before I could say a word though, she rose, her hands clenching and unclenching at her sides. "When I met Marlene I already had a book contract in hand. I was young and foolish and I was impressed with her fame, you know, the Tiffany Blake books and all that. How was I supposed to know her partner was the one really writing them? Anyway, I guess you could say I was a bit starstruck? When Marlene offered to introduce me to the right people, of course I was flattered."

"And did she? Introduce you to the right people?"

"For her purposes, yes." She tugged at a loose curl. "What I'm going to say next is off the record, okay?" I nodded and she went on, "When I first started out, I admit it, I was a spoiled rich kid. In lots of ways, I still am. My parents were wealthy—not Bill Gates wealthy, but pretty close—and as their only child, I never wanted for anything. As a result, I garnered the reputation of 'empty-headed playgirl' around our Pebble Beach neighbors for years. And then, two weeks after I turned eighteen, my parents died in a car crash. It was a tragic time in my life, and a wake-up call. I started thinking I should do something with my life, you know? Because if I died tomorrow, what would people remember me for? The way I polished my nails? The fact I could wear a different outfit every day of the year? I started dabbling in a few things, and lo and behold—I discovered not only did I like to write, I had a distinct talent for it. I got myself a private tutor, and took a couple of courses in creative writing at USC. Then one day I got my courage up and sent one of my manuscripts off to a New York agent. Imagine my surprise when he not only liked it, he signed me right up. Two months later I had my first publishing contract. Then I went to a RomCon and met . . . her.

"Marlene was really friendly to me at first, and she seemed like she wanted to be helpful, you know, giving me pointers on my career, things I should do, yada yada. She talked me into dumping my agent and signing with this other guy—what a giant mistake that was! He cost me more deals than he got for me. I finally wised up and sent him packing. Later on I learned Marlene had deliberately referred me to him so he would sabotage my career. I supposed I should be flattered she was that jealous of my ability.

"But that's not even the worst part. When I was fifteen I had a fling with my history teacher. Stupid, I know. He got me hooked on drugs—the hard stuff. It took my parents' death to get me clean. Anyway, after my book became a hit I got involved with a guy who was also a supplier. I didn't write for two years, but good sense eventually kicked in and I got clean again. It bothered me, and I made the mistake of confiding in Marlene. Big mistake. She delighted in holding it over my head. My platform is my squeaky clean image that I was a poor little rich girl and I made it in the industry on hard work and my ability. If the truth about my past ever surfaced, my fans might all turn against me."

I laid my hand on her arm. "You don't know that for sure. After all, you're human. People make mistakes."

She shook her head. "I can't afford to take that chance. Not anymore. I recently found out my accountant has been stealing me blind the last few years. Turns out I do need the money I make from my romance series, now more than ever." She ran a hand through her hair, tugged absently on a curl. "When she set up this meeting, I knew darn well what it was going to be about. Anyway, I called her, offered her a half million dollars if she'd leave me out of the book. It would have left me totally broke, but I felt I had no choice."

I shifted in my chair. I liked Scarlett, but I couldn't discount the fact that what she'd just told me was a great motive for murder. "What did Marlene say?"

"She said she'd consider it, and let me know her final answer at our meeting, but"—her slender shoulders lifted in a shrug—"that never happened."

"So you never met with her in person?"

"No. Trust me, I'm not the only one who had issues with Marlene. If you ask me, that smarmy lawyer had problems with her, and Sable St. John couldn't stand her either. As a matter of fact, I overheard her on the phone one day last month. She was telling someone that St. John and her agent, Anabel Leedson, were conspiring against her, and she wasn't going to stand for it." Scarlett sighed. "You know what they say, sometimes having no agent is better than having a bad one. And trust me . . . Marlene was plenty angry at both of 'em." She frowned. "I told all this to that detective this morning at my hotel."

My heart skipped a beat. "Do you remember the detective's name, by chance? There are a few working this."

"To tell you the truth, I wasn't paying much attention when he introduced himself. He was darn good-looking though. Very movie star-ish. Black hair and eyes, and he had a nice build."

Oh, yeah. Samms.

"Anyway, he asked me where I stayed while I'm on tour. I told him I usually just stay at my condo in Pebble Beach, but it's being renovated, so I've been hanging with a friend of mine in Monterey. Then he asked me where I was between midnight and three a.m. night before last, and I told him we were practically up all night in her den, watching a Jimmy Stewart marathon on a cable channel." She smiled faintly. "The last movie was a good one. Jimmy Stewart broke his leg, and he's laid up and bored, so he snoops on his neighbors with binoculars and ends up witnessing a murder. I can never remember the name of it though."

"Rear Window."

"Oh, right." She beamed at me. "It's a classic movie, but it's just so unbelievable. Who in their right mind would witness a murder and then goad the killer on like Stewart did?" She shook her head. "I mean, no one does that in real life. Hello, it's like drawing a target right on your back, you know, a real invitation to murder."

I couldn't have said it better myself.

Sixteen

I wished Scarlett luck with her life and her new book and beat feet out of there before either Bonnie or Milton could pin me down. After all, I had a return engagement there at seven with Sable St. John. Hopefully by then both of them would be off shift and not around. Running into Bonnie again would definitely be awkward.

I mentally reviewed what I'd learned on the ride back to Cruz. I found myself believing the girl when she said she hadn't killed Marlene, no matter how desperately I might want not to. She just didn't strike me as the murdering kind, although from her story, she'd have plenty of reason to.

I didn't know what Desiree's secret was and I didn't want to. I found myself thinking not so kindly thoughts about the late Marlene McCambridge. How could she do this to people she'd befriended, and who'd trusted her?

If I could get my hands on that manuscript, I'd burn it myself. Better that than to have it fall into the hands of that publishing house who would, no doubt, milk it, and Marlene's death, for all it was worth.

I switched off the radio and drummed my fingers on the steering wheel. "One suspect down. Two , maybe three to go."

"Merow."

I gripped the wheel and turned my head, very slowly. Nick was sitting up straight in the backseat, his tail fanned out like a black plume. He flicked it slowly back and forth as our eyes met in my rearview mirror.

"How on earth did you get back there?"

"Yowl–yurgle!"

I noticed something else too. A circle of red, white and blue crystals hung around Nick's neck. One of Chantal's newest creations, no doubt. I inclined my head toward his neck. "Very patriotic."

A loud hiss was his response, and then he launched himself

gracefully over the console and arranged himself in my passenger seat. He lay down, head on paws, blinked twice at me, and then closed his eyes.

I'd long since given up on figuring out how Nick did the things he did. For that matter, I'd long since given up on thinking that Nick was an ordinary cat. There was clearly a lot more going on with him than met the eye, and I had the feeling I was better off *not* knowing just exactly what that might be.

"So you got tired of trying on collars and thought you'd track me down? I'm actually kinda glad you're here," I told the cat. "Mind if I bounce some theories off you?"

He winked one eye open.

"Good. I just interviewed Scarlett Vandevere. She seems like a very nice person, and apparently she's not our Miss Anne Onymous. She's been staying with a friend. They even watched *Rear Window* on late-night TV."

Nick snorted.

"Yeah, I tend to doubt alibis that depend on another person's corroboration, but apparently Samms went to see her earlier today, and apparently hers passed muster."

Nick's eyes closed. Apparently if Samms was satisfied, he was too.

"Scarlett said there wasn't any love lost between Marlene and Sable St. John, and Morley Carruthers, either. Scarlett said Marlene accused St. John of conspiring with her agent against her. I wonder what that was all about."

Nick rearranged himself on the seat and started to purr.

"Well, maybe we'll find out soon. That's why we're meeting Jenks at the stucco house."

At the mention of Jenks's name, Nick made a growly sound in his throat. Then he gave his head a vigorous shake and thumped his tail twice against the leather upholstery.

"Yes, I know Jenks isn't your favorite person. What can I say, Nick. Some people just don't get cats. To be honest, he doesn't impress me much either. But he's a pretty resourceful guy. I'm hoping he can figure out a way to charm our mysterious inhabitant into letting us in. It's starting to look to me that Ms. Onymous is Anabel Leedson."

Nick sneezed.

I wondered briefly what Daniel and Samms would think if they could hear me carrying on a conversation with my cat. Probably that I'd gone batshit crazy. Ollie and Chantal, now, were a different story. In fact, I'd heard Chantal remark on more than one occasion that Nick seemed to be following our conversations. Whether he did or not, I often found it helped me to sort things out, particularly when I was dealing with dead bodies.

Both Nick and I could claim a certain amount of expertise in that area.

I made the turn onto the road and a few minutes later the roof of the stucco house came into view. I glided the SUV to a stop about fifty yards from the house. Jenks was nowhere in sight. I sighed as I realized I hadn't asked him what type of car he drove. Not that it would matter much, as there was little or no traffic down this road anyway.

I reached over to absently stroke the top of Nick's head. "Maybe we should have called Ollie," I murmured. "He came in handy the last time."

Nick moved closer to me and rubbed his furry black-and-white face against my arm. "Errrup."

"Yes, I'd rather have Ollie here too. For all I know, Simon Gladstone could show up here. He's not someone to fool around with. If Daniel had his photo, you can bet there's a lot more going on *there* than meets the eye."

Nick put his paw on my leg, stretched and gave me a head butt on the chin. Then he started to purr.

I gave him a quick scratch behind one ear, then switched the car off and leaned my head back against the rest. Simon Gladstone had been hired by someone to steal those appointment pages. And even though Samms would never admit it, I was relatively certain the second appointment book had been intended as a trap. Simon was undoubtedly working for someone. I felt safe crossing Scarlett off that list. That left Morley Carruthers, Dooley/Sable, and . . . whoever's initials had been erased from the original book.

The sound of my phone chirping cut into my thoughts. I dug the phone out, glanced at the caller ID, and clicked Accept. Before I even spoke I heard Hank's deep voice rumble over the line. "Hey, Nora. What have you been up to?"

"Deep in a mystery, as usual," I said and laughed. "I'm assuming you have some news for me?"

"Ah, gone are the days when we'd just call to chat." He chuckled. "Although I must say, at least the assignments you give me are interesting. That one was no piece of cake."

"I know. The photo was dark. I'm sorry."

"Fortunately, my contact at the lab was able to rise to the occasion. I'm emailing you a copy of the altered photo, but I can tell you that your hunch was spot-on. There was something erased under that DS."

Bingo. "Could you make out what was written there?"

"Nora, Nora, I told you, I only deal with the cream of the crop. Of course he could. It was another set of initials."

I was fully expecting to hear him say AL—so I gasped when he added, "NE."

"NE, huh." My head was spinning. None of my current suspects had those initials. "I owe you big-time, as usual."

"You certainly do and one day I might even collect."

"So can I press my luck and ask for one more favor? Can you check with one of your contacts in the Boston area for any crime families who might possibly have some sort of tie to a hit man who goes by the name of Simon Gladstone—not his real name, I'm sure—and possibly Marlene McCambridge as well?"

I explained about Simon, the address book, and Daniel's showing me the photo. "I'm thinking someone sent Simon Gladstone here on a mission, and even though Daniel couldn't come right out and say it . . ."

"You're certain it's someone of interest to the FBI." Hank let out a low whistle. "A photo would be best, but text me a detailed description of the guy and I'll see what I can come up with."

"I know you will. I've missed working with you, Hank."

"And I you. Any chance you'll give up your new profession and come back to Chicago?"

I laughed. "About as much chance of me doing that as you winning the lottery. Do you still buy a dozen tickets each week?"

"I've cut back to a half dozen."

"Well, you need to come to Cruz and visit me. I'll even make up a special sandwich in your honor. A nice steak sub."

"You sure know how to tempt a man." He chuckled. "Maybe in the summer. Crime takes a bit of a break then."

"Does it really?"

"No," he admitted. "But I sounded convincing, didn't I?"

We exchanged a few more pleasantries and then I ended the call, and texted him as detailed a description as I could remember. When I'd finished, I glanced at my watch.

Five fifteen. I drummed my fingers impatiently against the armrest. Jenks was late.

I dialed the *Cruz Sun* and was told he'd left for the day. The girl who'd answered the phone seemed in a talkative mood. She was glad to impart the information that he'd said something about running "an errand of mercy," which I assumed was me. Since he'd never given me a cell number there was no way for me to contact him, so . . . I slid the phone back into my bag and looked at Nick.

"Guess he found himself a hot story. Oh, well, that means it's you and me, big fella."

He sat straight up, and I could swear the corners of his lips tipped up, just a tad, the equivalent of a kitty smile.

"We should be okay, just as long as we don't run into Simon Gladstone. Come on, let's move."

We exited the car and trudged up the long driveway to the front door. Once again, I rang the bell. Once again, the sounds of a dove cooing, a donkey braying and a tiger snarling met my ears.

Once again, no one answered.

"This time, we're not taking no for an answer," I muttered. I wasn't as adept with a credit card as Ollie was, but I was certain I could manage in a pinch. I motioned to Nick and the two of us circled the house. It seemed to be shut up tighter than a drum; no curtains moved at all. I pressed my ear to the back door and stood for a few minutes, listening.

Nothing. No sounds of life anywhere.

I was just about to admit defeat for the third time when Nick suddenly took off like a shot across the yard. It took me a minute to realize he was heading for the garage.

"Nick, come back," I shouted. When he kept on running, I gave up and started after him. When he was about twenty feet away, he suddenly hurled himself like a missile through the air and landed on the windowsill. He stretched his forepaws up and started to paw at the glass.

"Nick," I cried. "Stop that. What are you doing?"

As I drew closer, I saw smoke coming out of the top of the garage door. I started to choke. The stench of gasoline was unmistakable. I hurried over to the window, pushed Nick aside, and peered inside.

The garage had been empty on my previous visit with Ollie. That wasn't the case now.

A white BMW sat square in the middle, and the door on the driver's side was open. A woman lay, one arm extended, half in and half out of the car.

And she wasn't moving.

Seventeen

"Oh my God."

It seemed pretty clear that the woman was dead, but I still felt the need to check. I circled around to the garage door and gave it a tug, but it wouldn't budge. Apparently something was blocking it. There was another door, off to the left. I tried that, but it wouldn't open either. Where was Ollie and his credit cards when you needed them?

I looked around. My best bet seemed to be the window, but one swift tug assured me this was locked tight as well. I looked around, searching for something, anything, I could use to break in, and spied a large rock. I hefted it up, hurried back to the window, and hurled the rock through the glass, holding my breath as gas fumes came rushing out. I fumbled in my pocket for a Kleenex, then took a deep gulp of fresh air before placing the tissue over my nose and mouth. Then, being very careful not to cut myself on any of the jagged slivers of glass, I unlocked the window and raised it, then lowered myself through the opening feet-first. Once inside, I moved swiftly to the door, curious as to what might be blocking it, and saw a doorstop wedged underneath. I thought about removing it, then changed my mind. The police would have to be called, and they wouldn't be happy with the broken window. Why compound it?

The fumes stung my eyes, and I could feel them start to tear. I blinked the moisture away and hurried over to the car. I reached inside and shut the engine off, then knelt beside the woman. Her eyes were open, staring sightlessly ahead, her lips frozen in an O of surprise. Her skin was pale, except for two bright spots of pink on each cheek, and there was a slight bluish ring around her lips. I put my fingers to the pulse at her neck.

Nothing.

I saw a purse lying a few feet away from the body. It was open, the contents scattered. I saw a wallet and reached for it. I opened it and the first thing I saw was a driver's license. I glanced at the photo and then at the name printed next to it.

Just as I suspected. The woman was Anabel Leedson.

I scratched thoughtfully at my ear. It was fairly evident she'd died from carbon monoxide poisoning. Add in the fact the window had been locked and the garage door jammed and it seemed to indicate she'd taken her own life. What would have made her want to commit suicide?

Or had she?

I glanced around the small building. Over to the right was another window. Granted, you'd have to climb up on the ledge to reach that one, but . . . it could be done, if someone were pretty agile.

Simon Gladstone was thin, wiry, and a fast runner. He fit the bill by my standards. It looked as if my theory about Anabel seeing the murderer might hold water, after all.

I started to cough and my eyes started to sting. I dropped the wallet, hurried over and stuck my head out the window, breathing in the fresh air. Once my eyes stopped tearing, I walked back over and picked up the wallet again. I opened the billfold. There were quite a few bills tucked in there, all twenties. I did a quick calculation. There was four hundred dollars in cash in the wallet. Well, rule out a robbery. I examined the other items, which consisted of a few business cards all from bookstores in the area. Each had a contact's name and phone number written there.

Well, that would substantiate that she'd come to California intending to set up a book tour for Marlene. My gut was telling me, though, that the tour was only a cover for some other, possibly sinister, purpose.

As I started to replace the cards I noticed one was stuck to the back of another. I pulled them apart and glanced at the bottom card. It was for a beauty supply store in Marina, about fifteen minutes away. On the back was a number. I pulled my phone out of my pocket, snapped a quick photo of the front and back of the card, then stuck it back in the wallet.

Next I opened the zippered compartment. Inside was a small

cardboard square and a slip of pink paper. I unfolded the pink paper first. It was a rental receipt from Century 21, signed by Joannie Adams and Rita Robillard, for the sum of eighteen thousand dollars for two months' rental of the brown stucco house. I let out a low whistle. Nine thousand dollars a month seemed an obscene amount for a rental to me, but in this hoity-toity area of Cruz it was most likely a bargain. I wondered what Marlene had paid for hers. If it was anywhere near that amount, no wonder Rita had been so desperate to close the deal.

I glanced at the name scrawled on the bottom. Anne Onymous. Well, that certainly seemed to cinch the fact she and Anabel Leedson were one and the same. I looked at the date. She'd signed it two weeks before Marlene had come to town. Three weeks after she'd been fired.

My brow puckered in thought. Why had she signed the rental before she knew what house Marlene had been going to rent? How had she known Marlene would choose the Porter house? I remembered Scarlett's assertion that Marlene had believed Anabel and Sable St. John were plotting against her. Could St. John have known Marlene's plans and tipped Anabel off? Were they in league, plotting Marlene's demise together?

I picked up the cardboard square. It looked like what was left of a business card; however, all the important information had been ripped off. There was a large staple in its center, and I turned it over. Stapled to the back was a small square of paper bearing the number: N657. There was some writing on the back.

"*Marowl!*"

My head snapped up and the papers fluttered to the ground. I'd forgotten all about Nick. I glanced around for a sign of the tubby tuxedo. He was squatting low, right next to the body. He put a paw out, rested it on the dead woman's chest.

"Nick!" I hurried over to him. "What in the world are you doing! Get off that body this instant."

He removed his paw and backed up, all the while watching me with his wide gold eyes. I started to walk back toward him, and his back arched, his tail fluffed, and he opened his mouth wide, showing me a generous expanse of fang.

"Ya-rowl!"

I took a step backward, and Nick's stance relaxed. I started to move toward him again, and got the same reaction.

"What? You want me to look at the body again?"

It seemed to me he inclined his head. I went back to the body and knelt down. Anabel's left arm was extended out, her hand open, fingertips brushing the concrete floor. Her other arm was twisted at her side, her hand inverted toward her stomach, almost as if she'd been trying to hide something. I leaned a bit closer and caught a glint of something twined between her fingers. I started to back away from the body, and then I caught Nick's eye. He was staring steadily at me, his tail thumping up and down against the concrete. His whiskers twitched, his rear end wiggled, and in the next second he was squatting next to me, his gaze focused on the object in Anabel's hand.

"Ma-row! E-ower."

I sighed, then moved closer and squatted down for a better look at the object entwined in Anabel's clutching fingers. It was a small initial E on a silver chain. The points of the letter were dotted with tiny diamond chips. As I stared at it, I heard Desiree's voice in my head:

"One day I saw her with a necklace. It was a pretty thing, a silver initial surrounded by a few diamonds. And when she saw me looking at her, she hid it right away in a pouch. Funny thing, though. You'd have thought it'd be an M, right? For Marlene or McCambridge? Nope. It was an E."

This had to be the same necklace, but how had Anabel gotten hold of it? I racked my brain. Marlene owed her money. Perhaps she'd given her the necklace in payment. Or Anabel could have stolen it from the house. Maybe after she'd killed Marlene?

I pulled out my phone and snapped several quick pictures of that too. As I finished, Nick's head suddenly snapped up and his ears flattened back. He uttered a low growl and bounded over to the window. I rose and followed him. I could see the front part of a convertible parked across the street. The next minute a slim form came hurrying up the drive. I leaned out the window and waved. "Jenks," I yelled. "Over here."

"Nora?" He sounded incredulous. "What on earth are you doing in the garage? What happened to the window?" He paused as his gaze rested on Nick and he took a step backward. "I didn't realize you'd have your crime-solving kitty with you." He sniffed the air and frowned. "What is that smell? Is that gasoline!"

His face paled as he looked through the window and caught sight of Anabel's body. "Is she . . . is she . . ."

"She's dead. It looks like carbon monoxide poisoning. Can you give me a hand out, please?"

"You broke the window? Why didn't you just open the garage door?"

"Someone wedged a doorstop there. I think I should leave it as is for the police. It's bad enough I broke the window."

Jenks cast a wary eye at Nick, who bounded out on his own, then streaked right past the reporter and arranged himself atop a nearby rock. As Nick calmly licked one paw, Jenks helped me out of the garage. "Well," he said and inclined his head toward the car. "I take it you found the renter?"

I nodded and finished brushing myself off. "It would appear so. I found a rental slip in her purse, signed Anne Onymous. According to her driver's license, she's Anabel Leedson, Marlene's former agent."

"Wow." Jenks scratched at his head. "So she committed suicide, huh? I wonder why?"

"Maybe," I murmured. "Or maybe someone just wants the police to think she did." I pointed. "There's another window in the garage, one above a ledge. Someone could have followed Anabel in here, knocked her out, started the car, wedged the door and locked the other window, and then gotten out that way, pulling the window shut behind him."

Jenks walked around the side of the garage and came back a few minutes later. "I see what you mean. There's a tree right by that window they could have shimmied down. But it would have had to be a pretty

137

agile person." He gave me a wry look. "That isn't something you can picture Desiree Sanders doing, can you?"

I shook my head. "Not in the least. Scarlett Vandevere is in good shape, but she's got an alibi for last night and today. From what I saw, Morley Carruthers is thin and wiry. I haven't met Sable St. John yet."

Jenks pulled a face. "Can you really picture Morley Carruthers shimmying down a tree trunk?"

"No, but people do strange things in desperate situations." I glanced around for my cat, who seemed to have pulled a disappearing act. "Would you mind calling it in? I need to find Nick."

"Sure," he said, but I could tell from the way his lips twisted into a half grimace he'd be happier if Nick remained MIA. He pulled out his cell and I looked around for my vanishing kitty, hoping that he hadn't found any more corpses. I caught sight of him, trotting down the drive toward my SUV. I hurried after him and found him sitting by the car, looking at me expectantly. Something white was in his mouth.

"What have you got now?" I bent down and retrieved Nick's prize. It was the corner of a business card I'd found in Anabel's wallet, with the other numbered piece of paper stapled to its back. I looked at my cat. "You took this from where I dropped it, didn't you?"

Nick's lips peeled back. "Er-owl!"

I hesitated. "Technically, I suppose this could be considered evidence. We should put this back, or at least tell the police, but since everything so conveniently points to a suicide, we both know they won't investigate any of this. They'll just make a note of her purse's contents and it'll sit in an evidence locker for God knows how long and then get thrown out. And I've got a feeling these might be important, somehow."

Nick's head bobbed up and down. "Yowl."

In the distance I heard the wail of a police siren. Too late now. "Good. We agree. We're felons together, Nick."

I shoved the paper into my pocket and gave Nick's head a quick pat; then, breathing a silent prayer that Samms was unavailable, I hurried back up the drive to greet the police.

Eighteen

As it turned out, there is a God. Samms was indeed unavailable, so another policeman had been assigned to come out and take our statements. I elected not to hang around and wait for Samms and his crew to come out and secure the scene, normal procedure until it was established Anabel's death was definitely a suicide. Jenks said he'd hang around and give me the lowdown later, so I drove back to Hot Bread. I pulled into the garage and let myself in the store through the back door. Chantal was in the kitchen area, just finishing cleanup. She took one look at my face and paled.

"No-not another body."

I nodded. "Anabel Leedson. As it turns out, she was the mysterious Anne Onymous."

"Anabel's dead?"

I looked up. Desiree stood framed in the doorway leading up to my apartment. I nodded. "I'm sorry, yes, she is."

Desiree placed one hand over her heart and swayed slightly. Chantal took her arm and guided her over to the table and chair by the refrigerator. Once she was seated, she dropped her head into her hands.

"Oh, Anabel!" she wailed. "Even though you probably framed me for Marlene's murder, I will miss you! You were such a good agent. Believe me when I tell you good agents are so very, very hard to find."

Apparently Desiree had forgotten all about her intentions of the day before to fire Anabel. I pulled out the chair across from Desiree and eased into it. "It appears she died from carbon monoxide poisoning. She was in a locked garage with the engine running. By the time I got there it was too late. She was gone."

Chantal frowned. "Suicide?"

"It would look that way. I had to break a window and crawl through to get inside. The door was wedged shut, and the other door into the garage was locked."

"So, she couldn't take the guilt of what she'd done to me," Desiree spat. "Did she at least leave a note, admitting her crime and clearing me?"

"I don't know. Samms hadn't arrived yet, so I don't know if they went inside the house or not. I imagine they would. Jenks stuck around. He said he'd give me a report."

Chantal looked straight into my eyes. "*Chérie*, I get the sense Anabel's death might not have been suicide."

"I'd say that vibe's right on," I answered. "I don't think so either."

Desiree turned her startled gaze on me. "But who would murder Anabel?"

"Well, it's possible she might have seen the killer, or maybe was in league with him." I repeated what Scarlett had told me about Anabel and St. John.

Desiree shook her head. "Somehow I can't picture St. John as a killer. Then again, before all this I couldn't picture Anabel as one either. Yet she had to be involved in all this. Oh, dear. I don't know what to think."

I pulled out my phone and called up the photos I'd taken of the necklace. "Does this look familiar to you?"

"Oh my God!" Desiree cried. "That's the necklace I saw her with! The very one." Her eyes narrowed. "Anabel must have taken it after she killed her."

"Not necessarily. Who did Marlene know with the initials *NE?*"

Desiree's brow furrowed as she thought, and then she shook her head. "None come to mind."

Another dead end. I pulled up the photo of the beauty supply card, then pulled the half card and square of paper out of my pocket and laid them on the table. Chantal picked them up to look at them. "This one," she said and held up the paper with N657 on it, "looks like it could be a claim check of some kind."

I tapped at the ripped card. This is obviously half of a business card. She did have cards in her wallet from various bookstores with contact names written on the back. So that does bear out what her admin told you, Desiree, about her arranging a book tour." I tapped the image of the card from Arlene's Beauty Supply with the edge of my nail. "This card was tucked in with the bookstore cards."

Desiree looked at the photo then shrugged. "Anabel loved those places. She always bought her dye, hair spray, even her hair dryers there. She always said they were cheaper than a department store or drugstore and good quality." Desiree's fingers lingered over the paper. "Now this one's real odd."

"I agree with Chantal," I said. "It could be a claim check. Maybe for a pawnshop?"

"What would she have pawned? And that writing on the back makes no sense at all," stated Desiree.

We all leaned over to study the writing:

in's

isals

roy, CA

5-1738

"The second word could be appraisals," Chantal offered. "Maybe she took the necklace somewhere to have it appraised?"

"Maybe," I said. "So a jewelry store?"

"I've never seen a claim check like this given out at a jewelry store. Some pawnshops do appraisals," Chantal said. "She might have wanted to kill two birds with one stone. Get it appraised and get some quick cash. What cities or towns end in *roy?*"

I snapped my fingers. "Gilroy. And that's not too far from here."

"So now we need to search for shops ending in *in's*, and with those last four numbers as part of their phone number?" Chantal asked. "I'll bet that's going to be harder than it sounds."

I walked over to my laptop and brought it back to the table. "One way to find out."

I keyed "businesses ending in *in's* in Gilroy, CA" into the search engine, and groaned as twelve pages of matches came up. I tried narrowing it down by the last four digits of the phone number. This time I was rewarded with ten pages. I scratched at my head. "You're right," I said to Chantal. "This is gonna take awhile." I glanced at my watch. "I still have another suspect to interview. Who knows, maybe he'll be able to shed some light." It was almost seven o'clock. I'd wanted to talk to Sable St. John at the bookstore tonight. It was going to be impossible to get there before his appearance started, but maybe I could get him for a few minutes on a break, or hang around till the store closed at eleven. I mentioned my plan to Chantal, who nodded.

"I'll stay here with Desiree till you get back. And if our pal Samms should show up, I'll call you right away." She pulled the laptop in front of her. "I'll continue the search. Maybe I'll get lucky."

"One of us should." I rose and picked up my purse. Nick had risen from his supine position in front of the refrigerator and stood, black tail waving. I pointed my finger at him and said in a stern tone, "You stay here, okay. Help Chantal."

His eyes narrowed, and then he let out a soft *grr* and sprang onto the table. He padded over to Chantal and positioned himself so that he had a good view of the computer screen. I walked over, bent down, and placed a kiss on the top of his furry head. "Good boy," I whispered.

He hunched his shoulders and growled softly.

Boy, was I going to pay for this later.

• • •

I didn't even bother trying to find a spot near the bookstore, I just went right into the Municipal Lot and parked on the deck. I didn't have to put any quarters in, since it was after eight o'clock by the time I got there. When I went inside the store I saw that the sign in the lobby had changed. Scarlett's was gone and this was in its place:

Book Signing
Seventy Degrees of Heat
Sable St. John
7–9 p.m.

Next to the book title was a headshot of Sable St. John. His dark eyes seemed to stare right through me. I pushed through the glass doors and immediately saw a cluster of women up on the second floor, near the railing where Scarlett had been set up earlier. There was much shouting and laughing coming from that direction, and I could see several women waving their copies in the air.

Well, fat chance of getting him off to the side. I'd probably have to wait till nine o'clock, although judging from the crowd, I was betting the signing would run later, an hour over at least. I decided to grab a cup of coffee while I waited, so I ambled over to the coffee bar, which was practically deserted. I smiled at the clerk on duty.

"Slow night, huh?"

He was a pimple-faced kid, either late teens or early twenties, and this was probably how he put himself through college. His name tag said *Alan*. He shrugged. "We're usually busier on a Wednesday. Tonight, though, everyone's enjoying the show."

I glanced up at the second-floor corner and ordered a mocha latte. "I see what you mean." As Alan made my drink, I attempted some conversation. "I guess today was pretty busy. There were two signings here, right?"

"Yeah. Usually we don't have two back to back like this, but *he*"— here Alan rolled his eyes skyward—"insisted, and our manager didn't want to say no. Sable St. John sells a lot of books. Even more now that everyone knows Sable's a he and not a she."

I paid for the latte but stayed at the counter, sipping slowly. "I wonder what the big rush was?"

"Apparently he's booked for some European tour, or something, and he's got to leave by tomorrow night. I've got to tell you, Milton was pretty pissed. St. John was originally scheduled for next Wednesday, and then he had to juggle everything around. Must be nice, to wield that kind of power."

"Must be," I murmured. A sudden trip to Europe? Had there really been a conflict at Book Haven, or was it just an excuse to get out of the country? And if so, why?

As I gazed upward, a tall blond man wearing a three-piece suit leaned over the railing. He beckoned to the clerk at the information desk. "Be a love," he shouted, "can you find any more copies of my book? I'm running out, and there are at least two dozen more ladies here eager for an autographed copy."

I frowned and turned to look at Alan, who was wiping down the counter and shaking his head. "That's Sable St. John? I thought he was a brunette? The photo outside . . ."

"Is an old one," Alan finished my sentence and nodded toward the balcony. "That's him, all right, although if you ask me, that hair's a wig. I bet he's really bald."

I frowned up at the man, still leaning over the railing. Of course, I was pretty far away, but that hair color looked the same as . . .

My cell chirped at that instant. I moved away to answer it. I flipped it on, and saw I'd gotten a text from Ollie. I breathed a sigh of relief at the first line:

Hair fibers do not match.

But my jaw dropped at the rest:

Lone strand is neither male nor female. Strand synthetic.

I shut the phone with a click.

Now wasn't that interesting!

Nineteen

I sat down at one of the tables, sipping my latte, my thoughts whirling. If Sable St. John's blond do was indeed a wig, then there was a good possibility that was where the strand of hair Nick had found at the scene of Marlene's murder had come from. It was possible he'd been the one Anabel'd seen skulking around the house. Had she confronted him, and he in turn lured her to the garage, killed her and made it look like a suicide?

Timing. I needed to know the timing. I dug my phone back out and dialed the *Cruz Sun*, then punched in the extension Jenks had given me. When I heard his harried voice I said, "Hey, it's Nora. I was just curious what happened out at the crime scene?"

"Oh, hey." His tone perked up a bit. "I was gonna call you just as soon as I finished the story. I'm almost done."

"Got a few minutes now?"

"Sure." I heard the sound of papers being shuffled around, and then his voice came again, sounding a bit clearer this time. "It was a good thing you left when you did. Your pal Samms came out about twenty minutes later. Of course, I had to tell him you were there and left. He didn't seem too happy. I expect you'll be getting a visit pretty soon. I'm surprised you didn't already." More papers were shuffled and then Jenks continued, "He took my statement, asked me a few questions, and then he wanted me to leave. Of course I didn't. I went back and waited in my car till the coroner showed up, and then I went back to the garage, ducked down behind a bush. I overheard the coroner tell Samms he had to do a formal autopsy, but as far as he could tell, it looked like a case of carbon monoxide poisoning. Samms asked about foul play and the coroner said he didn't see any visible bruises, which would indicate the victim would have been knocked unconscious before getting in the car."

Hm, that seemed to knock my murder theory out for now. "Anything else? Did they look for a note?"

"Samms and his men searched that garage top to bottom. No note. Then they went into the house. I followed them and hid in the shrubbery behind the rear entrance. They were in there maybe forty, forty-five minutes. When Samms came out he looked pretty grim. He had something clutched in a baggie in his hand. I couldn't see what it was."

"Could it have been a suicide note?"

"That's what I'm thinking, because then he called to his men to wrap it up. I didn't see them put any crime scene tape up, but then again I pretty much had overstayed my welcome. I hotfooted it back here to write it up for the evening edition and then I was going to let you know."

"Thanks, Jenks. You've been a big help."

"Does this mean Marlene's murder is wrapped up? That Samms will be making a statement declaring Anabel Leedson her killer?" There was an almost hopeful note in his voice. I knew the feeling and could sympathize. He wanted to be the one to get an exclusive.

"At this point, I'm not sure. From what you just said it seems the logical assumption."

"I sure would like to scoop that story, if it's true. It would definitely make it up to me with my editor for having to sit on the story about Marlene's death, which by the way, Samms was pretty skimpy on details with."

"I think he was trying to avoid as much sensationalism as possible. And I promise, if I have anything to say about it, you'll be the first to know the whole story."

"Fair enough. Let me know if you still need my help."

"Will do, and thanks."

I disconnected the call and glanced up at the balcony again. The crowd seemed to have thinned out. I looked at my watch. It was a quarter to nine. I squared my shoulders.

Showtime.

• • •

"Who shall I make this out to?"

There were no copies of *Seventy Degrees of Heat*, but I managed to snag one of the bestseller before it, *Sixty Points of Lust*, on my way over to the book signing corner. I made certain I was the last one in line, and waited behind an overweight woman with hair the color of an overripe tomato and listened to her gush at the author for a good ten minutes before he politely nudged her on. I thought I saw a glimmer of relief in his eyes as he took the book from me, opened to the first page and held his pen aloft.

"I guess this is a pretty long night for you?" I asked.

"Ah, no night is too long for my faithful fans," he said. His smile stretched from ear to ear. I took a good look at his hair. Up close, it looked pretty fake to me. Almost as fake as his bronzed California tan.

"Miss?" Sable's voice broke into my thoughts. "Who would you like it made out to?"

"Oh, sorry. Nora. Nora Charles. Actually"—I leaned in a bit closer to him—"I have a confession to make. I'm really not a fan."

He'd just finished writing 'Nora' and he paused, pen in air. He had a slightly insulted look on his face. "You're not?"

"No." I pulled my press pass out of my bag and flashed it at him. "I'm a reporter, and I was hoping for a few minutes of your time?"

"A reporter?" The injured look vanished, replaced by an almost gleeful expression. He set the book and pen aside and pushed back his chair. "Why didn't you say so, my dear? Nancy!" He motioned to a tall girl wearing dark jeans and a dark green polo shirt with the bookstore name emblazoned over her left breast. "Be a dear and get us two coffees, won't you?" He turned to me. "How do you take yours?"

"Cream, no sugar."

"Two light and sweet." Nancy hurried over to the escalator, hopefully to catch Alan before he called it quits for the night, and Sable St. John took my arm and led me over to a love seat wedged in between two bookcases chock-full of mystery novels. "The store is closing soon, and the signing's officially over, so no one will bother us here." We both sat down and he put his arm over the back of the love seat, leaning in slightly toward me. "Well, I'm all yours, my dear. What would you like to know? What my favorite food is? Drink? How I get these salacious ideas?" He bounced both eyebrows suggestively.

I opened my tote and removed a pad and pen. "Actually, I'm more interested in your relationship with the late Marlene McCambridge."

For an instant his face clouded; his eyes darkened, and I thought I saw a vein bulge in his jaw. A second later, though, he was all smiles and ebullience. "Marlene." He said the name on a long sigh. "What a tragic end for such a paragon of literature." He put his hand up to his eye as if brushing away a tear. "She will be missed, indeed she will."

"But not by you?"

"Why, whatever do you mean? Marlene and I were close, quite close."

"Yes, I understand you met her at your first romance convention. She introduced you to your agent."

"My first agent," he amended, his lips settling into a slash. "I've since traded up."

"I heard he was a scumbag."

"Scumbag doesn't even begin to describe him. I'm sorry, but I can't use the proper adjectives in mixed company." He gave me a hard stare. "Is that what you're after? Some sort of sensational story on how I secretly hated Marlene? If that's your aim, I'm afraid you're going to be sadly disappointed. As I said, she and I were quite close."

"Oh, I'm sure you were. You were so close that you told her your most confidential, deadly secret."

His eyes widened and his skin, beneath all that tanning spray, paled. His tongue darted out to slick across his bottom lip. "Who told you that?" he rasped as he jumped up from the love seat, almost colliding with Nancy, who'd approached silently, two large coffees in hand. "Oh, my dear," he cried, reaching out a hand to steady her. "I am so sorry."

"No problem." She set the coffees down on the small table in front of the love seat, regarding us with an anxious expression. "Is everything all right here?"

"Of course it is," he said, his smile getting wider. "Why wouldn't it be?"

Her gaze flicked in between us. "You look upset," she said. "And Milton will have my head if things don't go smoothly tonight." She glanced at her watch. "Your agent will be here soon."

"There are no more fans waiting for books to be signed, correct?" As Nancy nodded, he motioned to me. "Then I would like to go into that lovely back room where I was before the signing started, with this young lady, for just a very brief interview. Will you see we are not disturbed?"

"Sure."

Sable St. John led me back to a very different room than the one I'd sat in with Scarlett earlier. This one was large and airy, with a window that faced the street. A deep-cushioned love seat sat in one corner, and in the other was a large vanity with a high-backed chair covered with a floral velvet cushion.

Hm, you could certainly tell which author rated higher. Whoever said sex sells sure wasn't kidding.

Sable closed the door and waved me toward the love seat. I sat down and he stood over me. His face no longer wore a pleasant expression; rather, his features had contorted themselves into a fierce scowl. He fisted both hands on his hips.

"What do you know about my secret?"

Well, of course I had no idea what his secret might be. I'd run a bluff, and from the looks of things it was a pretty good one. I decided a frontal attack was my best defense. "Anabel Leedson is dead," I said.

His fists uncurled, then curled again. "What did you say?"

"I said Anabel Leedson is dead. She was found in the garage of a house she'd rented in Cruz earlier tonight. She died from carbon monoxide poisoning." I paused. "An apparent suicide."

He didn't say anything for a few minutes, and then he slowly shook his head. "No, that's not right. Anabel would never take her own life."

"How well did you know her?"

He let out a bitter laugh. "Quite well, better than anyone imagined. Remember, I told you I had gotten a different agent."

Now my eyes widened. "Anabel was *your* agent?"

He nodded. "And a damn fine one she was, too."

"Is that why Marlene accused you and Anabel of plotting against her? Because Anabel took you on as a client?"

He laughed. "Marlene thought the whole world was plotting in some form or another against her, so probably the answer is yes. I know Anabel told me she wasn't happy about it, although it's beyond me why she would even care." He leaned in a bit closer to me. "Marlene accused us of having an affair. Can you imagine? I mean, I was fond of Anabel, just not in a sexual way. Her feelings for me, well, that's another story. But I did nothing to encourage her, I assure you."

I bit down on my lower lip, studying him. I looked at his hair again. Abruptly I jumped up and pulled at a strand of his hair.

"Ow!" he yelled and jumped back. "What did you do that for?"

I sat back down. Definitely not a wig. That hair was all his.

"I'm sorry. You dye your hair?"

He fluffed the ends back, glaring at me. "You could have just asked me that," he growled. "Actually, this is my natural color. I'd dyed it brown, but I got so tired of keeping it up. Anabel was a bit tentative about it, but the women eat it up. She was tentative about me admitting Sable St. John was a man, too, and that turned out better than we dreamed." He let out a long sigh. "She was such a worrywart, but she was always making plans. We planned this European tour together." He dropped onto the love seat beside me, scrubbing at his face with both hands. "It can't be true. She can't be dead!"

I laid a hand on his arm. "I'm sorry. I hate to ask you this, but . . ."

"You want to know where I was? I've been doing PR all day. Interviews for book websites, blogs, stuff like that. Then I did an impromptu personal appearance at a small bookstore the next town over. You can check that. Then I came back here and I was with Milton till he left, and Nancy all evening. Oh, I've got an alibi, trust me. I didn't kill Anabel. I would never have harmed her. Now Marlene, well, there's a different story." He held out his hand. "Before you get any ideas, I didn't kill her. Trust me, no one warranted killing as much as her, and I'm not sorry she's dead. But me kill her?" He shook his head. "Not only do I not have the nerve, could you imagine me in prison? On death row? I'd never survive."

Now *that* I could believe.

I leaned toward him. "I'm going to be honest with you, Mr. St. John. I used to be a reporter, but I'm retired from that line of work. I do, however, assist the police from time to time."

He nodded slowly. "And you're assisting them with Marlene's murder?"

"Your name was in her appointment book. The day of her death, you had a meeting with her."

"Yes." He ran a hand through his hair, making some of the ends stick out, nutty professor style. If I'd doubted it was a wig, that gesture sealed the deal. "Marlene was writing a tell-all book about her life, and about several people she knew who had secrets. I had a little problem with alcohol when I met Marlene. My tongue would get a bit loose at times. Long story short, I shared something with Marlene I shouldn't have, and she was going to reveal that in this book."

"Might I ask what this secret is?"

He shook his head. "I've learned my lesson. What I will tell you, though, is that Marlene had secrets on people that some would consider shady, maybe even dangerous."

"Dangerous?" I narrowed my gaze at him. "You mean like the mob?"

He looked at me for a long moment, then shrugged. "I really can't say," he said at last.

"Okay, so you told Marlene this secret in a weak moment, and she was going to reveal it in this book. Was it someone you worked for when you were Dooley Franks? Someone with the initials *NE*?"

He shrugged again, but a flicker of some emotion crossed his face for a brief instant and then was gone. "I'm sorry. I can't say one way or the other."

"You wouldn't happen to know if Marlene herself had dealings with that person, would you? Most likely of a personal nature?"

"Trust me, I'm the last person Marlene McCambridge would apprise of her personal affairs," he spat. "If you want information, why not talk to her lawyer, Carruthers? Now there's a likely suspect if I ever saw one. They argued like cats and dogs, especially these last few weeks. I saw him once, leaving her office. His face was beet red. He looked mad enough to kill." Unexpectedly he reached over and gave my arm a pat. "You're a bright girl. Maybe this will help you. When I saw Anabel the other day, she was speaking to someone on her cell and she sounded quite agitated. She was trying to track down someplace called Stein's Estates and wasn't having much luck. Seems the number she'd been given had been disconnected."

"Track it down, you say? She wasn't familiar with the place?"

He shook his head. "It didn't seem that way."

Hm. Then that half card and claim check couldn't have belonged to her. "Thank you, Mr. St. John. You've been a very great help indeed."

I hurried out of the room and down the escalator to the main floor. I was unsure how to categorize St. John. I'd have to reserve judgment on him for now. I glanced at my watch. It was almost ten o'clock. I exited the store and paused, fishing in my bag for my cell to call Peter to tell him to see if he could try and find anything on a Stein's, when suddenly a heavy hand came down on my shoulder. I turned around slowly, and stared into Leroy Samms's face.

"Well, well, Nora Charles. Just the person we wanted to see."

"We?"

I glanced over my shoulders. Daniel had emerged from the shadows and was standing close behind me. "We had a feeling we'd find you here," he said.

So here I was, sandwiched in between both of the men in my life . . . and neither one of them was smiling.

Twenty

In spite of the fact both Samms and Daniel looked as if they'd lost their last friend in the world, I put on my brightest, widest smile.

"Well, fancy running into you two. I was just about to call you, both of you, actually. I was here having a little talk with Sable St. John. He told me some pretty interesting stuff about Anabel, and about the secret Marlene had on him."

Daniel and Samms exchanged a look, and then Daniel reached out and grabbed my elbow. "We have to talk."

"Great. I like good conversation." I glanced back toward the store. "They're closing soon, but I think there's an all-night coffee shop two blocks down."

"This conversation is best had where we won't be overheard," Samms said, his lips tightening into a thin line.

"Oh. Well, I suppose we could go back to Hot Bread. Chantal and Desiree are there, though."

"We can deal with that," Daniel said. He motioned toward a sleek black sedan parked in a No Parking zone. "Let's go."

"Wait." I hung back. "My car's over in Municipal."

Samms's fingers dug into my elbow, a sure sign there was no point in arguing. "That's okay. I'll send someone to pick it up. You can ride with us."

• • •

Chantal was bent over my laptop when I entered Hot Bread about a half hour later. She looked up when she heard the door open and tossed me a brilliant smile.

"Ah, *chérie!* I think I found what we were looking for. In Gilroy—"

She stopped speaking as I shook my head and put a warning finger to my lips. A second later Samms and Daniel came in. Chantal shot them both a bright smile. "Good evening, gentlemen. Here for a late-night snack?"

Daniel shrugged out of his jacket, tossed it carelessly across my back counter. "I could go for something," he admitted.

"I could go for a blueberry banana smoothie," said Samms. "That's a delicious healthy snack. Too bad someone I know doesn't have a smoothie machine in her shop."

I pulled a face at him. "I've got some Greek yogurt in the fridge. I can mix it with berries. That's a nice healthy snack. Or, if you can wait a few minutes, I can whip up some bruschetta on ciabatta."

"Or"—Chantal had been rummaging in the refrigerator while we were talking, and now approached the table, platter in hand—"we can just keep it simple with some grapes and cheddar cheese."

Samms rubbed his hands together. "That'll do."

Chantal set the tray down in the middle of the table and resumed her seat in front of my laptop. Daniel sat on Chantal's left, Samms on her right. I took the remaining chair directly across from Chantal. I waited until Samms and Daniel helped themselves to cheese and grapes and then said, "You two wanted to talk. The floor's yours."

I looked at Chantal. "Where's Desiree?"

Chantal's gaze flicked from me, over to Samms, then Daniel, then back to me. "They did not tell you?"

"Tell me what?"

"The DA dropped all charges. Peter came and took her back to the Cruz Inn about an hour ago."

My mouth dropped open and I started to rise out of my chair. Samms took a bite of cheese, swallowed, and leaned partway across the table, his intimidating cop stance. His finger shot out, jabbed at my nose. "Sit down."

I remained standing. I put my hands on my hips and glared at the two of them. "The two of you knew Desiree was cleared. When were you going to tell me?"

He ignored my question and countered with one of his own. "You went back out to that house today, didn't you?"

I folded my arms across my chest and stared sulkily ahead. "You know darn well I was there."

Samms flopped back in his chair, drummed his fingers on the tabletop. "You went out there even though we both told you it was dangerous territory you were treading on, and that you should stay away." He popped a grape into his mouth. "Didn't you learn anything from the last time you pulled a stunt like this?"

I spread my hands. "What can I say? Old investigative reporter habits die hard."

Samms snorted. "Just as long as the investigative reporter doesn't," he said. He folded his hands in front of him. "We found a suicide note, and what appears to be a confession."

My head snapped up. "You did? What did the note say?"

"The usual: that she could no longer live with what she did, even though she'd gladly do it all again to protect innocent people. It was signed *Anabel*."

I looked at Daniel and directed my question to him. "Sounds a little ambiguous to me. Are you certain she wrote it?"

"Handwriting matches." It was Samms who answered. "We also found a pair of high-powered binoculars under the living room sofa."

I nodded. That pretty much substantiated my belief that Anabel had been spying on Marlene. The murder angle, though, I found a bit tougher to swallow. "While I'm happy to see Desiree exonerated, neither of you really believe that Anabel killed her and then committed suicide, do you?"

"Honestly?" Daniel looked me square in the eye. "No."

"But you're both convinced Desiree's innocent?"

"Of murder, yes. Of panicking and suppressing evidence, not so much."

"Suppressing evidence?"

"The bloody clothes she had cleaned, for one. And she moved that body looking for something, although she wouldn't say what. To be honest, I wouldn't put ransacking those rooms past her, either."

"So, if you think Desiree's innocent, and you don't believe Anabel killed Marlene, then who do you suspect? Wait, let me guess . . . Simon Gladstone?" When both men remained silent I said, "Sable St. John intimated Marlene knew secrets about dangerous people. Do you think that this Gladstone could have been ordered to kill Marlene, and when he realized Anabel had seen him, he had to take care of the loose end?" When they remained silent, I let out a triumphant cry. "I'm right, aren't I?"

Daniel took both my hands in his. "What I'm going to tell you and Chantal never ever leaves this room. We've had Marlene McCambridge under surveillance for a while. The FBI received a tip that the book Marlene intended to publish had a chapter in it that revealed confidential information about a Boston mob boss we've been after for a while. Nico Enerelli."

"Nico Enerelli? Then he must be *NE*!" I cried. I thought of the necklace with its diamond-encrusted initial *E*, and things began to make a bit more sense. "They were an item, weren't they? He spilled secrets during pillow talk, and she put them in her book?"

"More or less. According to our source, Marlene thought she and Enerelli were getting hitched," Samms said. "He broke it off, and you know that old adage about a woman scorned. Apparently he'd thought he'd paid her off to keep her mouth shut, and then he found out he was going to be the star chapter in her new book."

"I wonder how he found that out," I mused. "Marlene wouldn't have been stupid enough to tell him, would she? I mean, if she'd hung around with him, been that intimate with him, she had to know revealing that beforehand would be like signing her own death warrant."

"Oh, Marlene was too clever to let Enerelli know what she was up to. However, she made the same mistake as the people she violated in her book. She told someone who tipped off Enerelli."

"She did? Who?"

Daniel and Samms just smiled and shook their heads.

"Okay, I get it. You can't say. But you can at least tell me if this guy Gladstone was Enerelli's emissary."

"Simon Gladstone's real name is Freddie Bartholomew and yes, he's performed many services for Enerelli, among lots of others. We believe Enerelli sent him here to get that manuscript and either destroy the whole thing, or at the very least the part about him. Unfortunately we have no evidence to back it up. Anabel's apparent 'suicide' tied up the loose ends all neat and tidy."

I blew out a breath. No one knew better than me that tying up loose ends was what the mob did best. "So . . . what you're saying is, it's over? You're not going to investigate any further?"

"On the surface, we've no reason to . . . at the moment," Daniel said. "Effectively, the case closed with Anabel's death."

"But that's not right," I burst out. "I don't for one minute believe that Anabel Leedson killed Marlene, or that she committed suicide, and you don't either, do you? You think Simon Gladstone killed them, for Enerelli."

"Unfortunately, we have no evidence to back that up, and without that, it's a dead end. Unless we can tie either or both to the crime, they'll walk."

I looked at Samms. "You found the right appointment book when you were at the crime scene and noticed that erasure, didn't you?"

He nodded. "We figured it might have something to do with Enerelli, and he'd send someone to destroy the evidence. Unfortunately, the wrong book stayed in the house. The guy I had guarding it, Tim Blackwell, noticed the error, but before he could do anything Gladstone surprised him and knocked him out and made off with the pages."

"Do you think he found the manuscript too?"

Samms scratched at his head. "Don't know. The upstairs was messed up pretty good. From what we know, Enerelli's pretty desperate to get his hands on that chapter."

"It names names and deeds, eh?"

"We're not entirely certain just what's in it, but we're hoping it reveals something that will enable us to finally put him where he belongs. A nice long stretch in prison." Daniel leaned forward. "I know you're pretty fearless, Nora, but Enerelli plays for keeps. We want you to promise to stay away from that house, at least until we're certain his goons are gone for good." Daniel captured one of my hands in his. "Desiree's been cleared, so that should mean your interest in this case is effectively over."

I clamped my lips together. "Not really. I promised Louis I'd write this whole affair up for *Noir*. Besides, I've invested too much time in it to back away now."

Daniel's lips twisted into a lopsided smile. "I kinda thought you'd feel that way. But I am worried about you, Nora. These people play for keeps."

"I'm probably aware better than anyone how the mob plays."

"Yes, I guess you are." He scraped his chair back and motioned to Samms. "We'd better get going."

"I'll be in touch with Peter tomorrow, after I speak with the DA. In the meantime, not one word to anyone about what's going down," Samms cautioned me.

I made a crossing motion over my heart. "You have my word."

Samms snorted.

Daniel gave me a quick peck on the cheek and followed Samms out the door. I closed and locked it behind them and sat back down opposite Chantal.

"You are not going to stay out of this, though, are you, *chérie?*"

"Heck, no." I took a quick look out the window, and as soon as the car pulled away, turned back to my friend. "Okay, now that they're gone . . . what did you find out?"

"I found a Stein's Estates and Appraisals in Gilroy. I was lucky, too. I got the manager himself on the phone. He remembered the transaction quite clearly." Chantal's voice bubbled with suppressed excitement. "It was Marlene who came in. He knew it was Marlene because his wife is a big Tiffany Blake fan, and he'd seen her photo on the book dust jackets. Anyway, he identified the number on that ticket as being from his shop. But here is the best part. She did not pawn anything. She put something in storage."

"Storage?"

Chantal nodded. "He takes items on consignment, and for a small fee he also stores articles for his customers."

"That's great work, Chantal!" I clapped my friend on the shoulder. "Did he say what the item was?"

"She brought it in a sealed box, so no, he has no idea. He thought it might be something heavy, though. He remembered her struggling with it a bit. He also said that she insisted on storing the article in his back room herself. She tipped him five hundred dollars for the privilege."

A scrabbling sound reached my ears. I looked underneath the table. Nick lay there, on his side, four Scrabble tiles in front of him.

"Hey, Nick. I wondered where you were."

He blinked at me twice, and then took one of the tiles between his claws and started to chew on the end.

I got down on my hands and knees and wiggled partway under the table. "Whatcha got there, bud? What's so delicious?"

I reached out and gently disengaged his paw from the tile, then scooped up the other three. He blinked again, then rolled over on his side.

Oh, yeah, his work was done.

I rocked back on my knees and laid the four tiles on the floor in front of me. A *b*, two *o*'s, and a *k*.

I didn't even have to think about what they spelled. I looked over at Chantal, a wide smile on my face. "Did the manager happen to tell you his store hours?"

"They are open nine to five tomorrow. Why?"

"Can you open for me tomorrow?" Even before she nodded assent, I punched in Ollie's number on my speed dial. When he answered I said, "Can you possibly pick me up around eight tomorrow morning? I need to get over to Gilroy, I'll explain everything on the way. Great. See you then." I hung up and took another look at the tiles spread across my floor, and at the furry white and black face, peeping out from underneath the table.

Chantal tapped her foot impatiently on the floor. "*Chérie*, you look like the cat who swallowed the canary. You have something up your sleeve."

"I sure do." I gave Chantal a mysterious smile. "I think I know what's in that box."

Twenty-one

Ollie picked me up at seven fifteen sharp, and I filled him in on recent events, including the fact I was hopeful the missing manuscript might soon be found. He was pleased to learn that Desiree was on her way to an acquittal, not so pleased to learn that the mob might be involved in both Marlene's and Anabel's murders.

"What happens if they do manage to catch Gladstone, and it turns out he didn't kill either one?" Ollie asked. "Do you think the DA would change his mind about Desiree?"

"I don't know," I said. "Anabel's death is still considered a suicide, thanks to the note. So to answer your question, hopefully not."

"You think it was a hit on Enerelli's behalf, don't you? Too bad we didn't know this when we ran into Gladstone." Ollie's fingers curled into a fist.

"Hey, calm down, Rocky. I'm glad we didn't, or you might have done something really stupid."

"Look who's talking," Ollie said and chuckled. "Face it. You were never above taking some liberties with the law to get a story."

I shrugged. "Yeah, well, sometimes taking a chance pays off. If a killer can be brought to justice, it's worth the risk, don't you think?"

"Indeed. As long as one doesn't get caught, that is." He wrinkled his nose. "Be it far from me to judge. I've taken a few risks in my time, and Nick Atkins, of course, was the king of risk-taking." He smiled, reminiscing. "Who do you think taught me how to break and enter?"

I swallowed and decided it was time for a change of subject. "I confess, I'd like to read that manuscript. If everyone's secrets are as damning as Scarlett's, then Jendine at Peachtree Press would be right. It has *New York Times* bestseller written all over it."

"Did Desiree tell you what Marlene had on her?"

I shook my head. "No. She said she told my mother, and my mother took it to her grave. She didn't volunteer, and I didn't ask. She's entitled to her privacy, I think. They all are, except maybe Enerelli. I sure would like to know what Marlene has on him."

"And so apparently would the FBI. Well, perhaps we'll find out soon enough."

I looked at him out of the corner of my eye. "You do know you didn't have to come with me today. If you're afraid this'll put you in danger . . ."

He stopped me with a brisk wave of his hand. "What sort of private eye would I be if I balked at a little danger?"

I chuckled. "This is the sort of case Nick Atkins would have thrived on, isn't it?"

"You betcha. Nick had lots of cases like this. Lord only knows what he's into now. I only hope he's safe. For all my grousing about him, he was a good partner, and a good friend. Kind of like you are now."

"Except I'm not your partner."

His smile stretched from ear to ear. "We can remedy that. Whenever you're ready, you just say the word. I'll take you, and little Nick, formerly Sherlock, too." He laughed. "You know, in some ways, that cat's a better detective than you or I could ever hope to be."

"Ollie," I said as I patted his hand, "you said a mouthful. Just don't say it around Nick. His head is big enough."

• • •

Stein's Estates and Appraisals stood on a quiet tree-lined street, in a large brick building that took up most of the block. Situated right next to it was a used bookstore that looked oddly out of place. I wondered just how much business it might do, since the sign on the door read *Closed* and the place was dark and looked locked up tighter than a drum. I paused before the window and peered in at the rows and rows of books, and at the lone gold tabby who lay in one corner of the window, sunning himself.

"Every bookstore has a cat," Ollie said behind me. "I think it must be a law."

I agreed, half wishing the store was open. Regretfully, I walked past the window, wiggling my fingers in farewell at the gold tom, and marched over to the oak and glass door that had *Stein's* etched across it in big gold letters.

A bell above the door tinkled as we let ourselves in. The shop looked like most of the secondhand shops I'd been in over the years. Clutter, clutter everywhere. Glass cases lined the walls, and there were rows and rows of shelves jam-packed with articles, some that looked really old and valuable, but mostly junk.

"One man's junk is another man's treasure," Ollie whispered as we made our way to the long counter at the rear of the store. There was a bell at one end. Ollie slapped his palm down on it, and almost immediately a curtain parted, and a tall, stoop-shouldered man emerged. He had black hair slicked back from his forehead, eyes blue and clear behind tortoiseshell glasses, and a clipped mustache above thin lips. He wore a shirt open at the collar, sleeves rolled up, and a pair of faded khaki pants. He rubbed his hands in anticipation as he approached us.

"Good morning. How can I help you folks today? Are you in the mind for some knickknacks for your home? Antique furniture? Maybe an Oriental rug?"

I cleared my throat. "I'm Nora Charles. My friend Chantal called yesterday, about the storage ticket." As he still stared me blankly, I asked, "Aren't you Mr. Stein?"

He gave his head a quick shake. "Nope, sorry. I'm Bud."

"Well, my friend spoke with Mr. Stein. He said he'd have the box ready for us to pick up."

Bud shrugged. "He didn't tell me about it, and I don't usually handle the storage end. I'm acquisitions. Mr. Stein should be here shortly, though. Would you care to wait?"

Apparently we had no choice. I nodded, and Bud vanished through the curtain again, leaving Ollie and me free to wander through the store. There was an archway leading to another showroom. We entered and found ourselves staring at rows and rows of antique furniture.

"Whatever else is in the main part, this showroom has good stuff," Ollie said, walking over to inspect a grandfather clock. He pointed to a set of matched chairs, done in blue upholstery with high backs, nearby. "Textured wool upholstery," he said, running his hand along the back of one of them. He tapped it with his finger. "Solid frame. They don't make stuff like this nowadays."

"Why, Ollie. I didn't realize you were such an antique aficionado."

He shrugged his broad shoulders. "It's a hobby." He moved over to a ceramic lamp with an ugly rose-colored shade. He picked it up, squinted at the markings on the base. "A Bollhagen with an original paper shade. Very rare." He glanced at the price tag dangling from the shade and abruptly set it back down. "Stein knows his stuff. It's right within range."

I bent over to look at the tag and gulped loudly. "Not mine, that's for sure."

We were examining a display of Stiffel lamps when a soft voice called out, "Miss Charles?"

I glanced over at the doorway. This man was short and squat, with a bald pate, watery green eyes, and thick lips. He wore a short-sleeved white shirt, no tie, and dark navy pants. He looked more like a professional poker dealer than an estate appraiser. He extended a hand, which I noted was grubby and sweaty. "Len Stein. You called yesterday?"

"My friend did. About Ms. McCambridge's storage item."

"Ah, yes." His hand went up to rub at the back of his neck. "I read about her death. The police are calling it a 'suspicious circumstance.' Makes me wonder if I should turn this over to the police. Could it be evidence of some sort?"

Ollie stepped in, flashing his PI license. "Actually, we've been authorized by the attorney to bring this box to him. It is part of Ms. McCambridge's estate, after all. I'm sure that he'll take care of notifying the police, if necessary."

Stein still looked dubious. Ollie patted his jacket pocket. "I have authorization papers. Do you want to see them?"

The man's watery eyes gleamed. "Yes, thanks."

"Sure."

Ollie whipped an envelope out of his pocket and handed it to Stein. Stein opened it, pulled out a sheet of paper, and spent quite a few minutes looking it over. At last he folded it, replaced it in the envelope and handed it back to Ollie.

"Seems to be in order," he said. "If you'll just wait here a few moments, I'll get your package."

He vanished through the doorway and I grabbed Ollie's arm. "What on earth did you show him? We don't have authorization papers from Carruthers."

Ollie shrugged, but his eyes twinkled behind his glasses. "I had a set of authorization papers from a case Nick and I handled awhile back. I brought 'em along, just in case they might come in handy. I figured he wouldn't examine 'em too close."

I shook my head and smiled. "You're a very enterprising man, Ollie Sampson."

"Not really. But after twenty-odd years in this business you learn to anticipate every angle, any little setback you might run into."

Bud stuck his head in the doorway. "You might want to bring your car around to the service entrance. That package is a mite heavy, and I can set it right in your backseat or trunk." He walked over to me, handed me a form. "Just sign this release, leave it on the counter with the claim check, and you're good to go."

Ollie pulled out his car keys. "Why don't you wait out front after you're done, Nora? I'll pull right up and we can go. I know you're anxious to have a look at what's inside."

Anxious? That was an understatement. I was on the proverbial pins and needles.

Ollie followed Bud out the door. I signed the form with a flourish, left it and the cardboard square on the counter, and then walked back into the main showroom. A bored-looking blonde girl was behind the glass counter, idly thumbing through a magazine. I paused to inspect a display of cat figurines and saw one that looked amazingly like Nick. I picked it up and held it in my palm for a moment, debating whether or not to buy it, when I heard the bell above the door tinkle. I didn't pay much attention, though, until I heard a growly voice ask, "I'd like to see Mr. Stein, please."

That voice sounded familiar. Where had I heard it before? I looked up and almost dropped the figurine.

Morley Carruthers was standing in front of the glass counter, and he did not look happy.

"He's busy with a customer. Can I help you?"

Carruthers drew himself up to his full height of nearly five foot seven, if that. "I need to speak with him. I believe he may have something that belonged to a client of mine." His hand dipped into his jacket pocket. "I have a letter of authorization . . ."

Oh, hell. I put the cat figurine down and beat a hasty retreat out the front door, arriving at the curb just as Ollie pulled up. I glanced in the backseat and saw a large brown cardboard box, heavily taped. I whipped open the door and slid into the front seat.

"Guess who's inside? Carruthers," I said. "With a real letter of authorization for the box."

Ollie didn't say a word, but the instant my seat belt was fastened, he gunned it down the street. I glanced in the side mirror just in time to see Carruthers race out of the store. His neck snapped this way and that, and his gaze settled on our car just as Ollie took the corner on two wheels. From the brief glimpse I got, he was definitely not a happy camper.

Obviously no one had ever told him the early bird catches the worm—or, in this case, the box.

• • •

We drove back to Hot Bread and Ollie parked around the corner in front of the side entrance to my apartment. Then he and I lugged the box up the stairs and deposited it in my den, under the watchful eye of Nick, who'd somehow vacated his favorite spot downstairs in front of the refrigerator to supervise. Ollie flopped down in my recliner and I retreated to the kitchen, returning in a few minutes with a bottled Evian for Ollie and a Corona Light for myself. Then I sat down in my overstuffed club chair, leaned over, and we clinked bottles.

"Here's to success," Ollie said, raising his bottle.

I took a long, deep swig, and then got up and went over to my desk for a pair of scissors. I crossed my fingers, then I made a clean incision down the center of the box and slowly opened it. Nick leapt onto the desk and leaned over so he could get a better look.

Nestled inside the box was an IBM Selectric typewriter. Seeing it brought back fond memories. I'd learned to type on one of those in high school, long before computers had come into vogue. I'd always felt a bit like Lois Lane when I'd churned out my assignments on the one my parents had bought for me, and a wave of nostalgia hit me like a slap in the face. Wedged in next to the typewriter was a wooden box.

There was no sign of a manuscript.

"Let's take everything out," Ollie said, and he grasped the wooden box, lifted it up, and set it carefully on the coffee table. I leaned over to examine it. The box was made of teak, in the shape of a bird—maybe a parrot, or a macaw—and intricate in design.

"It looks like a puzzle box," I said.

"What kind of box?"

"Puzzle. It's also called a trick box. It can only be opened through some obscure or complicated series of manipulation. My Uncle Phineas had one. I used to love to play with it when I was a kid."

Ollie laughed and rubbed at his forehead. "Liked solving puzzles even then, eh?"

"Oh, yeah." I smiled, reminiscing. "My uncle loved magic, and anything remotely mysterious. He introduced me to 'em. Some require only a simple squeeze to give up their secret, and others, the more intricate ones, require the subtle movement of several small parts to open the box. Many of them had a good luck charm inside, sort of a reward for breaking the code. It could get a bit sticky. The correct series of movements to open a box can range anywhere from two to fifteen hundred moves."

"About fourteen hundred ninety nine too many movements for my taste," Ollie said. "We may never find out what's inside."

Nick lofted from the desk onto the table with a loud *thunk!* He sashayed over, round bottom wiggling, to give the box a sniff, then tapped at it with his paw. He leaned down and butted his head against the hard wood, rubbed his whiskers over the edge.

Ollie chuckled. "Nick seems to like your puzzle box."

"Of course he does. He's a real cool cat. Maybe he can figure out how to open it."

Nick stretched out, took one edge between his paws, and started to gnaw at the wood.

"Hey, what are you? Part beaver?"

Ollie was getting quite a kick out of Nick's antics. "Cats love to gnaw at wood and old books. Used to piss his former owner off royally."

"I'm not too thrilled right now, either." I gently disengaged his paws from the box and set it up on a high shelf. Then I jabbed my finger in front of his face. "That could be a valuable clue, Nick, it's not a snack," I said, in as stern a tone as I could muster. "And chewing is definitely not the way to open it."

Nick gave me an injured look and hopped down to the rug.

Ollie stretched his arms out. "Well, I guess this was a bust, eh? I know you were pretty certain you'd find the manuscript in here. I have to admit—I'm disappointed too. I was kinda looking forward to seeing what sort of dirt Marlene was preparing to dish out."

"Well . . ." I set down the box and turned my attention back to the typewriter. "We still might find it."

"What do you mean?"

I tapped the edge of the machine. "This is an original, non-correcting Selectric II. They used ribbons made of polymer tape rather than the old-style cloth ribbons of manual typewriters. And unlike the cloth ones, the polymer ribbons could only be used once and were then discarded. In fact, it presented a security issue in some environments, since it was possible to read the text that had been typed on the ribbon. You could see the light characters against the darker ribbon background."

"In other words, you can lift a copy of the book from the ribbon."

"Precisely."

Ollie looked at me approvingly and rubbed his hands. "Well, what are we waiting for?"

My heart pounded as I snapped off the hard-sided cover and laid it aside on the table, then gripped the front portion of the typewriter and raised it up. Both Ollie and I let out a yelp of dismay at the same time, and even Nick saw fit to utter a low growl of annoyance.

There was no cartridge in the typewriter. It was empty.

Twenty-two

"Darn," I said, after the initial shock had worn off and subsided to a throbbing ebb of crushing disappointment. "I was so certain, too."

The corners of Ollie's lips were drooped down. "She must have destroyed the ribbon, or else hidden it somewhere. Crazy like a fox," he muttered.

I pushed the heel of my hand through my ringlets. "Doesn't make sense. The police found nothing when they searched the house. Gladstone apparently found nothing. Anabel was trying to locate Stein. She was searching for this box, too, so even if she ransacked the house, she couldn't have found anything, either, so *where's the darn book?*" I narrowed my eyes and started to pace. "Marlene put these things in storage for a reason. She wouldn't have paid five hundred dollars for the privilege if she didn't have a good reason, right? But what could that reason be? The logical assumption would be she wanted to hide something very important. Something she thought someone might be after."

Three pairs of eyes—green, gray and gold—traveled upward to rest on the shelf where the puzzle box lay.

I shook my head. "It's obvious the manuscript can't be in that box. It's way too small."

"Perhaps not the manuscript itself," suggested Ollie. "Perhaps she hid a clue to its whereabouts."

"Such as?"

He shrugged. "A map, showing where she did hide it. Or perhaps she put a key inside, to a safe deposit box."

"Now that would make sense." I eyed the box on the shelf. "I know from past experience figuring out the proper sequence of moves to open the box could take awhile. How about I go downstairs and grab us some sandwiches to munch on while we're trying to figure it out?" I rubbed my stomach, and heard a loud rumble. "I only grabbed a slice of toast this morning. I was too excited to eat."

"Me too. Sounds great." Ollie settled himself in the recliner, and Nick hopped up onto his lap and started to purr loudly. "Food sounds good to Nick, too."

"Food always sounds good to Nick," I said and laughed, "but I'll fix him something too."

I left Nick sprawled across the big man's lap, purring away as Ollie gently rubbed him on the white streak behind his left ear, his favorite spot. I hurried down the stairs and through the door that led to the back entrance of Hot Bread and peered into the main store. There were a few customers scattered about, some standing in front of the TV, others seated at tables. Chantal was at the counter, ringing up a sandwich for Henrietta Watson, who'd been with Dr. Price since I'd been in knee-highs and pigtails. Chantal glanced over her shoulder, saw me, and hurried over, her arms waving in dramatic fashion.

"Thank goodness you are back, *chérie*! It has been crazy today." She rolled her eyes. "Breakfast was brisk, and the lunch crowd has been steady since eleven a.m. Your regulars, plus it looks as if you've gotten some newbies as well." She gestured toward my double-door refrigerator. "All the specials and salads are gone. You're low on whole wheat, and the last roast beef is in the case. I think the novelty of the TV has finally worn off. They are actually coming in now and ordering food instead of just congregating by the counter."

I put my arms around the slim brunette and gave her a big hug. "You know, I do appreciate all you do for me, and I probably don't say it often enough, but I do love you, you know that, Chantal."

"Ah, *chérie*, and I love you too! What are friends for, if not to help each other out?" She glanced over at the counter, which was bare of waiting customers, and asked, "How did your morning go? I have the feeling it did not go as well as you'd hoped."

"And you would be right, as usual. Ollie and I skipped lunch, so I need to make some sandwiches. Come help me and I'll fill you in."

As we prepared a small tray of ham and cheese, tuna and chicken cutlet sandwiches, I told Chantal about the morning's events, ending with the empty typewriter and puzzle box. "So Ollie and I are going to see if we can figure out the secret to opening it," I finished. "Maybe Marlene hid something of some value inside it, or hopefully a clue as to what she did with her book."

"Hm." Chantal spread a ciabatta roll liberally with mayo, then added a thick layer of ham and Swiss. "It does seem odd, to hide a typewriter when you've already removed the ribbon. Is the typewriter itself valuable?"

"Not really. I've seen them on eBay for around a hundred, hundred and fifty. I have no idea what her reasoning could have been for putting it in storage. Now, the puzzle box could be a different story."

Chantal handed me the platter of sandwiches. "What will you do if the box turns out to be a dead end?"

"Cry? Throw things? Seriously, though, Anabel was trying to locate that box, so she must have known something valuable was inside. And since it isn't the typewriter . . ."

I broke off speaking as the bell above the door tinkled. I glanced into the shop and sucked in a breath as I recognized the man making his way to my counter—Morley Carruthers! His long face wore a pinched expression, and his shoulders drooped more than usual. In short, he didn't look happy, not at all.

Chantal shot me a questioning look. "I get the feeling this is someone you'd rather not see."

"That's Marlene's lawyer, the one who also came for the box. Bud no doubt told him about us taking it." I motioned to her. "See what he wants."

She nodded and moved off. I slipped into the storeroom, leaving the door open just enough so I could see without being seen.

"Good afternoon," I heard Chantal say. "Can I help you?"

"I'm looking for the owner. Ms. Nora Charles."

"She is not here right now." Chantal swept her arm toward the blackboard. "Can I interest you in one of our lunch specials? Today we have a lovely Greek salad . . ."

Carruthers's hand waved about like a baton. "No, thank you. It's very important I speak with Ms. Charles. Will she be back today?"

"Um, that's hard to say. She is not here. She left on a business trip today."

"Oh. Well, when will she be back? Tomorrow?"

"I am not sure."

I saw Carruthers pick up one of the printed take-out menus from the sidebar that listed the store hours and slide it into his jacket pocket. He withdrew a small card and passed it across to Chantal. "Please give her that when she returns and have her call me, no matter what time."

"Certainly. Are you positive you would not like something? A cup of coffee, perhaps?"

He shook his head. "Some other time. Make sure she gets that, now. And tell her I'll be waiting for her call." He turned on his heel and stalked out, letting the door slam behind him. I waited a few extra minutes just to be on the safe side before emerging from my hiding place.

Chantal handed me the card. "Such a pleasant person."

"He's interested in that box, too. Ollie and I just missed him at the consignment shop."

"Well, I can tell you this." Chantal leaned closer to me. "That man has lots of secrets himself. Lots of them. I felt the vibe loud and clear when he handed me his card. He is not someone to fool with, *chérie*. I would even venture to say he knows a great deal more about all this than he is letting on." Her eyes widened.

"For all we know, Carruthers could be the murderer."

• • •

Ollie and I worked on the puzzle box for a good three hours, took a break, said good night to Chantal, and then worked on it for another two before we admitted defeat. The intricate piece of teak just didn't seem inclined to give up her secrets to us and we'd tried every position and move imaginable, even some that weren't. It was close to eight o'clock when we finally decided to call it quits. I walked Ollie downstairs. Nick was God knew where. He'd gotten bored watching us and had taken off hours ago, presumably to work his charm on Chantal for some more leftover tuna, having scoffed up the bowl I'd brought him.

"Lock your doors and your windows," Ollie cautioned me. He hadn't been too thrilled when I mentioned Carruthers's visit.

"He's not going to come and attack me, Ollie. That would be a bit obvious, don't you think?" I went over, picked up my tote, and dug out a print I'd made of the front and back of the card from Anabel's purse. "Mind checking this out for me?"

Ollie took the paper and squinted at it. "Arlene's Beauty Supply?"

"It was in Anabel's wallet. See the number in the second photo, that was on the back of the card? It's probably nothing, but she had it tucked away for some reason."

He folded the paper, slid it into his pocket and gave me a quick peck on the cheek. "Remember, don't open your door unless you're absolutely certain you know who it is."

I clicked my heels and gave him a mock salute. "Yes, sir."

I watched him drive off, then locked the downstairs door and walked back through Hot Bread, making sure the rear entrance, side entrance and front doors were locked securely. Satisfied no one could get in without my knowing about it, I hurried back upstairs and into the den . . . where I stopped and stared.

I'd left the puzzle box right on top of my desk. It wasn't there.

"Nick!" I yelled.

No sign of the cat, either.

The den phone rang, and I hurried over. Seeing Hank's number, I scooped it up. "Hey, what's up?"

"Got some information for you," he said without preamble. "You asked me to do a little checking into crime families that might have some connection with Marlene McCambridge, right? Well, she and Nico Enerelli were involved."

"Right. They were lovers."

"Until about a year ago, when their relationship abruptly ended. And from all accounts, it was Marlene who ended it. Now, this Gladstone fellow . . ."

"Is really Freddie Bartholomew, and he has worked for the Enerelli family."

"You take all the joy out of this job," Hank said and sighed.

"Actually, blame Daniel. He decided to be forthcoming."

"Yeah? I bet he wasn't entirely forthcoming. He didn't tell you the name of his FBI source, by chance."

"You found that out?"

Hank sounded smug as he asked, "You know Morley Carruthers?"

I wrinkled my nose. "He's the FBI source? You're kidding!"

"Sadly, I'm not. Carruthers has worked off and on for the Enerelli family for years. Apparently his father before him did, and grandfather, you get the picture. That's how he became Marlene's lawyer. He took her on as a favor to Enerelli, and when they broke up he kept her on, much to Enerelli's chagrin, but what he was really doing was spying."

I gasped. "Like a double agent! And Marlene didn't know?"

"I think she may have suspected, but she couldn't prove anything. Or maybe she was so confident she just didn't care. Anyway, in the last few months it appears the grass has been looking greener to Morley. He's been playing both sides of the fence. This is where it gets good. Apparently Marlene confided to him what she'd written in her tell-all about Nico, and he blabbed it to Enerelli."

"Isn't that a breach of lawyer-client confidentiality or something?"

"I guess it doesn't count if the client doesn't know, or knows and doesn't care. Anyway, about a month ago Carruthers went to the FBI, promising to spill the goods on Enerelli—if they'd get that manuscript back. Seems Morley's got his own little chapter in there as well. That's when your guy Daniel and Samms started setting up shop. In the meantime, of course, Carruthers is also working for Enerelli, promising to get the book for him."

"Is that part of the sting?"

"No one's quite sure. I can tell you this, though. The FBI doesn't exactly trust Carruthers. There's talk that perhaps Enerelli isn't even involved, that Carruthers might have hired Bartholomew independently. There's also talk that Carruthers is tired of working behind the scenes, that he might be planning a little takeover on his own."

I whistled. "So Enerelli might be the next victim, eh?"

"Right now, that's only supposition. In the meantime, the manuscript is MIA. It hasn't turned up at the editor's office as Marlene promised, and in light of her death, they're getting antsy now. Offered Carruthers a big finder's fee if he can produce it. Seems they have a huge publicity campaign planned, which will be a total waste with no product."

"So her death doesn't change anything as far as releasing it?"

"Are you kidding? They're more anxious than ever to acquire it. They've already sunk high six figures into it, money they'll never be able to recoup without sales."

"The advance." I sighed. "Fat chance they have of getting any of it back."

"Just be careful, little girl. You know, if you do manage to locate that manuscript, you'd better get it and yourself under armed guard immediately. These are desperate and dangerous people you're dealing with. I'll keep my ear to the ground, and if I hear any more, I'll give you a holler."

I hung up and dropped into my recliner. This information definitely cleared up a few things. Daniel's informant was Morley, and Morley was still working for Enerelli. Morley'd tipped Enerelli off as to what Marlene'd written about him, so Morley had to have seen the manuscript, or at least the part about Nico . . .

"Darn it all, Nick, what have you done with that puzzle box?" I yelled.

Nick's head peeped out from underneath the small love seat in the den. "Merow," he yowled.

I dropped to my knees in front of him. "Look, buddy, I won't get mad, I promise. Did you take that box?"

Nick's head disappeared and a minute later the box slid out from under the love seat, followed by Nick. I picked the box up and took it back over to my desk, where I just stood for a few minutes, staring at it.

"I've tried everything I can think of. Ollie and I even looked up moves on the Internet. This box is certainly true to its name. It's the biggest puzzle I've ever seen."

Nick leapt onto the desk and sat, looking down at the puzzle box. He reached out, gently tapped at the parrot's head.

"You think I should give it one more try, huh? Well, okay."

I picked up the box and turned it over in my hand. The parrot beak seemed to lay a little differently than the rest of the piece and I wondered why I hadn't noticed it before. I hooked the edge of my nail underneath the beak and pushed from side to side. Nothing. I started to set it back down but Nick's paw lashed out.

"Okay, okay, I'll keep trying."

I studied the box a minute, trying to remember all the different ways I'd heard of to uncover the secret cavity. Finally I pressed down on the beak and moved it counterclockwise in a circle once, twice . . . I almost dropped the box as a small drawer shot out from underneath the parrot's claw.

Nick turned around twice. "Meower."

"I guess you were right, Nick. I just had to keep at it. Thanks."

I peered inside the drawer, saw something long, black and silver. I reached inside and pulled it out, and my breath caught in my throat.

Nestled in my palm was a flash drive. I pulled my laptop over, booted it up, and slid the flash drive in. After a minute, one file came up: a file labeled *Memoirs*.

Nick sidled up to me, gave me a headbutt on the chin.

"Well, it looks as if Desiree was wrong," I said, giving his head a pat. "Marlene did write her book on a computer after all."

I pulled out my chair and sat down, my heart beating madly in my chest.

I was about to find out just what all the fuss was about, and what had gotten two people killed.

Twenty-three

Marlene's writing style was what some would call dry, and yet she had a definite flair for getting her point across. I skimmed through the first ten chapters, which mainly recounted her early life, her childhood, her abuse at the hands of a drunken uncle.

Then came her meeting with Desiree, Dora at the time. Even though I confess I was curious as to the nature of Desiree's secret, I deliberately skipped the next couple of chapters. If Desiree had wanted me to know her secret, she would have told me. My mother had pledged to keep it. I saw no reason to violate that confidence.

The rest of the book wasn't written in chronological order. It appeared to be more or less ramblings, observations that Marlene had written down when the mood suited her. I decided that it read more like a diary than a novel. Whoever had been selected as its editor would have a massive task ahead of them.

I found the chapter about Scarlett and skimmed through it. Every detail was there, just as she'd told them to me; except the way Marlene wrote it, Scarlett came off as cold and calculating rather than put-upon. She'd been right. If it were allowed to be published this way it might do serious damage to her career.

Sable St. John's chapter was riddled with innuendo, but no names were named. Marlene hinted at Sable's (Dooley's at the time) being employed by a "major crime figure" and detailed some interaction with drugs, illegal firearms, even the smuggling of not only gems but illegal aliens, yet only hinted at the fact Sable might have offed a thug or two at the "mcf's" behest. I decided that not only was his chapter a bust, but it was even doubtful that Enerelli was the crime lord for whom Sable'd worked. The feeling remained though, that Sable knew more about Enerelli and his dealings than even he liked.

Then—at long last—the chapter about Enerelli. I started to read this with great interest. You could almost feel the electricity generated between Nico and Marlene, it was so palpable. The sparks fairly flew off the page. There were many scenes with sex so explicit, I could feel my cheeks (and other areas of my body) growing hot, and I am not a prude by any means.

It seemed to me as if there were a genuine love between them, at least in the beginning. Then it was evident Marlene grew tired of Nico, and what she called his "dependence on her." She grew irritated with his "neediness" and "constant seeking of approval"—particularly in the bedroom. She even intimated that he sought her counsel on family matters—and even though she didn't come right out and say it, I could tell just what was implied.

And yet, that wasn't the worst of it . . . for Marlene.

Despite her waning interest, she still considered Nico her man. And, apparently, "her man's" eye had begun to rove . . . big-time.

Maybe because he sensed she was tiring of him, or maybe because it was just in his blood, the reasons were never fully explained, but Nico cheated on Marlene, and not with just anyone.

With Lila St. Claire.

I had heard the name before. Twenty-odd years ago, Lila St. Claire was one of the most beautiful women in the world, as well as one of the most powerful. She was a madam, and not just to anyone. Her clientele included mayors, senators, mob bosses and even the occasional small-time hood or hit man. Lila was successful because to her, sex was just a business. Love never entered into her transactions.

Until she met Nico Enerelli.

Although I found I couldn't quite agree when Marlene likened their romance to that of Rhett and Scarlett or Megan and Father Ralph (four of my favorite literary characters, no less), the metaphor was clear: doomed and forbidden. Lila and Nico had a mad, passionate fling, and then . . . just like that . . . it was over. Lila apparently came to her senses, sent Nico packing, and he went, tail between his legs, back to Marlene.

Seven months later, Lila St. Claire mysteriously disappeared. People thought she'd gone to a fat farm, because after breaking up with Nico she'd apparently started to pack on the pounds. When she returned to her Boston apartment four months later, she was her old spunky self, and reed-thin.

Her explanation of hiding out at a fat farm to battle her depression and get back in shape apparently satisfied everyone but Marlene, who spared no expense to track down what she termed to be "the truth," and which she finally found in the form of a birth certificate from a small hospital in San Mateo, California.

A baby, eight pounds, seven ounces. Mother: Lila St. Claire. And under the section labeled *Father*: Nico Enerelli. The sex of the baby wasn't mentioned.

It had taken Marlene many years and practically all of her monies to finally get hold of that birth certificate, which had been very well concealed. Even after she and Enerelli had finally called it quits, even after they pledged undying friendship to each other, and that each would keep the other's secret, even though they'd done everything except take an oath in blood. Marlene had plotted, and planned, and waited for the day when she would have her revenge on the man who had the audacity to sleep with another woman when he claimed it was *her* he loved, and her alone.

And now millions of people would get to read about it, as well.

I skimmed through the remaining pages of the book, but the identity of the child was not revealed. I had an idea Marlene was probably waiting until the very last second to fill that in.

I got to the end of the book, and closed the file. I pulled out the flash drive and sat for a long time, holding it.

Well, Jendine had been right. This would make one helluva book, and it would make every bestseller list that had ever been created.

It had been written in such a way as to ridicule Enerelli, to paint him as a man with no control—which was very dangerous in his line of work. But the person it would ruin most was the poor progeny of Lila and Nico.

I found I had many unanswered questions. Had Nico known about his child? Lila St. Claire had died shortly afterward. Had she ever told him? I wasn't too familiar with the Enerelli crime family, but I did know that Nico had never married, and had no children. He had a nephew, Donato, who was being groomed to eventually take over.

That opened up another can of worms. If Donato knew he had competition somewhere out there, might not he have wanted to silence Marlene before the truth could be told? Maybe it was Donato who had hired Freddie Bartholomew.

I rose, still clutching the flash drive. It was time to turn it over to the pros. Daniel and Samms would turn cartwheels to get this, I was sure. Maybe after I gave it to them and they had a chance to look it over, they'd be so grateful they'd be happy to overlook just how I'd come to have it in the first place.

I thought of Carruthers. How much of all this did the lawyer know? I was betting a lot, maybe even the identity of the love child. He was pretty anxious to get his hands on all this, too, but for very different reasons. It made me wonder, as well, how much Anabel knew of all this. As Marlene's onetime agent, had she somehow managed to sneak a peek at the work in progress without her client's knowledge?

Either way, it was moot. Anabel was dead, whether it was because of what she knew about the manuscript or because she knew who'd killed Marlene. Hank was right. It would be prudent of me to get this out of my hands and into those of law enforcement before I became the next target.

I rose from my chair and reached for the landline phone at the exact same instant Nick's back stiffened. He cowered on the desktop, back arched, every hair standing on end. His ears flicked back, flattened against his skull, his gold eyes almost protruded out of their sockets, and his lips peeled back, revealing his sharp fangs and pink tongue.

He looked every inch the picture of your typical, scary Halloween cat, and in the next instant he was gone, a black-and-white blur racing out of my den and vanishing down the hallway, his nails clicking on my hardwood floor.

"Nick," I wanted to call after him, but his name came out sounding more like a strangled sob. The flash drive fell from my suddenly nerveless fingers, rolled partway underneath the desk. I wasn't one to be scared, yet right now I felt the sensation of fear so acute it was like an ache in the pit of my stomach. There was a pricking sensation at the back of my neck—the sensation of eyes, cold and unfriendly, boring into the base of my skull—and then a hand clamped down across my mouth and I felt myself being jerked backward, feet leaving the floor.

"Don't move a muscle," a silky voice hissed in my ear. "Or you're a dead woman."

I inclined my head to show I understood. He spun me around and dropped me—plop! Right on my recliner. I had to swallow around the giant lump in my throat before I could speak.

I'd expected to be looking at Simon Gladstone, but this man was his total opposite. He was much taller, and impeccably dressed in a three-piece gray suit made of some silky material. A light pink handkerchief protruded from his jacket pocket, and I could see expensive cufflinks of thick gold on the cuffs of the crisp white shirt protruding from the sleeves. He had a swarthy olive complexion, jet-black hair, and hooded eyes that reminded me of a cobra's ready to strike. He raised his arm to fix his sleeve, and as he did so I could see the cufflinks more clearly. They were big yellow initials. An *N*, and an *E*.

"Nico Enerelli!" I gasped.

He made a little bow. "In the flesh, Ms. Charles. You should be flattered. I rarely call on clients personally."

"Clients?"

"Just a little term I use." I could detect a slight Italian accent as he spoke. Nico tipped his head. "I think you know why I'm here, don't you, *bella?*"

Anger replaced the fear. "I know you're trespassing on private property. How did you get into my house?"

His hand dipped into his pocket and removed what at first glance appeared to be a pocketknife, but he flicked his wrist and I could see it was something much more deadly—a long, stemmed, sharp razor. He held the weapon aloft in his left hand, and wiggled the fingers of his right. "Like I said, you know why I'm here. Give it to me."

"I—I have no idea what you're talking about."

"Of course you do," he snapped. "You and I both know that all that drivel about not liking to type on a computer was just lip service. I know Marlene put the book on a flash drive."

"And how do you know that?"

He looked at me as if I were someone with a mental deficiency. "She told me, of course. She could not wait to dig it into me." His gaze locked with mine. "You've read it, right? Then you know how much trouble it will cause within my family if that truth ever gets out."

"The truth about your illegitimate child."

"My son." Nico nodded. "Marlene told me that much, although she never told me any more details. Morley knows, and I will deal with him next. But right now, I need to destroy the evidence." He wiggled his fingers again. "The flash drive, please."

I shook my head. "I—I don't have it."

He laughed lightly, his thick lips parting to display pearl-white teeth. "Of course you do. You got the box. Marlene hid it in the box. I know that. I gave her that box. It's the only place left it could be. You had to have found it and I'm sure you would have wasted no time in looking at it." He swished the blade before my eyes. "I do not want to hurt you, but trust me, you do not want to anger me. Now give it to me."

I cleared my throat. I couldn't hand over the flash drive, because if I did, what reason would he have to keep me alive. Dead men tell no tales. "I guess I should be flattered that you paid me a personal call, instead of sending your goon."

"I had no choice. My goon, as you call him, got himself arrested. He went back to that house to give it another once-over, just in case. The FBI was on him like a cat on a mouse." He dragged a hand across his chin. "They will most likely charge him with Marlene's murder, and Anabel's."

"And did he? Kill them?"

Nico shrugged. "Who's to say? Freddie can get very excitable."

"But he was acting on your orders, correct?"

He stared at me, and his expression was one of genuine puzzlement. "My orders? Is that what you think?" He made a tsking sound. "Why would I order Marlene's death? In spite of our differences, I loved her. Why else would I put up with her crap? And why would I want Anabel killed? I only met the woman once."

"There's a possibility she might have seen Freddie enter the house the night Marlene was killed."

"So what if she did? I told you, I did not tell him to kill Marlene. My hands are clean. And if it should turn out Morley is behind all this, well, I promise you he will pay. Now . . ." He wiggled his fingers. "Enough small talk. Hand it over."

"Even if I were to give you the flash drive, how do you know there isn't another copy somewhere?"

"Silly girl . . . Marlene told me she only made one copy. And I know she did not like clutter. She would never print out an entire copy of the book unless she had no choice." He held out his palm. "Give it to me."

Out of the corner of my eye I saw Nick pad quietly into the den. He hopped up on the desk, and then in one graceful leap he was on top of my bookcase. He padded over to my brass bust of Edgar Allan Poe and stood beside it, his tail fanning out behind Poe's head almost like a black raven's wing.

I looked at Enerelli. "You gave Marlene an initial necklace."

He nodded. "Yes. It actually belonged to my grandmother, Elena Enerelli. I'd given it to Marlene early in our courtship, when I'd hoped she might consent to make my family name her own. It was but one of many presents of jewelry."

"It was clutched in Anabel's hand when I discovered her body."

"She must have stolen it from Marlene. They had many arguments lately over money." His brows suddenly drew together. "You're stalling, aren't you? Why? Help is not on the way, Ms. Charles."

True. My help was sitting on top of the bookcase, waiting for . . . for what, exactly? Nico waved the razor in the air. "I do not wish to harm you, but I will if I have to. We've wasted enough time. Where is the flash drive?"

My eyes strayed to the spot underneath the desk where I'd dropped it. Nico caught my action, followed my gaze.

"Ah," he murmured, and bent over to pick it up.

Nick chose that moment to raise his forepaws and push the bust of Edgar Allan Poe off the shelf. Enerelli heard the slight noise, because he raised his head—and bam! Edgar Allan hit him square on the forehead. He went down with a low groan.

I leapt up and darted over to the desk. I jerked open the left bottom drawer, rummaged around until I found what I'd jammed in there one day: a pair of handcuffs, a souvenir from the Chicago PD when I'd quit my job. *"Here's something to remember us by,"* Lieutenant Peterson had said. *"You never know, Nora. They could come in handy."*

I'd have to send Lieutenant Peterson a thank-you note.

I snapped a cuff on Enerelli's wrist, then snapped the other one around the desk leg. Then I whipped a roll of masking tape out of the other drawer and slapped it right across the crime boss's mouth.

I jumped as I heard a heavy pounding on my front door. Now what?

"Nora." It was Daniel's voice. Almost dizzy with relief, I took the stairs two at a time and practically fell into his arms.

"Chantal called. She had a feeling you were in danger."

God bless my psychic friend. "Enerelli. Upstairs. He tried . . . he had a razor. He was going to kill me."

"Good Lord."

He took the stairs two at a time, one hand on his gun, the other on his phone. I followed at a slower pace. When I reached the den Enerelli was still unconscious, but Daniel had his wrists and ankles cuffed and he was propped up against my recliner, his head lolling to one side.

"He got a pretty good conk on the head." Daniel bent down, picked up Edgar Allan. "How did you manage that?"

"I didn't," I said, and pointed to the top shelf, where Nick sat. The nails of one claw were extended and he was giving it a through washing, probably to remove all traces of dust.

Daniel shook his head. "I swear, one of these days I'm deputizing him."

"At least you appreciate him. Samms thinks he's a nuisance."

He grinned, then his expression sobered as he asked, "What was he doing here?"

I leaned down to retrieve the flash drive, which I dropped into Daniel's hand. "Marlene's book."

He stared at me. "Do I want to know how you got this?"

"Probably not."

I heard the squeal of tires outside and glanced out the window. Two black sedans came to a screeching halt at my side entrance. Samms got out of the first sedan and hurried toward the door. A second later I heard heavy footsteps pounding up the stairs. I felt faint, suddenly, and sank into the love seat. Daniel was beside me in an instant. He took my face between his hands.

"You okay?"

"I will be," I sighed. "This isn't over. Enerelli told me he didn't order those hits. He said he didn't kill Marlene, and he didn't kill Anabel."

"Of course he's going to say that." Daniel looked at me. "You don't believe him, do you?"

"Honestly, I'm not sure. But if he is telling the truth, you know what that means. Their killer is still out there."

Twenty-four

After Daniel and Samms had taken Enerelli away, I called Ollie to fill him in on the evening's events. "I had a feeling I should have stuck around," he said when I'd finished. "Are you okay?"

"Yes, at least physically. I'm just not entirely satisfied the right murderer has been apprehended." Nick jumped up on my lap. I rubbed the fur on the back of his neck and sighed. "I still feel as if something's missing. Something important."

"Well, get some rest. You'll think of it. Things always look better the morning after."

We talked for another few minutes and then I hung up. I sat back in the recliner, my eyes closed, fingers drumming against the chair arms. I felt a movement on my chest and opened my eyes. Nick had shifted his position so that he was sitting straight up, staring at me. His tongue came out, swiped across his lips.

"Merow."

"Hungry? Well, I guess you deserve a snack for your heroic actions. That was good work, Nick. If not for you, I'm not sure what Enerelli might have done. He said he wasn't going to harm me, but . . ."

He leapt off my lap, and I got up, went to the kitchen, and got a can of sardines down from the cupboard. I spooned half the contents into a bowl and set it down on the floor. "Enjoy. You earned it."

He gave me what one might term an appreciative glance, and then hunched over the bowl and started slurping. I washed my hands in the sink and then went back into the den. I picked up the puzzle box from the shelf where I'd laid it and sat down, turning it over in my hands.

I'd told Ollie I felt something was missing, and now I knew what it was that bothered me: Marlene's omission of the name of Nico and Lila's son.

I'd never met Marlene, but from what I'd read of her book I could tell the woman was a stickler for details. No way would she do all that research, write all that down, and not finish the job. She'd left the son's name out—why? Was it a bargaining chip between her and Enerelli? Or . . .

Between her and the son?

I did a quick calculation. The affair had taken place thirty-six years ago; that would mean the son was born sometime in the early nineteen eighties. Lila had gone away to have the baby, but she most likely wouldn't have gone too far. An enterprising woman like her would have wanted to keep tabs on her business.

So . . . a boy born in the early eighties within a fifty-mile radius of Boston. A boy that would have been placed immediately into foster care.

I sighed. Like searching for a needle in a haystack. And yet, I'd bet every last cent I owned Marlene had managed to find out his identity.

A slight scuffling sound made me look down. Nick had finished his snack and was under the desk, batting around more Scrabble tiles. I pushed my chair back and leaned down.

"Hey, Nick. What have you got?"

He batted one tile across the polished floor toward me. I picked it up. An *R*. Next an *E* and an *O* came flying at me, followed by a *C* and a *V*.

Nick stretched himself full-length and folded his paws, X-shape, in front of him. A real "my work here is done" kind of pose.

I laid the tiles on the desk and started to move them around. *Vocer.* Hardly. *Crove.* Nope. *Cover.*

Well, that one made sense.

I bent underneath the desk and looked at the cat. "Cover? What kind of cover, Nick? A book cover?"

Nick's eyes flicked toward the cardboard box I'd placed in the corner of the den, and the proverbial lightbulb flashed on over my head.

"The typewriter cover!"

Nick purred loudly.

I moved over to the box and pulled back the flaps. I reached down, lifted up the side clips, and stepped back, turning the hard-side cover

over in my hand. The top portion of the case had a large clip that could be used to hold papers; it was empty. I ran my nail along the inside and felt a slightly raised edge. I brought the cover over to the desk, grabbed a letter opener, and slid the point underneath the raised lip, then pressed down. There was a soft *pop* and then the surface raised, just about a half inch, revealing a small cavity inside.

There were papers jammed in there.

I knew the letter opener wouldn't do the trick, so I quickly went downstairs into Hot Bread's kitchen, returning a few minutes later with a sharp, serrated double-edged knife, which I jammed into the opening. The knife cut through the plastic as if it were butter, and a few seconds later I held in my hand a small cache of papers, bound with a thick rubber band. I pulled the band off and carefully laid the papers on the desk. The top sheet only had a few words written there, in a bold scrawl:

Notes on Nico's Son

I debated for a moment calling Ollie, or Daniel, or even Samms, but then my curiosity got the better of me. I squinted at the cramped, spidery writing. Marlene certainly was no ace when it came to penmanship. I was able to make out a name: North Andover Foundling Home. I booted up my computer and typed it into the search engine. The North Andover Foundling Home was a charitable institution, founded in the early 1900s, that was primarily a children's home established for the education and maintenance of deserted and homeless young children. It operated mainly on grants from many philanthropic individuals, and there followed a long list of names. I skimmed them, finding none of note, and then a sentence near the bottom caught my eye: *Foundling Hospital provided through a grant made possible via the estate of Lila St. Claire.*

I turned again to the handwritten notes. There was a date underlined, January 5, 1985, and then some words I simply couldn't make out, with another notation: *LSC real name: Miranda J. Paulson.*

I picked up my phone and dialed Hank's number. When he answered I asked, "How fast do you think your source could get me the name of a baby boy, born at the North Andover Foundling Hospital in Massachusetts on January 5, 1985?"

"Is that all?" He didn't even bother to disguise the sarcasm.

"The mother's name would either be Lila St. Claire or Miranda Paulson. I'm not sure which one she'd use."

"Lila St. Claire? *The* Lila St. Claire, the famous madam?"

"None other."

He let out a low whistle. "How'd you find out she had a kid?"

"I didn't. Marlene did. I'm thinking she might have tracked him down, maybe even blackmailed him to keep his name out of her book. I finally found the manuscript. It was on a flash drive hidden in a puzzle box. Chapter 18 reveals Lila and Nico Enerelli had a child out of wedlock—a boy—but doesn't give a name."

"You're thinking maybe this son murdered Marlene?"

"Maybe. I had a visitor tonight. Nico Enerelli himself."

"Oh, no," Hank groaned. "What happened?"

"He wanted the flash drive, but Nick managed to knock that bust of Poe on his head before he could harm me."

Hank let out a low chuckle. "Are you sure that cat's not part human?"

"To be honest, no, I'm not," I admitted. "Anyway, before he got knocked out cold, Nico did say he didn't order a hit on either Marlene or Anabel."

Hank snorted. "Yes, and crime bosses always tell the truth."

"Oddly, I think he was. Like I said, how fast do you think you can get me that info?"

"I'll do my best."

Hank hung up and I pored over the notes again. Down at the very bottom of the page was a phone number: 555-978-0651.

I frowned. That number seemed familiar. Either I'd dialed it recently, or I'd gotten a call from there. I picked up my cell phone, thinking how fortuitous it was I didn't erase calls out of memory until it got full. I scrolled down the list, and then I saw it:

555-978-0651
Cruz Sun

The only person who I'd called from the *Sun*, and who'd also called me . . . was Jenks.

I set down the papers. What did I know about Jenks? He was new to Cruz, only here a few weeks . . . as a matter of fact, he'd come to town right around the same time Anabel had rented the house. He was a reporter, and Marker had given him the assignment of a story on Marlene . . . He'd never heard of the woman before that morning in Hot Bread, when Alvina had filled him in.

Or so he said.

I dialed the *Cruz Sun* and got the switchboard. I asked to speak to Mr. Marker. A few minutes later, I was connected with Connie, his assistant.

"Hey, Nora. What's up?"

"Hey, I just thought I'd check in with Mr. Marker," I said, thinking fast. "He'd wanted to do an article on Hot Bread, and I've been putting it off, but now . . . now I might be ready."

"Gee, that's great. Want me to connect you with Aldo Greenstein? He's the local food reviewer. He had really nice things to say about your dishes at the library fundraiser, so I'm sure he'll be thrilled to know you're interested in a full-page spread."

"Um, yeah, that'd be great. But I'd still like to speak with Mr. Marker first, if that's possible."

"Not really. Mr. Marker won't be back until next week. Would you want to wait that long?"

"Back? He's been away?"

She laughed. "Yes, the last three weeks, and it's been heaven. His wife made him take her on a monthlong cruise to the Greek Islands."

I gripped the receiver more tightly. "So Marker hasn't been in the office for the last three weeks?"

"Nope. Not that I mind working for him, you understand, but . . . he can be a bear at times."

"Demanding, yes. I know the type." I swallowed. "But he's been in touch with the office, right? Doling out assignments?"

"Hah, are you kidding? His wife would have his head. Jenny McNamara and I have been handling that end, and not too shabbily, I might add."

So Jenks had lied about Marker's wanting to do an article on Marlene. "Did you by any chance give Paul Jenkins an assignment to write an article on Marlene McCambridge?"

"Heck, no!" There was no mistaking the surprise evident in her tone. "Why would I give the Phantom something like that to do?"

"The Phantom?"

She giggled. "Yeah, that's what we call him, 'cause since he's been hired, he's out more than in." Her tone took on a hard edge. "Has he been telling people he's a reporter?"

"He's not?"

"Heck, no! He works in the morgue, night shift. As a matter of fact . . ." I heard the sound of papers shuffling and then she said, "Yep— he called in again tonight. I thought I heard Greta grumbling about having to pull a double in the break room. Sure, she could use the overtime, but sometimes a night off is worth just as much, ya know? Conroy ought to fire his ass, except we've been so short-staffed. I'm sorry. I shouldn't speak out of turn. What did you need Jenks for? Did you need something looked up?"

"No, no. I'll call back next week, thanks."

I clicked off and rested my chin in my hands. So Paul Jenkins wasn't even a reporter. He had a press pass, but I knew from experience they were easy to duplicate. He'd come to Cruz three weeks ago, around the same time as Marlene. And Marlene had the number for the *Cruz Sun* written on these notes.

Something else niggled at me, some memory at the back of my brain. Something that had seemed a bit off, but I couldn't quite put my finger on it.

My phone rang. I answered without looking at the caller ID. "Well, that was fast."

"Glad you think so." It was Ollie, not Hank. "I forgot to tell you I heard back from Arlene's Beauty Supply. They were able to trace that number. It was for a rental, of an ash-blond pageboy wig. It was paid for in cash, so there's no credit card record. The clerk was able to give only a vague description of the renter. It was a man with long reddish hair, who wore glasses. That's it, sorry."

I felt my stomach lurch. I thanked Ollie and hung up and then sat for a few minutes, staring at the papers spread out before me, and at the phone. And just like that, it came to me, the elusive something that had been gnawing at me, teasing my memory. My lips thinned to a straight line.

I could call Daniel and Samms, and tell them my suspicions, but unfortunately I had no concrete proof to back them up. Juries liked solid evidence. It made convictions much easier.

So, I had two choices. I could alert the FBI and let them take care of it and run the risk of a killer skipping out, or I could try to get that proof myself.

I looked at the phone, and then I looked at the pile of papers in front of me. Then I let out a slow breath and reached for the phone.

Twenty-five

J enks showed up in front of the Porter house right on time, at precisely ten o'clock. I met him in front, and then we walked up the front steps and into the foyer. Jenks looked mildly surprised when I locked the door.

"For privacy," I explained. "Even though this isn't considered a crime scene anymore, you never know when someone might come wandering by, you know, a fan of Marlene's looking for some sort of souvenir they could sell on eBay."

"I'm glad I checked my messages," Jenks said. "I don't always. So have I got this straight? You're telling me that Anabel *isn't* the murderer?"

"That's right."

"But they found a suicide note."

"Forged," I said crisply. "By the real murderer, to tie things up neat and tidy with a big pink ribbon, so that he could get away unscathed and unpunished."

"I see." He shifted restlessly from one foot to the other. "Don't keep me in suspense. You know who the murderer is?"

"Nico Enerelli came to see me tonight, razor blade and all. He wanted the flash drive I found in Marlene's puzzle box."

Jenks shook his head, and some of that silky red hair spilled out of the hasty ponytail he'd caught it up in and hung limply to his shoulders. "Wait, you're losing me. What's a puzzle box?"

"It's a box that can only be opened by a series of movements. Marlene had one, and she was satisfied enough that her manuscript would be safe there. She didn't type it out, like Desiree thought. Marlene must have either borrowed or rented a computer. It's all on a flash drive."

A muscle in his lower jaw worked. "And Enerelli got away with it?"

I shook my head. "No, he didn't. Thank God the FBI showed up in the nick of time. They've got the flash drive now."

He was silent for a long moment, digesting this, and then he said, "So Nico Enerelli had Marlene murdered to get the manuscript, and then his henchman murdered Anabel why? Because she'd seen him? And made it look like she'd murdered Marlene and then committed suicide so the case would be closed?"

"You're partially right. The killer murdered Marlene to get the manuscript, which of course he didn't find because she'd hidden it in the puzzle box and taken the box to storage. He wore a blond wig to disguise himself, but then he found out that someone who knew him had seen him. So he killed her and then made it look like a suicide, so the police would be satisfied and not look for anyone else." I reached into my pocket and pulled out the card from Arlene's Beauty Supply. "You really shouldn't have rented the wig under the name you're using now."

I had to hand it to Jenks, he was one cool cucumber. He seemed unfazed by my accusation. Nothing changed: expression, demeanor, or voice. "I'm sorry, I don't understand."

"Sure, you do. Now, I can tell you that the police and the FBI don't know what I know. You weren't named in the manuscript, and right now I have no intention of going to them."

One eyebrow lifted. Still, he remained silent.

I tucked a strand of hair behind my ear in an unconcerned gesture. "You know, it's tough in this economy to make a go of a business. Hot Bread's been slowly coming back into the black, and I figure one good shot in the arm is all I need to turn a substantial profit this year. That's where you come in."

His mouth twisted into a leering expression. "Pardon?"

"I figure in exchange for my silence on your parentage, you can make a capital donation to my store. One hundred fifty thousand," I said in a voice that didn't waver at all, despite the butterflies fluttering about in my stomach. "I figure that's a darn good price, bargain actually, to let you get away with murder."

He shook his head. "You're crazy," he mumbled.

"Not so much." I opened my tote and took out the notes I'd retrieved from Marlene's typewriter. "Marlene went through a lot of trouble to find out your real identity. How did you feel when she tracked you down, told you that you were going to be the star chapter in her tell-all book?"

He smiled at me then, a smile similar to the one a lion gives a gazelle before it pounces. "She didn't even have the guts to tell me herself, at first. Anabel did."

"Anabel knew what was in the book, then."

He nodded. "She did. Marlene needed Anabel's help to make the connection with the publishing house. Once that was established, she told Anabel to take a hike. Anabel, of course, knew about the advance and demanded Marlene pay her back what she owed, and Marlene, like the snake she was, refused. So then Anabel decided to enlist my help. She got in touch with me, told me what Marlene had planned. Then I decided it was time I made some plans of my own." He glanced around the room, then returned his gaze to me. "How did you come to the conclusion I had to be the murderer?"

"Several things, actually. The card from Arlene's Beauty Supply, with the rental number on the back. Then there were Marlene's notes, of course, and the manuscript alluding to an illegitimate son. I called the *Cruz Sun* and found out that you're not a feature reporter, that you work in the morgue, although probably not for much longer. What really cinched it was when I remembered something you said the day after the murder."

His gaze narrowed. "What was that?"

"You were talking about stopping by the house for your interview. You said Samms wouldn't let you in, but he gave you a statement. Police never give out all the information to the public. That was one of the first things I learned when I started on the true crime beat in Chicago. I found out later that Samms didn't tell anyone how Marlene died, just that they'd found her dead. He was trying to prevent an influx of media sensation that he felt might impede his investigation. Yet, you told me that Marlene was half of the goose that laid the golden egg, and you didn't shoot it in cold blood without a good reason. There was only one way you could have known she was shot."

His jaw tightened. "It's always something simple that trips one up, isn't it. I wasn't lying about the good reason part, though. I had the best in the world. I was kept from my birthright."

I stared at him. "You would actually *want* to be acknowledged as the son of a gangster?"

He shrugged. "Why not? The Enerellis have money, position and power. I've had to struggle for most of my life. I went to her, told her I knew what she planned to do, and I said it didn't bother me in the least. My father would be forced to publicly acknowledge me at last. Then she said she had no intention of hurting him in that way, she wasn't going to reveal my identity. She said that's why she halted her investigation, because of the position it would put him in. It would destroy his family. Can you imagine her saying that to me?" He balled his hand into a fist, pounded it against his chest. "What a joke. *His* family. I was—I *am*—his family!"

He started to pace back and forth. "She said he was coming the next day, and she was going to give him the papers she'd unearthed, among them my birth certificate. I was enraged, but I didn't let on. I went out, rented that wig, and came back that night." His lips twitched, as if he were recalling something pleasant. "I cut the lights. Anabel had told me Marlene hated the dark. She had a flashlight, and when I came up to her, at first she thought I was Desiree. By the time she realized her mistake, it was too late." He cocked his hand, moved his thumb as if pulling a trigger.

"You killed her."

"Oh, of course I killed her," he said impatiently. "And then Anabel called me, and said she'd seen someone going into the house, but they didn't walk like Desiree. I told her Desiree was guilty as sin, but she didn't believe me, and then she found out I rented the wig, so I decided why not? Kill her too, and make it look as if she couldn't hack the guilt over Marlene. Bingo! Everyone's happy."

"And to think I actually asked for your help," I murmured.

"Yes, that was convenient. Enabled me to sneak in and plant the note and binoculars. I really wasn't late getting there." He smiled smugly. "And you want money to keep quiet? Do you really think I have money to pay you to keep quiet?"

"I'm sure you can get it."

"Who are you kidding? You're not someone who'd resort to blackmail. You're the person who fights on the side of truth and justice. This is a setup, isn't it? Where's your FBI boyfriend? Outside?"

I swallowed over the giant lump in my throat that threatened to choke me. "No. I'm alone."

"Pity." He flexed his hands in front of him. "Guess this'll be a crime scene again, when they find your cold, dead body lying here. Me, I'll be long gone. I quit that dead-end job before I came here."

He took a step toward me. I took two steps sideways and back. One eyebrow quirked, and he took another step toward me. I veered to the right, just out of his reach.

"The FBI has Enerelli in custody, and Bartholomew too. I know they're not sterling citizens, but is it fair for them to suffer for your crimes?"

"That's an odd sort of justice, wouldn't you say? They couldn't be pegged for all the crimes they did commit, so now they'll suffer for ones they didn't. While I'll be off, living my life. I haven't much money, but it's enough to get myself a new identity, start my life completely over, knowing I've gotten my revenge on my no-good birth father at last."

He lunged for me again, and this time I wasn't fast enough. He grabbed me and twisted my right arm cruelly behind my back. I let out a yelp and then brought the heel of my shoe down hard on his instep. He yowled and let go of my arm, and I made a dash for the door. Just as my fingers touched the knob, he dragged me back against his body, his arm around my neck this time. He pressed in, cutting off my air supply. I struggled to catch a breath, and jabbed my elbow back and into his ribs. It connected, but not hard enough to get him to release the chokehold he had on my neck. Little pinpricks of light swirled around my vision, but I knew I had to act fast or I was a dead woman. I was just readying the heel of my hand to try and connect with his nose when I heard him gasp. He released me and took two steps backward, staring at the window. I rubbed my bruised neck and followed his gaze.

A cat stood silhouetted in the window, its large gold eyes fixed right on Jenks. It's back arched, and the mouth opened in a hiss, revealing razor-sharp fangs. The animal reared up, pawed the window with its sharp claws, making a screeching sound against the glass.

"Cats! I hate 'em. I always knew they were bad luck," Jenks whimpered.

He turned on his heel and ran out of the room.

I looked back at the window. The cat was gone.

A second later I heard a shout: "Stop. Police. Stop or we'll fire."

Then I heard a gunshot.

I ran to the door and opened it just in time to see Samms snapping handcuffs on Jenks's wrists. The guy's red hair was fluffed out all around his head, like a fiery halo, and he was trembling. "Damn jinx," he muttered. Daniel stood just behind them, replacing his gun in his holster. I looked at him questioningly.

"Warning shot," he said, patting his side. "He went right down on his knees."

I glanced over on the lawn. Nick sat there, calmly licking one paw, looking about as threatening as a neutered tiger.

Samms pulled Jenks to his feet and then glanced at me. "I have to say, I had my doubts but your plan worked."

"I knew if all else failed, the sight of Nick might get to him," I said. "I remembered how nervous he got that day in Hot Bread, when he first saw Nick, and then again when I found Anabel's body. Plus, he said he thought black cats were bad luck." I felt for the tiny transmitter taped to the underside of my sweater, pulled it off and pressed it into Daniel's hand. I fisted both hands on my hips and cocked my head at the two men.

"Now, as far as you two are concerned, I have only one complaint. Why did you wait so long?"

Twenty-six

It was a beautiful Saturday afternoon, and Hot Bread was closed for the rest of the weekend. I'd decided that my near-death experience with both Enerelli and Jenks deserved some "me" time, aka well-deserved R&R. I'd gotten my dad's old gas grill out of the basement and fired it up, and now the fragrant aroma of grilling hamburgers, hot dogs, and steaks filled the air. Ollie had appointed himself assistant chef and stood over the grill, spatula in hand, while Chantal and I brought out pitchers of sangria, lemonade and iced tea and bowls of chips and salsa to munch on. Peter and Desiree were seated at the table, and Desiree looked the happiest I'd seen her. She looked up with a wide smile as I poured her a glass of lemonade.

"So it's really over? And Enerelli had nothing to do with it?"

"The only thing Enerelli's guilty of is breaking into my house and threatening me," I said. "And I've decided not to press charges." Heck, it was never good practice to piss a crime boss off, not unless you were one hundred percent positive he was going away to the Big House for many, many years.

"Gladstone was only really guilty of breaking into the Porter house and ransacking it, and taking those appointment pages. Even though Marlene had erased Enerelli's initials he didn't want to leave anything there that could possibly lead back to him. And, of course, Gladstone searched for the notes and birth certificate Marlene claimed to have on Jenks," Peter added.

"Speaking of the birth certificate," Ollie remarked as he flipped a burger over, "does anyone know what happened to it? It wasn't in those papers you found, was it, Nora?"

I shook my head. "Nope. I'm thinking maybe Marlene destroyed it. It was, after all, the only real shred of proof that Enerelli and Lila had a son, and the only way Jenks could ever have laid claim to his birthright.

Marlene knew admitting he'd had an illegitimate son would destroy Enerelli, so it might have been the one decent thing she ever did."

"And this Paul Jenkins?" Desiree asked stiffly. "What happens to him now?"

"Well, if he gets a judge who shows some mercy and doesn't condemn him to death row, he'll be serving a nice long stretch in San Quentin for the double murders of Marlene and Anabel."

We all turned as Daniel came into my yard, followed by Samms. Daniel had a bakery box in his hand, and Samms a large paper bag from Creed's Deli. Chantal and I hurried over to relieve them of their burden.

I peeped inside the sack Samms handed me then shot him a quizzical look. "Macaroni and potato salad?"

He grinned. "One can never have enough."

Chantal, meantime, had peeped inside the box Daniel had brought. "Ooh, strawberry shortcake. How did you know it's Nora's favorite?"

"I didn't," Daniel said with a grin. "It just happens to be mine, too." He gave a quick glance around the yard. "Where's the star of the hour?"

"You mean Nick?" I gestured with my thumb. Nick was right at Ollie's side, looking longingly at the burgers and steaks he was heaping on my good platter. Ollie broke off a small piece of hamburger and tossed it to Nick, who grabbed it between his paws and began to eat greedily.

"Jenks had such an obvious distaste for cats," I remarked. "I figured at the very least Nick's appearance would rattle him. As it was, he popped up at just the right time."

Nick glanced up at me. The look in his eyes plainly said, *as usual.*

"Once again, he saves the day," Ollie sang out. "Let's eat."

He brought the huge platter of meat over to the table, followed by Chantal with another platter of bread and rolls. Then everyone started to dig in. Once sandwiches were made and glasses refilled, Desiree asked, "What will happen to Marlene's manuscript? I'm sure Peachtree Press is champing at the bit, waiting to publish it. Marlene might have shielded Enerelli, but she surely didn't do the same with me, or Scarlett, or Sable St. John."

"We could get a court injunction," suggested Peter. "It would delay things, and maybe we could reason with the publisher."

"Those people only reason with dollar signs," Desiree said. She grimaced and put down her hamburger. "Suddenly I've lost my appetite."

"Well, don't," Daniel said. "The FBI has appropriated that flash drive. It might not touch on Enerelli's illegitimate son, but there's plenty in there to make things very uncomfortable for him and his crime family for years to come."

Desiree's eyes widened. "Can you do that?"

"Marlene knew her manuscript contained issues the FBI would consider sensitive, however, she never approached the bureau with her intent to publish. As such, the FBI has the authority to censor material if it might pose an issue for "public safety." It will have to be gone over with a fine-tooth comb." Daniel closed one eye in a broad wink. "Trust me, that manuscript will be tied up for review indefinitely."

Desiree frowned. "But can't the publisher appropriate the parts that have nothing to do with FBI business?"

"Well, there's the rub. It seems as if all of your secrets, in one form or another, touch on areas sensitive to the FBI." Daniel looked Desiree right in the eye. "I'm not at liberty to say any more, but I think you get the idea."

She was quiet for a few minutes, then put her hand over her heart. "I do. Oh, thank God!" Then she grabbed her hamburger and took a huge bite.

"Looks like all the loose ends are tied up," I remarked, squirting ketchup on my burger. "The manuscript will die a slow death in the hands of the FBI, Enerelli and his cronies will get what's coming to them, Jenks has a nice long stretch in the slammer to look forward to, so what's left?"

"I can think of something," sang out Chantal. "A certain envelope you shoved in your drawer from a certain very grateful head of our museum's board of directors."

I gave my head an emphatic shake. "I am *not* opening Violet's envelope until she returns. She specifically asked me to wait, and I have no intention of violating her trust."

"You may have to trust a bit longer." Daniel cleared his throat. "I heard that she and Alexa have extended their stay in London another two weeks."

"Oh, no. Who told you that?" I demanded.

"Lance. Alexa made an overseas call to him last night. Seems Violet is in the midst of chatting up the curator of a big museum in Essex for a new display."

"And she was supposed to be on a vacation. Oh, well." I shrugged and ducked my head, hoping no one noted my disappointed expression. "It doesn't matter. I'm still waiting," I said, but my tone didn't carry as much conviction as before.

Daniel and Samms exchanged a glance. "As stubborn as a mule," Samms observed.

"It's a Charles family trait," I responded with a curl of my lip.

"Tell me about it," Peter chuckled. "Speaking of Charles women, Lacey graduates soon. Has she told you what her plans are?"

"No, but I expect I'll find out soon enough."

"She's doing a great job with the sketches for St. Leo," Samms said. "You know, they might be persuaded to hire her full-time."

I raised a brow. "Really?"

He nodded. "Last I heard, it was in their budget. If you want, I can put in a good word for her."

I smiled. "That would be great if you could. Thanks, Samms."

"Don't mention it." He shifted his weight to his other foot. "So, Red, are you planning to look into some less dangerous hobbies than crime solving?"

"Why should I, when I'm so good at it?" I got up, ducking my head to hide my grin, and walked over to the grill to put some more hamburgers on. As I laid the patties on the grill, Daniel came up to me.

"I've got to thank you. If not for your quick thinking, Enerelli might have gotten off unscathed. As it is, we've got some good stuff on him. Not enough for a conviction yet, but enough to make him sweat."

"I'm glad."

He reached out and took my hand. "If you're feeling up to it, that offer of dinner and a movie tomorrow still stands."

"Are you kidding! Of course I am." I looked over at the table, where Samms was engaged in conversation with Peter. "So, what's the deal with Samms? Is he going to stay on the Cruz force, or is he part of the FBI?"

"Oh, he's definitely part of the FBI," Daniel said. "However, he may stay on the Cruz force a while longer to break in the new head of Homicide, who I understand won't be arriving until sometime next month."

"Oh, goody," I muttered.

Samms looked up and caught my eye. He raised two fingers in a salute.

Daniel went back to the table and Chantal came over with another platter of rolls. "You do know that Samms has been watching you with Daniel, right?" she whispered.

I shrugged. "He probably knows he was the subject of our conversation. Daniel told me Samms is going to remain as head of Cruz Homicide for at least another month."

"Really? Well, isn't that interesting? Maybe you can get involved in another murder and work closely with him again."

I gave her a look of mock horror. "Chantal! Bite your tongue!"

She tossed her head. "Well, murder seems to be the only way you and Samms can get together."

"It's kind of drastic, don't you think?"

"Maybe, but you resist any other opportunity to give him a chance. Mark my words, all Samms needs is one little sign from you and he will waste no time asking you out."

I glanced over at the table, at the dark head bent so close to the blonde one in conversation. "Okay, let's say you're right, and I give Samms an 'all clear,' won't that make things awkward between him and Daniel?"

"I doubt it. They are two grown men. Besides, a little competition never hurt anyone. Daniel has not asked you to be exclusive, has he?"

I shook my head. "No."

"Well, then. There is no reason for you to tie yourself down to one man. You owe it not only to yourself but to them, to be sure of your feelings."

I laughed. "Okay, I'll think about it."

She gave my arm a quick squeeze. "Do yourself a favor. Don't think too long."

• • •

Later, after everyone had gone and I'd cleaned up, I went behind the back counter and pulled open the middle drawer where I'd shoved Violet's envelope and stood for a few minutes, turning it over in my hand, putting my mixed feelings about Daniel and Samms on the back burner, at least for now. Nick had followed me and now he hopped up on the counter and lay down, paws crossed. He inclined his head toward the envelope. "Merow."

"Right. What harm could it do to just take a peek? Chantal did say it would be something useful, and if it's not a smoothie maker . . ."

I put a pot of tea on, and when it started to steam, held the envelope over it so the steam would loosen the glue. An old trick, but effective. Inside the envelope were some folded papers. I removed them and spread them on the counter.

The top was a letter in Violet's handwriting:

> *Dear Nora:*
> *I know you didn't want to take money, so I tried to think of something fitting for you, something that you would never get for yourself, something that would adequately*

express my gratitude.

Whether you want to admit it or not, you're a pretty good detective. Such ability should be nurtured, and I think deep down you agree with me.

Please accept the enclosed in the spirit in which it's intended. I shall be forever grateful to you for using YOUR gift to reunite me with my Alexa.

Sincerely,

Violet

Underneath was a receipt for a ten-week course given by the Lockwood Agency, entitled *Fundamentals of PI Work*. It also included taking the exam to become a licensed PI in the state of California.

Both the course fee and licensing fee had been marked "Paid in Full."

I put the papers down and looked at Nick. "Well, what do you think of that? Violet thinks I have what it takes to be a pro investigator. I know Ollie does, too." I slid Nick a glance. "I don't even want to think how thrilled Louis will be. Guess I'll have no more excuses for not writing that series he wants on PI work, right?"

Nick tipped his head back and let out a sharp yowl.

I laughed. "Okay, then. I guess we'll give it a whirl. Who knows, I might learn something useful. It could come in handy if you and I are going to keep on being 'body magnets,' as Samms puts it."

I gathered up the papers and tucked them under my arm, then walked around to the front to make sure everything was locked securely. As I turned I noticed the pile of mail, neatly placed on the far corner of my counter. I picked the pile up and thumbed through it idly. There were the usual magazines (two issues of *Soap Opera Digest*, no less!) advertisements, bills (yech!) and . . . a postcard. The picture on the front was of the *Queen Mary* in Long Beach, about a five-hour-and-change drive from Cruz. Nick hopped up on the counter and reared on his hind legs to paw at the card.

"Yer-*owl!*"

"Yes, I see it. Who could be sending us a postcard from the *Queen Mary*, Nick?"

I laid the card on the counter and stroked Nick's head with one hand while I turned the card over with the other. My heart beat wildly in my chest as I read the three words scrawled beneath the description of the *Queen Mary*, in a handwriting that had become familiar to me over the months thanks to the journals now in my possession:

Good Job.
"N"

From the Recipe Book of Nora Charles

Megan Fox (aka Monte Cristo)

3 slices bread (white preferred, but it can be any type)
mayonnaise, as needed
2 slices cheese (Cheddar preferred, but it can be any)
2 sliced chicken breasts
3 large eggs, beaten
1/4 cup milk
2 tablespoons vegetable oil
1 tablespoon unsalted butter
powdered sugar for garnish
jam (optional)

On a work surface, lay out 2 slices of bread and spread with mayonnaise. Top each slice with 1 slice of cheese and 1 chicken breast. Put the third slice of bread on top of one stack, and flip the remaining stack on top, cheese-side down, to make a triple-decker sandwich.

Using a knife, cut the crusts off the sandwich (this helps to pinch and seal the ends). Wrap the sandwich tightly with plastic wrap and refrigerate for at least 30 minutes and up to 6 hours. (Wrapping the sandwich in plastic wrap compacts it and prevents the egg batter from seeping in in the next step.)

Combine the eggs and milk in a bowl. Heat the oil and butter in a skillet over medium-high heat. Unwrap the sandwich and dip it in the egg batter, to coat evenly. Gently place it in the skillet, and fry, turning once, until golden brown and hot, about 5 minutes total.

Cut the Monte Cristo in half, transfer it to a plate, and garnish with powdered sugar. If preferred, spoon some jam (any flavor, blackberry is what Nick prefers!) over each half and serve immediately.

Brian Austin Green Sandwich

Follow the same directions as above, except substitute sliced ham for the chicken breast.

Jimmy Fallon Breakfast Sandwich

1 egg
2 slices ham
2 slices yellow American cheese
2 slices bread or roll
tomato slice
bacon bits

Fry the egg, and right before it's done, cover with ham slices and American cheese. Put on bread or roll and garnish with tomato slice and bacon bits.

Howard Stern Breakfast Sandwich

2 eggs
Canadian bacon
bagel
crumbled cheese

Fry the eggs and bacon. Slice the bagel and toast to a golden brown. Place the eggs and bacon on the bagel, crumble cheese on top.

About the Author

While Toni LoTempio does not commit—or solve—murders in real life, she has no trouble doing it on paper. Her lifelong love of mysteries began early on when she was introduced to her first Nancy Drew mystery at age ten—*The Secret in the Old Attic*. She and her cat pen the Nick and Nora mystery series, and they also write the Purr N Bark Pet Shop mysteries, which will be continued soon with book two, *Killers of a Feather*. Catch up with them at Rocco's blog, catsbooksmorecats.blogspot.com, or her website, tclotempio.net

Made in the USA
Las Vegas, NV
22 September 2021